The Alchemy Press Book Of Ancient Wonders

The Alchemy Press Book Of Ancient Wonders

Edited by
Jan Edwards and Jenny Barber

The Alchemy Press

The Alchemy Press Book of Ancient Wonders

Copyright © Jan Edwards and Jenny Barber 2012

Cover painting © Dominic Harman

Layouts: Peter Coleborn

First Edition

ISBN 978-0-9532260-8-5

Published 2012 by The Alchemy Press by arrangement with the editors and authors. All rights reserved.

The Alchemy Press
Cheadle
Staffordshire
ST10 1PF, UK

www.alchemypress.co.uk

Copyright Information

Contents

For the Alchemy Writers

There shrines and palaces and towers
(Time-eaten towers that tremble not!)
Resemble nothing that is ours.

Edgar Allen Poe
"The City in the Sea" (1845)

INTRODUCTION

Kari Sperring

ANYTHING CAN BE a wonder, from the memory of an elderly man (Ray Bradbury, *Dandelion Wine*) to a soft drink bottle falling from the sky (*The Gods Must Be Crazy*), from a micro-processor to an historic bridge. When we think of a wonder, our minds go most often to the great buildings of the past – the pyramids, the Taj Mahal, Stonehenge – but the human mind can make almost anything wondrous. The Bradbury novel mentioned above is a case in point. Nothing very dramatic happens over its course: it is an account, in the main, of a single summer in the life of a boy in his teens. Yet despite the absence of pyramids and dinosaurs and spaceships and dragons, it is filled with wonder, with that sense that we all possess of the numinous, the liminal. A year on the cusp of turning towards the fallow months; a boy on the cusp of adulthood: the wonder lies in the writing, in the ways that Bradbury uses his words to draw us into the mind and emotions of his young protagonist.

And that, perhaps, lies at the heart of wonder, that sense of ambiguity, of mystery, of 'how does that happen'? In our post-enlightenment world, the natural world – from an erupting vol-cano to the pattern of spots on a ladybird's wing – remains astonishing and beautiful, but perhaps we no longer wonder at them as much as our predecessors did. In the backs of our minds, scientific explanations about tectonic faults and volcanism, camouflage and survival, loiter, reminding us of ourselves and our achievements. We turn not to gods and mysteries to explain them, but to geology, biology, chemistry. We are more comfortable with scientific answers than human ones – or more comforted, anyway.

The Taj Mahal and the pyramids are beautiful and awe-inspiring: we wonder at how they were built, how they sit in their landscape, at their human dimension. We know their history, or some of it, but their significance transcends that – they are layered over with the wrappings of all the stories that we tell ourselves about them.

This current collection is filled with such wonders: ancient constructions whose meanings are occluded from us by time and distance, but whose power, whose attraction for us, remains powerful. Why did ancient men erect menhirs and stone circles? We do not know, not completely. We reach for explanation – funerary monuments, markers of nobility, places for ceremony or magic. But we can never been entirely sure. There are gaps, spaces where story and wonder slip through. Adrian Tchaikovsky reminds us here that stories – and history is itself a collection of stories – are mutable, that the explanations they offer us may change with time and necessity, may be lost, may be rewritten in new and dangerous ways. The same point about the mutability of story is made by Shannon Connor Winward, though in her story knowledge is lost and recoded in new ways. There are a lot of forgotten histories here, a lot of old explanations discarded – perhaps foolishly – by our scientific modern age. Human time is shallow in geological terms, but – as several of the stories here point out – we are remote from our ancestors and their meanings are not ours. Their beliefs remain oblique to us, but we discard them at our peril, as several protagonists in this collection learn.

Meanings shift, are reworked, but the older levels remain and may come back to haunt or harm or change us.

Many of the wonders recounted by the authors in this anthology are frightening, but not all are harmful. The harm lies in how we approach them, what we expect from them, and what we do. Pride precedes a fall for Anne Nicholls' protagonist, but in Aliette de Bodard's story, the heroine's persistence and humanity strengthen her in the face of an inhuman enemy. Several tales revisit famous legends – the Odyssey, the Arthurian cycle – or bring members of other cultures face to face with the British past, in order to cast new light on familiar myths and places. Peter Crowther's story brings us a wonder that is temporary, mutable, built of the power of human need and hope, while Pauline Dungate offers a glimpse of how wonders change over time. Stolen lovers and friends who choose the past over the hardships of the present, sacrifices and battles, births, deaths and betrayals, old stories and new needs, loneliness, greed, love and madness. We walk with wonders everyday, through the power of curiosity and imagination and our human tendency to make stories about what we fear, what we desire, what we wish to understand. This collection offers new glimpses into the wonder we all feel: enjoy.

BONES

Adrian Tchaikovsky

BETWEEN THE SCARF and the hood, hardly anything of Elantris' face was exposed and still he was breathing grit, every blink grinding the stinging particles into his eyes so that he thought he would go blind before they reached Dust Port.

"Is this a sandstorm?" he demanded of the man in the locust's forward saddle, leaning forwards to yell in his ear.

"Sandstorm'd strip your flesh from your bones!" The rider's amusement was plain. "First time in these parts, then?"

"Domina Hastella never wanted to visit before," Elantris yelled. The man's back was offering no insights. "Which means you found something?"

Their locust dipped and dived, some current of desert air slipping out from beneath its wings. For a moment the pair of them could only cling on and let the labouring insect regain its hold on the element.

The rider cursed the beast, swatting at its antennae for emphasis. "Found lots of things," he called back. "But yes." When not proving a surprisingly able locust-wrangler, the man in the forward saddle was an academic, a Beetle-kinden named Fordyce Gracer, a student of the buried past.

Elantris recalled waiting for Gracer in a shabby town of white-walled, flat-roofed buildings where south had been the desert, only the desert, like the edge of the world: vast, ground-down stretches of broken, rocky country standing barely proud of the sea of sand. If there was some habitable place on the far side of that barren ocean, nobody could swear to it. Even airships that had tried to brave the storms and the heat and the abrasive air had either come back in defeat or not at all. *Surely nothing of any value to man lies that way,* had been Elantris' only thought. And yet not true: here were Elantris and, on the locust ahead, his mistress Hastella, two Spider-kinden come all this way to inspect her family's investment.

"It didn't used to be like this," Gracer bellowed. He seemed to be guiding the locust lower, but the blowing sand kept Elantris from taking a look as he hunched in the Beetle-kinden's wind-shadow.

"Like what?" he managed.

"We've known for a while this wasn't always a desert. Sea was much closer, and we've found where rivers were. It was green, all this."

"So what happened?" To Elantris it sounded like something out of the old stories, that some ill-worded curse could parch a whole country to this death-by-dust.

"Time happened," was Gracer's curt reply. "Things change. You go digging around the place as much as I have, you realize that. But in this case it's a good thing. When the desert came, it buried a lot of fascinating stuff, and that stuff's still there. So long as it's out of the wind, you'd be amazed what secrets the desert keeps."

Then the locust had spread its legs, although its wings flung so much sand up that Elantris could not even see the ground. A moment later the insect came to a clumsy, skidding stop, hopped a few paces as though uncertain, then folded its wings primly.

"Welcome to Dust Port!" Gracer boomed. "Dig's just a little

way on. You'll learn to love it, just like we have!"

A moment later the wind lulled, the dust swirling and sinking, revealing a camp of tents and slope-sided shacks ringing a stand of stunted trees that Elantris thought must be a watering hole. Gracer was waving at a train of animals winding its way in from the far side, a half-dozen round-bodied beetles with ridged, black shells, laden with boxes and barrels but stepping lightly enough that he guessed the containers were empty. A little logic suggested that the caravan had been sent to Dust Port from the dig site for supplies.

Elantris dismounted and made it to the other locust just in time to help his mistress down. She was sufficiently swathed in silks that he had no clue to her mood, but then even her bare face was seldom a good guide to that. They were both Spider-kinden, but Hastella was pure Aristoi, a distant scion of the Aelvenita family that was paying for Gracer's research. Her Art always hid her true thoughts deep behind her mask of watchful patience.

So has he finally found something to repay the investment? Elantris wondered. When Hastella had ordered him to arrange the journey she had not seemed keen, so much as resigned.

Elantris was just a poor secretary: letters, music and a little divination on the side. What would he know?

Gracer was heading off for the caravan. Beetles like him were tenacious, robust and found everywhere, just like the insects they drew their Art from. They got caught in Spiders' webs like any other prey, though, and now Gracer's little struggles had attracted the spinner's notice.

Hastella watched him go, then gestured imperiously for Elantris to follow her over to a ramshackle collection of wood that turned out to be something like a taverna. There, he procured some watered wine from the leathery-skinned Fly-kinden proprietor and brought it over hesitantly.

"It won't be much, Domina," he murmured. "I think it has sand in it."

She hooked her veil down so that he would receive the sharp edge of her expression. "If there's anything within ten miles that doesn't have 'sand in it', it's news to me." Still, she took the wine and downed it without a flinch, which was more than Elantris could manage.

He looked about the close slope-ceilinged confines of the taverna's single room, the stifling air glittering with dust motes where the sun crept in. There were a couple of big Scorpion-kinden sitting in one corner: waxy-skinned, bald men with snaggling underbites and claws on their hands. A scarred Spider woman reclined nearby, wearing armour of silk and chitin, and with a rapier displayed prominently at her belt. Most of the rest of what passed for the taproom was taken up by a dust-caked party of Flies and Beetles and a single sullen-looking Ant-kinden, all glowering at Elantris when they caught him looking their way. In Dust Port you kept your curiosity to yourself.

"You think I'm mad, of course, to come out here," Hastella said softly.

He started guiltily. "I would never…"

"Gracer is quite the scholar, you know. He believes what he does is important. He's right, though perhaps not quite in the way he thinks."

"Mistress, forgive me, I don't even know what he does, what anyone could be doing out here."

"The past is a book, and knowledge is never wasted. A grand discovery, an ancient palace, a city from time before record lost to the sands, these things buy status and prestige for him as a scholar, for me as his patroness. For the Aelvenita as my kin. And sometimes men like Gracer turns up something genuinely in-triguing – some scrap of ancient ritual that might be put to use, some antique blade still sharp despite the ages… Knowledge is never wasted. But, like good wine, it is sometimes best kept to those who appreciate it. After all, Master Gracer would scrabble in the earth with or without the patronage of the Aristoi. Better that we pay for his hobby, just in case it profits us. Just in case he finds something remarkable…"

"Mistress, can I ask … what was it drew you here, really? You wouldn't say…"

"No, I would not. Not back where the foolish lips of a secretary could spread the word." Her cold look did not endure, seeing his hurt expression. "Very well, Elantris, as we've arrived." She reached into one of her many pouches and produced a folded paper. "Feast your eyes."

For a long time he stared at the sketch, turning it and turning it and trying to understand what he was looking at. In the end he was forced to confess his ignorance.

"It's a skull, Elantris. A drawing of a skull."

As though the sketch had been one of those trick images, abruptly he saw it, the line of the jaw, the eye socket, the teeth; he had never seen such teeth. "A skull of *what?*" he asked.

"That's just it," Hastella confirmed. "Nobody knows." Her gaze might have been fixed on some image that existed only in her mind, but Elantris fancied that, while he studied the sketch, she had been staring at the two Scorpion-kinden, and that they had been looking back, yellow eyes fixed narrowly on the Spider Arista. *Brigands?* was Elantris's alarmed thought. Scorpions hereabouts were not noted for their genteel or law-abiding ways.

Interrupting his thoughts, Gracer ducked in, spotted them and ambled over, managing a creditable bow before Hastella. "Domina, we're ready to head to the dig site. You may fly the last leg if you wish, but we have a howdah for you if you prefer a more comfortable ride on the beetles."

"So kind, Master Gracer, and I accept." She favoured him with one of her warmest smiles, the kind she reserved for truly useful underlings – and which Elantris himself saw precious few of.

GRACER'S DIG WAS out where the bones of the earth jagged from the dusty ground, tiers of barren, red-rock uplands rising higher and higher until they broke free of the abrading hand of the sand to form the true mountains that spiked the horizon. It was stark, uninhabitable, malevolent country, and yet even here people lived. Riding atop one of the pack beetles, Elantris saw huddles of huts that must count as villages, corrals of animals.

"What did they raise here?" he asked Gracer.

"Crickets, beetles," the man explained. "The local varieties barely need to drink from one tenday to the next. The herders let them out before dawn, and their carapaces catch the dew like cups. If you know what you're doing you can fill your water-skin from them."

"And you say this place was once green!"

"Look ahead." Gracer's finger hands drew out landmarks from the stepped and broken terrain. "See the land dip there? Follow the gully up. That was a river once. People lived here, many people. This land wasn't just good enough to keep them alive, it was good enough to fight over."

"How do you know?"

The Beetle-kinden's teeth flashed in his dark face. "Because of what we found, young Spider. Because of what brought your mistress here."

Monster bones? But it was plain that Gracer meant more than that.

The dig itself was a large tent backed onto a sheer rock face, surrounded by a collection of smaller shelters, all dust-coloured, patched canvas looking as though it had suffered there for decades rather than just under a year. The motley collection of people who came out to greet them had rather the same look. Elantris's image of academics was the elegant and sophisticated, debating some point of abstract interest in an Arista's parlour, not this pack of weathered, villainous men and women, their hardwearing clothes layered with dirt and their hands calloused from the spade and the pick.

Gracer was making introductions, but the names passed Elantris by – even though he knew Hastella would recall every one. Instead he was just looking from face to face, wondering how one would separate a scholar from a fugitive killer just from the look. A half-dozen were Beetles like Gracer, stocky, dark and powerful, and there were a couple of Elantris's own kinden as well as three Flies and a lean Grasshopper woman employed to look after the locusts.

Elantris could see how such a team would function out here, the strengths each would bring. Every insect-kinden had its Art, the abilities it drew from its totem. The Flies would bring swift reflexes and the wings they could manifest on demand, able to scout the sands as swiftly as the saddled locusts. The Spiders drew on their archetype's patience and presence. The Beetles had their rugged endurance, and the Grasshopper must own that most ancient of Arts, able to speak with her kinden's beasts. Elantris watched her commune with them before walking off to their pen with the great creatures trailing meekly behind her. Without Art the merely inhospitable would have become uninhabitable.

Art aside, the barren surroundings and the looming rock face oppressed Elantris, loaded with an invisible threat that plucked at the edge of his mind. He felt as though some predator was laired there, crouched within those cliffs having drawn the substance of the desert before it as a blind, to entrap the incautiously venturesome. He glanced at Hastella, but her smooth composure admitted nothing of her thoughts.

And besides, this was one reason she kept him at her side, despite his more general failings. He had good eyes for the invisible, and what was history if not a great edifice of the unseen?

I shall have harsh dreams here.

He came back to himself because Gracer was guiding his mistress towards the largest tent, and presumably she had invited him to show her his finds, or else he was just too enthusiastic for propriety. Elantris followed hurriedly, catching the Beetle-kinden's words.

"We've dug a selection of trenches, and we hit stone everywhere: foundations, loose blocks, all of it worn by the sand but still recognisable as the work of human hands. No idea how far it extends – that would take far more labour than we have – but I think at least several hundred inhabitants, potentially well over a thousand."

"Where are these trenches?" Hastella asked him.

"We've marked locations and recovered them, otherwise the sand will destroy anything we leave exposed. A day or so here and you'll feel the same way, Domina." A jovial chuckle. "However, in *here* we've exposed the entryway to a dwelling set into the cliff. The entrance had been carved into the rock and then choked with sand and rubble, maybe actively filled in. People knew there was something here, though. We came here following travellers' tales."

"What did they say?" Elantris blurted out. Gracer and Hastella stared at him and he coloured. "About this place? What did they say?"

Gracer shrugged. "Some nonsense. They're not fond of it. Who would be? Nothing but dust here now – not like it was all those years ago. Thousands of years, Domina, five, ten... I've never seen anything like what we've found here – what we're still finding here. It's from before any history, from before even stories." And, with that, Gracer stepped into the largest tent, forcing his two guests to follow.

Inside, the heat was stifling, as though the very gloom radiated it. The slope of the ground within was steep where Gracer's team had dug down to the level of the old, that point in the sands that history had sunk to. There, the shapes of the past emerged from the dry substrate like ships from fog, and Elantris saw the angled lines of walls that had been ground down to mere stubs, the scatter of fallen blocks, carven sides effaced, worn almost smooth. At the far end of the tent, lit up by twin lamps, was a gateway, a crack in the rock that had been widened into a low rectangle of darkness, flanked by uneven, lumpy columns or, no… Elantris recognized the contours: statues cut into the stone. There the swell of hips, there elbows, shoulders. Time had played the headsman, though: barely even a stump of neck was left,

"We've collected a lot of odd artifacts, potsherds and the like, all unfamiliar styles," Gracer explained. "But you probably want to see the guardians."

There were a handful of pits dug there, covered with sheets against the dust that still got in, to hang in the air and prickle the throat and eyes. With a showman's flourish, Gracer drew the nearest one back, revealing—

For a moment Elantris was convinced he saw living flesh, movement, locking eyes with a fierce, ancestral glower, but there were only bones left of this ancient warrior. Bones, and the tools of his trade. An irregular lump of reddish corrosion was an axe-head, according to Gracer. A near-identical blot was a knife-blade. The armour had fared better, loose scales of chitin still scattered about the ribs, and curving pieces of some sort of helm placed reverently next to that yellowed skull.

"We've found more than twenty so far, buried before this

gateway," Gracer explained, "doubtless we've not found them all. Soldiers, guardians, sentries left to watch the threshold, interred with care and respect."

"What kinden?" Hastella asked him.

"Impossible to say." Gracer frowned, the dissatisfied academic. "You must know, from a skeleton alone the kinden is usually impossible to tell, unless Art has made modifications to the bone structure, like a Mantid's spines or a Scorpion-kinden's claws. The thing is, most of the old sites I've worked on, there's usually some fairly strong pictorial evidence to suggest who the locals were – statues of beetles, spider-web motifs, those mantis-armed idol things you get. Go back a couple of thousand years and that's usually the principal decorative motif. Here – nothing of the sort, not on the stones, not the walls – it all seems to predate that period entirely. Our dead friends here had some personal effects, and we've found a pendant with what might be a bee insignia, and a shield that's been embossed with fighting crickets, but it's circumstantial… Who were they? We don't know. We also found the remains of some dead insects close by, again apparently buried with full honours – two fighting beetles, a scorpion, but again, it doesn't necessarily follow that the people here were any kinden we know today. But you didn't come all the way to our humble hole in the ground to see these dead fellows, Domina."

"Show me," she told him sharply, reminding the Beetle-kinden of his station. Gracer bobbed, grinning, and headed for the doorway, snagging a lamp as he went and beckoning for them to follow.

Once inside, Hastella had gone still, so Elantris squirmed past, careful to avoid jostling her, and became so involved in proper decorum that he only saw the *thing* when he straightened up.

He let out a brief, strangled yelp and sat down hard, heart

hammering as fast as beating wings. Gracer whooped, typical coarse Beetle, and even Hastella had a slight smile at his expense. Red-faced, Elantris picked himself up and backed away from the skeleton Gracer's people had assembled beyond the doorway.

They must have set this display up to impress the woman paying their wages. They had gone to some lengths to wire and strap the thing together, and had sunk bolts into that antique ceiling to suspend the thing. It was an impossible monster.

It was bones, just bones like the men outside, but no man this. It had been posed on its hind limbs, rearing up like a mantis, its forelegs – arms? – raised as if to strike down with their crescent claws. Its spine had been reconstructed into a sinuous curve, and Hastella's sketch had not done that head justice. Elantris looked up at it, that broad, heavy skull with jaws agape, baring its long, savage fangs.

The whole beast looked to be about the size of a man but ferocity dwelled in every bone of it, as though without the wire and the cord it would have lunged forwards to tear the throat out of any mere human.

"Is it a human of some unknown kinden, perhaps?" Hastella suggested, for there was little in the world that carried its bones on the inside, after all. There were humans, and there were a handful of species domesticated by them: goats, sheep. Nothing like this beast dwelled in the world any more, and for that Elantris was profoundly grateful.

"Probably not, Domina," Gracer told her. "The relative proportions of the limbs suggest that it went on all fours, and the skull... My anatomist tells me that it has a lot of attachment points for muscle – not a bite you'd want to get in the way of – but a far smaller brain-space than ours... It's something new, Domina."

"But this reconstruction, it's speculative," she offered.

"Ah, well, no." Gracer had that smug look universal to academics with the answers "The skeleton was found not quite in this, ah, dramatic pose, but still complete – tucked just around the doorframe. There wasn't much interpretation required. If you would wish to take it back, Domina, as a gift from us in appreciation for your support, it would make quite the conversation piece, perhaps?"

He was being too familiar again, but Hastella seemed content to let him get away with it. "Show me more," she directed.

The next chamber was a great, long hall, and for a moment Elantris had to stop, swaying, his eyes bustling with shadow movement that had not been cast by Gracer's lamp: hurried flight, the thrust of spears, a tide of furious darkness, the silhouettes of monsters. His ears rang with distant howls and screeches, hideous and alien.

He realized the hand on his shoulder was his mistress's, and bowed hurriedly. "Forgive me."

She was studying him, though, and he understood unhappily: *So, she brought me here for my eyes, then.* He had medicines for when the seeing dreams became too insistent, but if dreams were why Hastella wanted him here then he would have to forego the cure and suffer.

The floor was littered with stone, irregular forms that eventually resolved themselves into the broken fragments of statues. Once he had understood that, Elantris felt he progressed through a stone abattoir. Everywhere he looked there were broken arms, legs, sundered torsos.

"No heads," he said, before he could stop himself. The other two looked back at him.

"Very good," Gracer said. "Yes, this isn't just wear and tear, and our dead lads out there weren't just taking a nap. There's holes in some of the skulls and shields, broken bones. They died defending this place, I reckon, and whoever got in here, they weren't gentle with the fixtures. We guess this walk we're on was lined with these statues, and they all got knocked over, and someone took care to hack off every head and cart them off."

"But why?"

"Symbolic, probably." Gracer shrugged. "My best guess."

At the end of the hall was another low, rubble-choked entryway, and a handful of Gracer's people were working at it, shifting the stones and setting in wooden props. "Ceiling came down here," the Beetle explained. "And that *was* just time, I think. We're almost through, though. Seeing as you're here, I was going to get my crew to go all night, and maybe in the morning we'll all get to see what's in there.

No! The thought struck Elantris without warning. *I don't want to know.* But he said nothing. Of course he said nothing.

"A perfect idea, Master Gracer," Hastella said warmly. "So good to find a man of your profession who understands proper showmanship. Perhaps, after my tent has been pitched, you might join me for a little wine, and we can discuss what else I may be able to provide for you and your team."

Hastella's tent was a grand affair, overshadowing the little billets of the scholars. Elantris got a separate chamber to himself, metaphorically if not literally sleeping at the feet of his mistress. He had thought she would want him to wait on her while she and Gracer talked, but she had sent him off around dusk, and he understood why. It was not that she cared about privacy, but that she wanted him to dream.

The temperature had fallen as soon as the sun crossed the horizon, and yet the day's heat still seemed to linger feverishly in Elantris, leaving him alternately shivering and sweating, fighting with his hammock, staving off the night as long as he could while the murmur of Hastella and Gracer's voices washed over him like waves.

He was standing before that crude opening again, in his dreaming. In the dark of the desert he could not see the restored heads of the statues flanking it, but he felt their stone gaze upon him.

He did not want to go in, and for a moment he felt that he did not have to, that he could still walk away and let the past keep its secrets. Then there was a rushing from all sides, and shadows were streaming past him, of men, of beasts, and he was carried helplessly with them.

He was racing down that hall, seeing the great flood of bladed darkness course on either side of him. He wanted to fight it, to resist it, but he could not: he was a part of it, it a part of him. He was responsible for what it did.

Ahead, the monster reared, bones at first but then clad in a ripple of fur and flesh. He saw those claws strike, the savage jaws bite down, flinging fragments of the dark on all sides. Then it was not a monster but a man in a monster's skin, face loud with loathing and hatred. There were many men, many monsters, creatures of the absurd, of the horrific: long-necked things with cleaving beaks; snarl-muzzled grey nightmares that coursed in seething packs; branch-horned, plunging things that used their antlers like lances. And the darkness was torn and savaged and brutalized by the monstrous host, but gathered itself and came again, pulling Elantris like a tide, forcing him into the jaws of the fiends to be torn and clawed and run through, over and over.

He awoke, crying and flailing and finally falling from his hammock completely – a real, physical pain to drag him from the morass of his nightmares. Looking up, he saw Hastella standing over him. How long had she been watching?

It was dawn already, the first threat of the desert sun just clawing at the eastern horizon outside the tent. "Tell me,"

Hastella said, and he did, all he could remember, a jumbled, near-incoherent rant of a story, and yet she listened all through.

Gracer had been optimistic, and his ragged band was still trying to safely clear to the next chamber through most of that day, leaving Elantris nothing to do save kick his heels and steal bowls of wine when he thought Hastella was not looking. He wanted rid of this haunted place. Every instinct told him to cling to his ignorance.

At the last, close to dusk, Gracer came, with much apologetic scraping, to say that they were ready, now, to break through. The delay had plainly dented his confidence as, even as they passed down the hall of broken statues, he was insisting that they might find nothing of great import. Now the moment had come, he was abruptly nervous that he might run out of material.

His entire team were standing there, shovels and picks and props in hand. Elantris squinted through that dark straight-walled aperture, seeing that there was a space beyond it but nothing more.

Like looking into a grave.

As thoughts went, he could have wished for something more uplifting.

"Olisse, you go first with the lantern," Gracer told a Fly-kinden woman. She nodded curtly and hunched down, shining the lamp through. She was just a little thing, like all her kind, barely reaching Elantris's waist. If the ceiling ahead was unsafe her reflexes, and the Art of her wings, would give her a fair chance to get clear.

She slipped under the lintel, barely having to duck, and the darkness within flurried back from her. Elantris shuddered, re-membering his dream.

There was a long moment of silence, in which they could see the light within waxing and waning as Olisse moved about. Then:

"Chief, you'd better get in here," came the Fly's hushed voice.

"We're all coming in," Gracer decided.

"Chief—" Elantris heard the Fly say, but Gracer was already hunkering down to duck through the doorway, and Hastella was right on his heels.

"Founder's Mark!" Gracer swore, his voice almost reverent. The other scholars were staring at Elantris, plainly expecting him to be next after his mistress. With no other choice, he scrabbled into the next chamber.

It was carpeted with bones. The chamber was wide and deep – deeper than the lantern would reveal, and everywhere was a chaos of ancient skeletons, heaped and strewn and utterly inter-mingled. Some were plainly human, whilst others – larger, heavier, stranger - must be the remains of more monsters, so that Elantris wondered if this had been some den of theirs, and these multitudes their victims back in the dawn of time.

We are well rid of such horrors.

Olisse was hovering overhead with the lantern, unwilling to touch down. Hastella was impassive, but Gracer regarded the ossuary with wide eyes.

"I never saw anything like this," he murmured.

By now Elantris had seen that, like the statues, one thing was missing. There were no skulls in all that chaos of jumbled bone, neither human nor other.

"How far back does this go?" Gracer was asking, and Olisse glided forwards, thrusting the lamp out, then letting out a startled curse. She had found an end to the slew of bones, and it was marked by a pile of skulls that reached close to the ceiling. The lamplight touched on the sockets of men and of fiends, the bared teeth of both united in decapitation and death.

What came here and did such a thing? Elantris wondered. The contrast between the orderly burial of the guardians without and the mound of trophies within was jarring, and as much as he tried to convince himself that this could just be the respect that some ancient culture accorded its honoured dead, he could not make himself believe it.

"Well, obviously it's going to take a lot of study, to sort this out," muttered Gracer, the master of understatement. "It could have been … a number of things."

A massacre, say it, Elantris challenged the man silently. *A massacre of men. A massacre of monsters.*

The Fly came down gingerly beside that great monument of skulls that towered over her. Some of the inhuman relics there had fanged jaws great enough to seize her entire body.

Elantris thought he saw it in the lantern-light then, even as Hastella was turning to go. Beyond that mound of grisly prizes, against the back of the cave wall: more skeletons, human skeletons, still intact and huddled together, and all of them as small as a Fly-kinden. Or a child.

Then his mistress was heading back for the surface, and he was hurrying after her, out into the gathering dusk.

She would not talk to him all evening, nor to Gracer; just sat in her tent and, perhaps, tried to come to terms with what she had seen. The scholars were uncertain what this meant. Gracer dragged Elantris off to their fire and plied him with questions he could not answer, angling for some insight into Hastella's mind. Elantris drank their wine and bore their inquisition because it kept him from sleep.

Even after the scholars had turned in, cramming themselves into their threadbare little tents, he loitered on, in the steadily deepening cold, staring at the canvas that hid that fatal doorway, mute witness to an atrocity ten thousand years old.

At the last, it was either drop on the chill sands or haul himself to his curtained-off corner of tent. When he had finally opted for the latter he found Hastella still awake, staring at him as he entered. He could never read her eyes, even at the best of times. These were not the best of times.

In his dream the darkness was receding like a tide, leaving only bones in its wake. The monsters were all dead now, and so were the men who had stood by them. In his dream he watched each of their skeletons hauled up, clothed briefly in flesh in the moment that the blade came down, in the moment that the scissoring mandibles cut, then the head was free and the body was left where it fell. He was in amongst the darkness. The weight in his hands was the great head of a monster torn from its body by savage pincers, its mighty jaws gaping impotently, teeth helpless in the face of history. He placed it with the others, on that gathering pile, and did his best not to look beyond.

In his dream he retreated down that hall and smashed the statues one by one, taking from those carven human shoulders the heads of monsters, the gods of a vanished people.

In his dream, he moved the stones to wall in that doorway in the cliff, blocking up his ears to the shrill cries of those they had left alive within. In his dream it was necessary. He had cast his lot, given his allegiance, and that made them his enemies in a war that only utter extermination could bring to a close.

In his dream he buried his comrades and their beasts, those who had fallen in bringing this final conclusion to an ancient rivalry. He heaped earth on the shattered wing cases of beetles, the broken legs of spiders, the serrated mouthparts, the snapped antennae of those who had brought survival and victory to his ancestors.

He started from his vision to hear Hastella re-entering the tent, wondering blearily what she could have been doing. Had she been into the dig site again? Had she stood, staring mesmerised at that great trove of the fallen and the dismembered? Had she pieced together some story in her head to account for it all, and would that story resemble his dream?

She was a hard woman, honed like a knife by the politics of the Spiderlands, where to be weak was to fall, where emotion was leashed and used, and ran free only behind closed doors. Had she been shedding tears over that host of the unknowable dead? Had she been drinking in the tragedy of ages?

He thought not. A humble secretary he, but he knew her too well.

In the first grey of pre-dawn she had orders for Gracer. "I want all your team working double time in the new chamber," she told him. "I want a catalogue of everything you've found. This is the greatest historical discovery of our age, Master Gracer. You have two days to conduct an overview and provide me with a report I can take back with me."

Was it academic prestige or financial reward that glittered in the eyes of Fordyce Gracer? In any event he had his complement on the move before the sun cleared the horizon, filing into that darkness with their tools and their sketchboards and their lanterns, eagerly tossing theories back and forth.

Hastella watched them go with a proprietary air, standing under the canvas of the tent that shadowed the doorway. "Elantris," she said, when the last of them had gone in, "pack my possessions. We leave shortly."

He glanced at her, then at the gaping socket of the opening. "Mistress?"

Her expression did not invite further inquiry.

As he stepped out into the sun he saw that the camp had visitors.

A couple of the scholars had stayed at the fire, preparing food. They were dead – and soundlessly – before Elantris came out, and the newcomers were already heading his way. They were

Scorpion-kinden, almost a score of them: huge, pale men and women in piecemeal armour, bearing spears and long-hafted axes, and with curving claws arching over their forefingers and thumbs. With them were a handful of their beasts, scuttling purposefully beside them, slung low to the ground beneath over-arching stingers and raised claws, each held in tight control by a leash of Art.

The brigands from Dust Port! Elantris thought, stumbling back into the tent. "Mistress!" he got out.

"I gave you an instruction," she snapped at him. "Go to it."

The light went almost entirely as a bulky figure shouldered in behind him, a Scorpion-kinden man fully seven feet tall. His eyes sought out Hastella.

"Go about your work," she said quietly. For a moment Elantris thought she meant him, but the Scorpion was loping past them both, heading for that shadowed entrance, and his men and his animals were on his heels.

"I don't understand," Elantris heard himself say.

"I think you do," Hastella said softly. "I think you have seen something of the past here, what was done of necessity by those who came before us. We are the Kinden, Elantris. We are the inheritors of the world, and that is the order of things. There is no sense confusing the academics with what might have been, or confounding them with what price we might have paid to ensure our survival. Such knowledge is not to be showered on the common herd."

"You knew…" Elantris whispered.

"Of course. Do you think this is the first such site? But such study is best undertaken covertly. Where men like Gracer are involved, there is only one way to guarantee secrecy."

There was a cry of alarm from within the cave, and then the screaming began. Elantris was trembling, staring into the beautiful, composed face of his mistress. She smiled slowly.

"I should have them kill you as well, I suppose, but you are a useful little tool, and I think I am fond of you. Now go and pack my bags, I'll have the mercenaries strike our tent."

He did so, numbly and, when he returned, the Scorpions were standing around Hastella respectfully – all so much bigger than she, and yet she dwarfed them with her presence and her Art, always the centre of her own web.

"I will send those I trust to further examine the site," she explained. "For now, block up this door. Let us seal away the monsters once again."

Too late, Elantris thought, watching them all, reliving the moments of his dream. *We are already outside.*

IF STREET

James Brogden

I NEVER THOUGHT it would be this boring, waiting to become a ghost.

The last few stragglers are leaving now, and soon there'll be nothing up here with me except rabbits and the wind. For a while, at least. If this were summer I'd have a problem. For a start, it wouldn't be getting dark much before ten, and even then there'd still be a handful of annoying teenagers come up from the sink estates of Telford determined to get shitfaced and shag each other in the overgrown hut circles. There's probably something poetically poignant about the idea of the youngest generation coupling on the same hearths as their Iron Age ancestors.

But it's winter, and the dark and the cold are coming on fast. I've got my thermos and my down-filled gilet and I wonder what the Cornovii will make of all my modern twenty-first century technology. They'll probably laugh their socks off. If they have socks.

Wind chill is a factor up here. The Wrekin is a good three hundred meters above the Shropshire plain, a stubborn hummock of volcanic rock overlooking what millions of years ago would have been a tropical lagoon. It stands apart from the other local clusters of hills like the Long Mynd, the Stiperstones, and folded-blanket ridge of Wenlock Edge. All of these features have disappeared into the deepening gloom leaving the lights of towns glowing in big orange splodges all over the landscape like the radioactive scars of a thermonuclear war. So many people, crowded so close together. It's no wonder we've all gone insane.

I can easily understand why the Cornovii built a hill-fort up here – apart from anything else, the strategic value of its position would have been enormous, and for precisely the same reason I can see why the Romans would have wanted to burn it. Their own city of Viroconium is down there somewhere, its grid pattern under the fields, all lines and squares and ruthlessly militarised efficiency. But I try not to think ill of the Romans. After all, they saved my friend Paul's life – if not his soul.

THERE ARE NO friendships quite like the ones you make when you're thirteen, and I'm certain that the way me and Paul Felton knocked around together confused the hell out of our parents and teachers. I was bookish, nerdish, and about as sporty as a draught excluder. He was on the football team as often as he was in detention, driven by an inexhaustible anger at everyone and everything. His dad had died in the Falklands and his mum's new boyfriend was a shit, but that was all I knew. Yes, I said we were friends, but there are things that thirteen-year old boys just don't talk about. What drew us together were two things: *Doctor Who*, and the old Roman road which ran through the park behind his house.

I say 'park': Sutton Park was, and I suppose still is, nearly two and a half thousand acres of municipal recreation space for cyclers, joggers, and horse-riders. It has seven lakes, ancient woodlands which haven't been touched since the Middle Ages, and it preserves a one-and-a-half mile stretch of Roman road called Icknield Street, which everywhere else is buried beneath concrete and tarmac, but in Sutton Park is hidden only beneath a thin skin of topsoil and grass. You could scratch away a few inches of dirt and stand on the same road that – with a bit of boyish imaginative license – carried legionnaires from the coasts of the Mediterranean up north to do battle with the marauding hordes of Pictish barbarians.

It fascinated us utterly. Paul and I had a pretty decent arrangement: he came around to mine to watch any episodes of *Doctor Who* that he might have missed due to things kicking off at home, and which I taped obsessively on our new VCR, in return for which I gained a certain amount of street cred for being friends with the school bad boy. We had a plan to save up our pocket money and buy a metal detector, absolutely confident that we'd find bits of armour, or gold coins or – best of all – rusted bits of weaponry lodged in old bone. But since Paul never got any money except the change he nicked when his mum sent him out for fags, and I was incapable of walking past a videogames arcade or a second-hand bookshop without spending every penny I had, it was slow going.

I think Paul must have finally lost patience with the plan, because late one evening he turned up at my place in a state of high excitement, covered in dirt and clutching something wrapped in a plastic carrier bag.

Mum opened the door to his knocking. "Paul? It's very late, dear. Is everything…"

"Hi, Mrs Cooper!" He grinned, launching straight past her and upstairs to my room.

"Paul! Shoes!"

"Yeah I know! Brilliant, isn't it?"

I don't suppose she bothered to spare a moment's thought trying to work out what he meant by that, since teenage boys plainly occupied a parallel universe only marginally connected to the real world; just so long as she reminded herself to make me clear up the mud he left behind. Which she did. Rule number one in the Cooper household: Your Guest, Your Mess.

He barged in without knocking. I was in the middle of making an Airfix model of an X-wing, which was only slightly less embarrassing than some of the other things he could have caught me doing.

"Check this out!" he said, and tossed the carrier bag onto my desk.

"Yeah, hi, I'm fine thanks, how are you?" I scowled, and opened it dubiously. Paul's finds were generally dangerous, often pornographic, occasionally illegal – and seldom safe to handle carelessly with bare hands. "It's a shoe," I observed, unimpressed.

To be precise it was a sandal, made of leather, a bit like the kind worn by our religious ed. teacher, Mr Holy-Molyneux.

"It's a Roman shoe," he corrected.

"Are you shitting me?" Instantly this had become a million times cooler.

"I shit you not. It is a Roman legionnaire's *caliga*. I found it on the Street." He didn't have to explain which Street.

"But it looks like new." I turned it over in my hands. I was no archaeologist – wasn't interested in any dates in history which had an AD after them – but I'd sort of expected leather which had been buried for two thousand years to be stiff and hard, or else disintegrating. This was neither. It was supple and shiny and – I gave it a sniff – yes, still stinky with Roman foot-sweat. Which, of course, it couldn't be.

"Bollocks," was my considered opinion, and threw it back at him. "This is a wind-up. Either you got this from a charity shop or you've been out mugging hippies."

"It is not bollocks! It's from a real, genuine Roman foot-soldier. He was marching along, part of it snapped – see that bit there? So he chucked it away and put on a spare."

"How can you possibly know that?"

Paul's eyes, usually dark and troubled, were on this occasion shining. "Because I saw him."

SUCH AN OUTRAGEOUS claim demanded testing, and an opportunity to completely take the piss out of him it couldn't be refused because, obviously, there was no way it could be true. So it surprised me how readily he agreed that we should take a look out on Icknield Street the following night. It had to be at night, he said, not because they were ghosts – and he punched me so hard on the arm when I made a few harmless *woo-oo* noises that the bruise lasted for a week – but because something about other people being around caused interference. It did occur to me that he might have taken the latest episode of *Earthshock* a bit too seriously, but I didn't fancy another bruise so I kept my mouth shut. That, plus, as I say, the piss-take potential.

We found ourselves sitting in a large bush in the freezing cold on a March night, munching sweets and jumping like idiots at every sound. Paul had chosen a part of Sutton Park as far away from any lights as he could get – not that there were many. From our hiding place the remains of the Icknield Street *agger* was a flat, black ribbon seemingly hovering above the ground, while the trees around us were dim rustling shadows against a sky the colour of orange charcoal. We saw several rabbits, something which might have been a fox, and shrank in terror at the approach of two human shapes, only to be disappointed when they stopped to kiss.

"Close-knit unit, are they?" I whispered at him, for which I earned another dead arm. "Right, sod it," I said. "I'm off."

"You can't go yet!" he protested.

I glared at him but I think the effect was lost in the dark. "I am not spending the night sitting in the middle of a bush watching people snog!" I hissed back at him. "It's pervy! Plus you keep hitting me!"

"Well you keep being a wanker, so sit down and shut up."

I did as I was told, and we resumed our voyeuristic vigil.

When we finally heard the legion, it was a bit like when you go scanning through the airwaves on an old radio and you pick up the faint thread of human speech but it's gone before you can be sure you've even heard it, so you crawl back slowly with the tuning dial listening for coherence to emerge out of the crackle and hiss which is the background noise of the universe. Not that I suppose anyone these days knows what a radio is, let alone a tuning dial. Nevertheless, out of the rustling of wind and foliage emerged a faint rhythmic noise. Unsustained at first, only a random-sounding *one-and-two-and*, just enough to set my heart racing so hard that I was afraid I was hearing that and nothing else. Then came *a-three-and-a-four-and-a*, and while I was straining to hear more I realised that it had resolved clearly into the unmistakable sound of many dozens of footfalls. Marching.

Marching towards us.

I clutched Paul. "What do we do?"

"Shut up!" He forced me back down with his elbows in the small of my back. "Lie still. Watch. Do not make A. Single. Fucking. Sound."

I did exactly that. The noise grew louder, came abreast of us, and resolved into a dozen other combined sounds: the creak of straps, the harshness of laboured breathing, muttered comments from one man to another, the heavy flap of their armour and the hollow clank of their gear. And the smell! A wide mantle of leather, sweat, wool, iron, piss, and spices swept after them, thick enough to insulate them from the cold on its own. If they were ghosts, then they were the most solid ghosts I had ever imagined.

I could see nothing more of them than a bristling mass in the gloom. The tips of their javelins reflected dully the same burnt-orange colour of the city sky, and I knew then without a shadow of a doubt that they were real. If their weapons reflected the light of *our* sky then they were in *our* world; they weren't ghosts or illusions. The only other plausible explanation was that they were the result of too little sleep, too many sweets, and too much *Doctor Who*, but I ask you, what thirteen-year old boy is going to side with plausibility over a park full of Roman legionnaires?

Paul and I managed to keep our cool until the last of them had disappeared into the greater darkness, and then we just lost it completely – whooping and yelling with excitement and jumping around madly so much that the locals in the houses bordering the park's edge could have been forgiven for thinking that an actual battle was being fought there. Then we made our separate ways home. Each of us got a bollocking from our folks, but it didn't make any difference; Paul was used to it and I was too wired to care.

It certainly didn't stop us from going back the following night. And the next.

"HOW DO YOU think they got here?" I whispered to Paul, as I peered out from our customary hiding place. "Where do they go to?"

We were watching a group of half a dozen of them standing around a flaming brazier, cooking pieces of unidentified small mammal on sharp sticks and generally slobbing about in a way which we imagined was little different to soldiers of any time. A few others were off to one side, gambling with a pair of dice.

"*From* is hard to say," he replied. "They look like local auxiliaries, from their face tattoos. Probably Dobunni. They were a pretty Rome-friendly lot, generally. *To* is easier. They'll be off up to the garrison at Viroconium to help keep the Welsh tribes from beating the crap out of each other. Or they could be really unlucky and get sent up to Hadrian's Wall to stop the Scots from beating the crap out of everybody else."

It was incredible how much research he'd done off his own back. Our history teacher, Mr Perry, wouldn't have believed it. In fact, to use an obscenity fashionable at the time, old Pezza would have shit kittens if he'd known exactly how well-educated Paul was making himself.

But there was the thing: I was focussed on the mechanism of how their very existence in the park could be; they could have been Mayans or Daleks for all I cared, but Paul just bypassed those questions completely, accepted the mystery for what it was and ploughed headlong into it. I still can't make up my mind whether this was due to him having too much imagination or too little – either way, at the time I almost envied him his single-mindedness. I had too many real-world distractions to keep me grounded: school, Dad just having been made redundant, and even a cautiously burgeoning interest in Samantha Corey from the Third Form Once the initial dazzle of Icknield Street's magic had faded, my mind needed to find some way of fitting its oddness with those other pieces of the whole puzzle for my place in the world to start making sense.

Take those soldiers chatting in the firelight, for example. Even though they were the only ones we could see, no way were they the only ones there. From their perspective the whole area must have been dotted with similar groups standing around similar fires. We knew this because every so often figures would come into view as they crossed the road, only to disappear on the other side like moths flying through a beam of torchlight. It was clear that something about the road was making them real; some interaction between its incredible age and our adolescent imaginations. Probably. Looking back on it now, I think it might have been fuelled by Paul's burning desire to escape his world whatever the cost.

"Heads up," he pointed. "Centurion's not happy."

Below us the soldiers' commanding officer was berating them. Apparently, bivvying in the middle of the road itself was a Very Bad Thing, because he was ordering them to move using the sort of profanity that you didn't need an O-level in Latin to understand.

We watched them hurriedly gather their things together and disappear off to one side, and then Paul scared the hell out of me by breaking cover and scurrying towards where they'd been standing.

I was aghast. "What are you *doing*?"

He paused long enough to grin back over his shoulder. "Salvage!"

"But what if they catch you?"

He ignored me and crept closer.

Over the last few nights we'd managed to collect a few scraps and bits of rubbish left behind when the soldiers had gone, and just as with the shoe he'd first shown me, they remained in pretty good condition – although we discovered that the longer we waited before picking anything up, the quicker it succumbed to the accumulated weight of time. If we left it as late as the next morning, there was generally nothing left but what an archaeologist would have to dig up with a trowel. Plainly, Paul had decided he wanted something as fresh as possible.

I watched, terrified and unable to breathe, while he crept up onto the slight rise of the *agger* and swept his hands to and fro in the dark across the ground where the soldiers had been shooting the Roman equivalent of craps just a few minutes before. He obviously couldn't see too well; he kept stopping, picking up small bits of whatever, feeling them and then chucking them away. Every molecule of my trapped breath wanted to scream at him to just get *out* of there, and then he waved something aloft triumphantly and came running back in a low crouch.

"Jackpot!" he announced, and fell into our bush laughing.

He'd found some coins. Three small, thin brass *sestertes*, missed as the soldiers had scraped together their belongings. He gave me one as payment for being lookout, he said, though I'd done nothing except kack myself – and kept the other two for himself, saying that he was going to find an expert who would tell him how much he could sell them for.

He didn't turn up to school the next day, or for several days after that. At the time I thought nothing of it, since his record for skiving was legendary, but when we next met at Icknield Street and I saw the state of him I knew that his disappearance had been down to something much less pleasant than playing hookey.

Both of his eyes were blackened and his lower lip was swollen and split open. He stood, wearing an oversized khaki jacket which he claimed to have belonged to his dead father but which I suspect came from an army surplus store, with his arms wrapped tightly about himself in a way that suggested physical pain.

"Jesus!" I said. "What happened to you?"

He took a while to answer. He'd never talked about his home life before but I think deep down he knew we wouldn't be seeing each other again, and for the first time in his life he opened to me, or possibly anyone.

"Brian," he spat. "Mum's boyfriend. Fucking prick. You know I said I was going to find someone who could value those coins for us? Well I asked Mum, which was stupid."

"Why?"

"Because she asked him, didn't she? Like, she couldn't tell that it was supposed to be just me-and-her business. So he finds out and he comes and accuses me of nicking them, doesn't he? I said where was I supposed to have nicked them from – a museum? Did I look like a bloody cat burglar? That got me this." He pointed to one of his black eyes. "I said I dug them out of the ground, dint I, and he said well you don't look much like fucking Indiana Jones either, and he gave me the other one." His voice was thick and tight, as if he was trying to choke back anger, or tears, or both. I didn't know what to say. What response could I have made which wouldn't have sounded pathetically in-adequate? Understand: there was no such thing as child-protection when we were kids. No ChildLine that you could call. If you went to the police with this sort of shit you were more likely to get a clip round the ear for wasting their time and taken straight back home where the pigs would nod understandingly about what an awkward troublemaking little sod you were, before leaving you to get a worse hiding than before.

No. There was nothing I could do. There was nothing Paul expected me to do, except one thing. He needed me on look-out one last time.

WE LURKED AROUND the park until nightfall before finding our customary bush and settling in to wait for the legion. It was raining, and our mood with each other was sour and tetchy.

"I don't see what good this will do," I whispered to him. "What's it going to prove? He'll still think you're a thief and a liar."

"Fuck what he thinks," Paul replied, with such cold and understated fury that it chilled my blood. "It's not about that. I just need a thing, that's all."

"What thing?"

But he refused to say.

This time when the legion marched past, with their armour

glistening in the rain like the carapaces of beetles, a portion of the steeply banked *agger* crumbled away to the side, causing half a dozen soldiers to stumble sideways, cursing, and a lot of ill-natured jostling as the men behind tried to sidestep around the sudden pothole and shoved into their mates. Orders were shouted, the chaos resolved itself, and when the men had passed a small detail of engineers were left behind with two guards to effect a temporary repair. Working by the light of a single lantern, they set to with shovels and poles, ramming hardcore back into the hole while the guards watched them in that attitude of surly boredom which we'd come to find familiar. They'd dumped their packs and weapons in a heap at the side of the road while they huddled against the rain in their woollen cloaks, and from the way I felt Paul stiffen next to me I knew without having to be told what he was after.

"No!" I ordered, far more assertively than I'd ever dared say anything to him. "Paul, just no. This is insane."

"A sword. A *pilum*. I don't care. Whatever's nearest. I'll wave it in Brian's fat fucking face and see how he likes it." Rain and the moving shadows of foliage played across his face, making it look like things were squirming under his skin. "I might see if he likes how it feels, too," he added in a dark whisper.

Before I could make a move to stop him, he'd gone.

Full credit to his sneakery: even I could barely see him, and I knew he was there. The dark clothes in which he was dressed must have been chosen deliberately for this, and all that I could make out was the pale blur of his face low to the ground as he crept like Gollum towards the silhouettes of the soldiers.

Still, he could never have hoped to pull it off. It's impossible for me even now, as a grown man – and especially a civilian – to understand the kinds of instincts which seasoned soldiers develop to keep themselves alive. Something in the animal hindbrain must wake up. Something which can detect the scent or air displacement of another human body, or the subtle change in the timbre of the sound of rain as it falls around a person. I don't know what made that soldier turn around and look straight at Paul just as he was reaching for the nearest pack. Maybe it was just dumb bad luck.

Paul froze, the worst possible thing he could have done, because the legionnaire didn't. Freezing in surprise can kill a man – or a boy. The legionnaire gave a cry of alarm and darted forward, grabbing Paul by his outstretched arm.

Don't ask why it suddenly occurred to me that this was a clever thing to do, but at this point I decided that I needed to rescue my friend, so I leapt out of hiding and ran yelling for the scene, just as the other Romans were turning in surprise. I managed to grab Paul's ankle as the legionnaire was pulling him up onto the *agger*, and for a moment my friend was caught in a bizarre tug-of-war between us.

The soldier's eyes locked with mine. I saw that they were brown, wide with bafflement at seeing me, and the sudden shock of his awareness communicated itself like electricity through Paul's body. What had those eyes witnessed – what scenes of an ancient world two thousand years lost to me and now just green mounds in the grass, but to him an everyday walking, talking reality? I was within touching distance of a mystery which felt like it might throw open the vaults of my soul, or destroy me utterly. The only time I've ever felt anything close to that was the first time I had sex – and here, now, sitting on top of the Wrekin, waiting for the Cornovii to arrive.

Then, with a sudden savage tug, Paul was gone, grabbed in a vicious headlock and rammed full body into the mud of the road, screaming my name.

One of the other soldiers had snatched up a *pilum* from the bundle of packs and had his arm cocked towards me. I watched rain drip from the weapon's pyramidal iron point, fascinated.

"Gaz, help me!" screamed Paul, though his mouth was muffled by the ground. "Help me! For God's sake, *please!*"

I mean come on – what did he expect me to do? Really?

I ran.

Just not quite fast enough.

At first I thought I'd tripped over something in the dark, because I pitched forward suddenly and nearly went headlong. Then I thought I must have snagged my foot on a root or a plastic bag or something, because my right leg was fighting some heavy resistance. A second later, when the pain began to burn in the back of my thigh, I figured it was a cramp. It wasn't until I reached back and felt the metal javelin-head hanging out of my flesh and its wooden shaft dragging along the ground behind me like an obscene tail that I realised what had happened.

In retrospect I was incredibly lucky. If that legionnaire hadn't been snap-throwing hastily, in the dark and the rain, the *pilum* would at the very least have skewered my leg completely, if not hit me in the torso and killed me outright. As it was, I was able to yank it out in panic and stumble a few more yards until shock dropped me like a sack of bricks. From that position, all I could do was watch numbly as the soldier who had hit me drew a short sword and stepped off the road towards me to finish the job.

He actually made it several yards past the road's ditch – further than we'd ever seen any of them come – before he stopped, looking around in puzzlement. I thought that maybe he'd come far enough to see something of our world: streetlights, perhaps, or maybe just the orange glow of the city sky, and wondered what great conflagration awaited him and his company beyond the night-time horizon. Then his face creased in pain and he screamed. Thankfully, darkness hid from my sight the full horror of what happened to him next, as two thousand years of cheated time fell on him in a few seconds, but for a moment I saw the agonised confusion of a young man who suddenly found himself to be a sallow and withered geriatric, before the flesh turned cadaverous and rotted from bones which themselves crumbled to powder. The leather bindings of his armour dissolved, its pieces blooming with rust even as they fell, and where they landed the ground swallowed them as if he had never existed at all.

A MONTH AFTER my grounding for having been idiotic enough to go climbing trees in the dark and falling onto some spiked railings, as my story went, I returned in broad, safe daylight with a trowel and a dug around the area where I thought I'd been hit – to prove to myself that it had really happened – as if the scar and the limp weren't enough; but I never found anything.

IT WAS AROUND ten years later, when I was in the final year of a postgrad course, that I came home to my bedsit one afternoon to find the door smashed open.

Worried that the burglar might still be inside, I edged in cautiously, but needn't have bothered; he'd probably heard me the moment I'd come through the front door two floors below.

"Gaz, mate, don't be afraid, it's me, Paul," called a gruff voice.

I found him sprawled at the table in my little galley kitchen, with the fridge door wide open and most of its contents on the way towards disappearing into his stomach. On the floor under the table was a large knapsack and a pair of hunting spears, and I saw an army-issue *gladius* at his side. He looked like life had been treating him harshly, and that he was thriving on it. He was huge enough to begin with, but his size was exaggerated by layers of leather, animal skins, and coarsely-woven fabric. The smell which came from him prowled the room like a beast. It was campfire smoke and the mud of long moorland marches with hard fighting at the end; it was ocean salt and tar and the perfume of sailors' whores; it was everything in between, a lifetime of adventuring. But his hair was neatly cropped and he was clean-shaven in the Roman style; and from his tanned and scarred face gleamed the bright blue eyes of my childhood friend. The boy who had loved *Doctor Who* and hated geography lessons.

"How did you find me?" I asked.

"Your mum's still in the old place," he replied. His voice was thickly accented; still Brummy but in a way I'd never heard before. "I was sorry to hear about your father."

I shook that one aside for a much more important question. "Where have you *been*?"

"Everywhere!" he laughed. "The road goes everywhere, old friend, and it took me with it. I joined up, can you believe that? I enlisted! They didn't want me at first, but I made myself useful, learned the language, learned how to look after their horses and their weapons." He laughed again. "Can you imagine the look on old Perry's face if he knew my Latin was now better than his?"

He chuckled at the thought and then subsided into a brooding silence. I didn't know what he was expecting of me. We were so alien to each other, it seemed impossible that there was anything we could chat about. The weather? Football? There was, in fact, only one meaningful thing I could say to him.

"Paul, the day you … left, I'm sorry I couldn't…"

"None of that," he cut me off. "Just don't. There was nothing you could have done. Leave it."

"So are you back then? For good, I mean?"

"Gods, no. This place is diseased. I've seen it a few times, passing by – you'd be surprised at now many thin places there are in the skin of the world, by the way – but I've never been tempted."

"Then why?"

"I've got my papers. The Empire's pulling out of this island and things are going to get nasty in the next few years, so I'm off up into Wales to find myself a nice strong place with some land and a few people I can trust. I came to see if you wanted to be one of them."

It was my turn to laugh. "Me? I'd be bugger all use as a farmer and even worse as a fighter."

Paul leaned forward, his face eager. "Oh, but you *know* things. There are always going to be strong arms; what we're going to be missing is strong heads. You were always the clever one. You can give us knowledge, make us stronger, help us survive what's coming. What do you say?"

"I don't know…"

"Because what can you do in this place?" He gestured around my bedsit in evident contempt. "What good can you do here except fill another desk and pay more tax until they let you die, another grey old man in a grey old country? Come to mine! It's green, and red with blood, and alive!" He slammed the table, making everything jump, including me. There was fire in his eyes, and what I had at first taken to be the warmth of friendship I saw now was the shine of battle. I was nothing more to him than an asset to be seized, a resource to be plundered like the contents of my fridge, and I felt genuine fear that his politeness had been just for old times' sake – he would simply refuse to take *no* for an answer and drag me off to his feral time, or else slay me where I stood for my defiance. I think he saw that in my expression – some reflection of what he had become staring back at him, because he subsided with a rueful chuckle.

"Ah well," he said. "I had to try. Can't blame a man for asking." He stood, gathered his things together, and paused at the door. "Have a good life, Gareth. Try not to regret too much."

Paul left, and I never saw him again.

UP HERE ON the Wrekin it's now completely deserted. For the moment. Every now and then I fancy I can hear a snatch of singing or child's laughter, and that is most definitely peat smoke I can smell.

Paul might not have persuaded me to spend my future in his past, but he did inadvertently set my life on the road which it has followed for the past forty years. What he said about the number of thin places in the skin of the world was quite true. I know: I've spent my life investigating them – everything from Mayan pyramids and the Nazca lines to stone circles, primeval forest glades, and even remnants of the old Birmingham back-to-backs which most people think have all been demolished – but the more of these ancient mysteries I've seen, the less I've been able to solve the greatest and most ancient of them all. The one called simply 'if'.

If I hadn't taken that job.

If I'd married that woman.

If I'd only chosen the road.

I look down from this ancient height to the Shropshire plain sprawled with the lights of towns and villages which one day will be nothing more than green mounds in the grass, but which at the moment are full of people enjoying the bright now of their lives and ignoring the wide darkness of time surrounding them on all sides, and I recall the look of terror on that Roman soldier's face as he found himself in an alien time, and I wonder how often that same look has been on my own face in recent years. And here they are come to meet me, out of the warm-orange doorways set below thatched conical roofs, with gold gleaming about their throats and smiles on their faces and songs in the voices. The Cornovii have come for me, and I am home.

PASSAGE

Shannon Connor Winward

SHE REMOVED THE first stone herself. She found it by touch, prodding with numb fingers until she fastened on one that would betray the others. Three and three and three more tumbled to the ground, their dull clacking thunderous as the crowd of people behind her held their breath.

Then there were hands beside hers, her brothers pulling down the stones, breaking through with their iron picks, shoving her aside when she stumbled.

She waited by the torches, swaying on her feet as more people came forward, hands crawling and sweeping until the last of the wall was pulled away and the mouth of the tomb lay open.

Someone whispered in her ear.

"Danu," it said, and something more, but the words were dissolving. Hands came to her throat, unfastened the pin she wore there. Her layers of warmth fell away. They took her shoes, her gown. They let her hair spill down her back in loose coils. She stood with arms outstretched, held in place as hands exposed her to the winter air.

She was so heavy. The drug they had dosed her with had begun to crystallize under her skin. If they let go of her she would fall, but they did not let go. They lodged themselves beneath her – mother, sister, friend. They took her shivering.

They moved her forward, bare feet dragging on the ground. She was clad only in her rings and torcs and the lightest dun shift, but she no longer felt cold.

Eoichaid did not look at her as he walked to the front of the gathering. The priest paused between the lintels of the entrance and etched sigils in the air, then passed into the tomb without a light. She watched the hem of his robe disappear into the black arch of space.

Danu leaned against her mother's shoulder. In the old man's absence, people dared to cough, whisper, shift their feet. Danu heard them, full of impatience and fear and something else. She rolled her eyes in all directions, but every face turned away from her. One in particular was missing – maybe watching, but not here where she could see him, not in front. Still, she looked for him until her vision grew blurred.

One of the women that held her shifted and stifled a complaint. As she moved, Danu's right foot turned out at an awkward angle. To Danu it looked alien, not her own flesh. Her head sank onto her chest, too heavy now to hold itself erect.

Danu heard her mother's ragged sigh, somewhere near her ear.

All at once, the ground below Danu's foot began to bubble and writhe. The earth peeled away like skin from bone and a large serpent emerged, a shiver of silver and black that curled into a fist of scales beneath her heel.

Danu felt – but did not feel – the gentle flicker of the serpent's tongue on the underside of her foot. She tried to raise her head to ask if the others saw it, but she had no strength. The serpent's head lifted instead, gliding over her foot and around her ankle, slowly inching its way higher and higher into her very core.

She felt the assembly draw close around her, though they had not moved. The priest returned from the tomb and had begun to call out to the people, and to the spirits of this place.

"Accept this … her crime … the right of kings…" The words fell like meaningless stones in Danu's ears, but she knew them all the same, for the serpent of the land was inside her, listening.

The serpent coiled in tight knots around her spine, moulding to her joints and limbs. Danu lifted her head, eyes of blue fire levelled on the priest as he threw hands to the sky, as he spread his arms in supplication to the mound and the hill and the valley.

The strength in his voice comforted the others on this dark, cold night, this turning point of the year when men believed they could harness power – but he could not fool her.

To Danu, the priest revealed his secret fear.

"Interloper," the serpent whispered from Danu's frozen mouth. Danu's mother went rigid, digging her fingers deep into Danu's arm. It would have pained her, if the flesh had still been her own.

Oblivious, Eoichaid gestured and called.

Three men – her brothers and, there, one other – separated from the assembly and moved towards her, to take her from the women.

They drew away her mother last. She plucked at Danu's wool shift. She smacked away their grip. She held Danu's cheeks until one of the men uttered gruff words – a plea, an oath. Mother tore something from her bosom and tied it around Danu's neck, then stepped back into the crowd.

Danu could not turn to look after her, nor could she feel the hands of the men that bore her, but her mother's pendant lay heavy and warm against her breast.

They stopped before the priest, at the mouth of the tomb. Eoichaid's small grey eyes shied away from hers, focusing on the line of her mouth instead. He forced her lips apart and placed a quartz stone under her tongue. He covered her mouth and nose with his wizened hand. He whispered, breath rank with mead, "For the people." His other hand swept across her with a sudden jerk, and Danu's throat opened.

As she bled, the serpent inside her loosened its coils. It slithered through the mouth of her wound, down her body, and back into the ground.

Her heart roared. Somewhere, she heard her mother's answer, keening.

Danu's body went limp. The men let her sink to the ground at Eoichaid's feet. One of her brothers swiped his hand across his mouth, concealing an unmanly sound. They laid her on her back, her eyes full of stars slipping silently, guiltily, over the horizon.

With his sickle spent and dangling at his side, Eoichaid waited for her life to empty itself. It took a long time. The blood that seeped from her grew sluggish, lacklustre. Eoichaid gestured.

The priest went first, then *he*, who held aloft a torch. Danu's brothers lifted her body and, with it suspended between them, followed.

Danu's friends and sisters came next, bearing gifts – her mirror and combs, clay jars and bundles, a bronze beaker. Without a word, the funeral party inched forward into the barrow, and the crowd behind them breathed a collective sigh.

Danu walked at the rear of the procession as the men carried her body down the corridor of stone. The priest stared straight ahead and the others watched the ground, unwilling to see any more than they must in this place of the dead, but Danu saw how the torchlight brought the passage to life. Symbols danced in the stones, at her sides and overhead – spirals and ovals and a thousand suns. The passage was the night sky, reigned in and narrowed so that they could touch it, if only they had the courage to lift their heads.

Danu lifted her head, and Danu touched the sky. It was hot and cold beneath her fingertips, solid and fluid. She felt a dawn of understanding humming just within the stone, but it was more than she could bear. She withdrew her hand.

When the passage opened into the central chamber, they moved quickly. One of her brothers, the one holding her feet, tripped in his eagerness to be finished. The necklace bounced from Danu's breast and dangled in the air, twisting and glinting in torchlight.

Under the priest's guidance they arranged her body in a foetal position within a low niche, just to the right of the chamber entrance. Eoichaid himself tucked her arms beneath her breast and angled her chin towards the back of the cairn. Her eyes were still open, and he could now look into them, now forgiving, now admitting in his secret thoughts how unsure he really was. How desperate. *The Gods reveal their will to no one.*

She turned a blind eye to him. Eoichaid took his hands away, and it was done.

The man who held the torch stepped forward. Eoichaid began to bark angry words, but the man silenced him with a snarl and the raised tip of his sword. The old priest said nothing more.

The man put his weapon away and stooped beside Danu. Gingerly, he plucked her mother's pendant from where it had trailed in the dirt and placed in between Danu's sticky, folded fingers.

His touch lingered. *I'm sorry. Sorry. Sorry*, said his heart.

He backed away.

She followed them out from the main chamber, back down the passage. Though the cairn was open and light from the torches tickled the floor, the world beyond the mouth of the tomb was hidden from her, covered in a heavy grey mist. One by one they passed through it, and left her. None of them looked back. He did not look back. He was moving quickly now, eager to get out and into the business of forgetting.

At the portal's edge, she stopped and leaned her head into the mist, listening to the sounds of the assembly dispersing, people heading back down the hill. A few stayed behind – she heard low voices, and scraping. Then with a heavy thud the first stone was laid in place.

They worked steadily into the night, tamping in wet clods of earth to cover cracks, closing the door between the worlds. At last, the wall was finished, and the folk could go home, comforted now with the knowledge that Danu was within. Danu had been offered.

Danu would protect them.

Danu turned and moved back to the chamber.

When she got there, a small, dark, bearded man was waiting for her.

"Interloper," he growled.

Danu froze. There were others in the chamber, as well: an old woman hunched on the floor, squinting at her with a squirrel-like face; another man beside her, a cripple with a knotty oak staff. He regarded Danu with curiosity. And yet another watched, too – somewhere. A shy, formless presence, lurking, perhaps within the walls.

"Look how tall she is," the old woman declared with wonder. "Look at all that bright hair!"

The cripple leaned towards her. "What do they call you?"

"Daughter," Danu replied. Out of habit, she lifted her chin. "Daughter of the King."

"What king?" queried the old woman.

"This is your name?" the cripple pressed.

"No, it is my rank."

"Trespasser," hissed the bearded man. His brown little eyes leered at her, darkly.

"This is not your home," the old woman said.

It was an observation, not an accusation, but Danu bristled. "It is."

"No, it isn't."

"Criminal!" barked the bearded man.

"I am not!"

"What is that you've got there?" the cripple asked. With a few quick, twisting steps, he picked up the bronze beaker they had left beside her body and poked a finger in its contents. He brought the finger to his mouth and smiled. "She's got beer!" he said brightly.

"Has she got porridge?" the old woman asked.

"Has she got a weapon?" the first man snarled.

"She has jewellery," came a soft voice from the recesses of the mound.

The bearded man wiggled his dagger at the niche where Danu's body lay. "She's getting blood all over the floor."

The chamber fell silent as the trio turned to look. Eventually, the old woman broke the stillness with a loud *tsk* of disapproval.

"I–I'm sorry," Danu blurted.

The cripple looked at Danu, his features softened with pity. "Do you not have fire where you come from?"

"Barbarian," the bearded man mumbled.

"Such pretty, pretty trinkets," the old woman chimed, changing the subject.

The cripple dipped another finger into the beaker and tasted thoughtfully. "It's been a long time," he said, slowly, as if in epiphany. He turned to look at Danu. "It's been a long time since they brought us beer."

"I suppose it has," Danu replied.

"She doesn't belong here," the bearded man insisted. "She isn't one of us."

"But I *am*."

The bearded man ignored her. "She's one of them."

"One of who?" asked the old woman.

"One of *them,* the new ones. The big ones, from the ocean."

"But I was born here," Danu protested.

"They pronounce things wrong. They swear allegiance to whatever man carries the biggest sword and they can't even dispose of their dead properly."

Danu opened her mouth to argue but closed it again, realising what the bearded man said was not untrue.

"They're all murderers! The lot of them," Bearded Man went on. "When they run out of enemies to fight they slay their own. Look!" he gestured to the lump in the niche on the floor. "They even slay their women."

"I was chosen," Danu said softly.

"They slay their criminals for sport," he told them, jutting his chin and eyeing her knowingly. "They play foot-games with their heads."

"I was cleansed," she whispered.

The trio regarded her in heavy silence. After a long moment, the voice in the walls asked, "Are you a criminal?"

Danu turned to the wall. "I loved wrongly," was all she said.

The voice in the wall was still for a while, its thoughts reflected in three pairs of unblinking eyes around the room.

When the voice piped in again, it asked, "How can love be wrong?"

Danu fidgeted with the bands of gold around her arm. Again, she could not answer. She could not argue.

The old woman shook her head. "Poor girl," she said. "You don't belong here."

"I do," Danu answered. "They've given me to you."

The trio looked at her quizzically. "Given you?" the cripple repeated. "Whatever for?"

"For the good of the People. To make the rain come. To stop the crops from failing. To protect the herds and bring us victory at war."

The trio stared at her, all with wrinkled brows. Then the bearded man began to snicker. The old woman's mouth twitched at the corners. The cripple hid his face behind a healthy drought from the beaker.

From behind her head, Danu heard a muffled giggle.

The bearded man lowered himself to the floor and retrieved a pair of bones from a niche in the wall. "Idiots," he said, shaking his head. "Barbarians. Every last one of them." He began rubbing one bone against the other – slowly, methodically, as if he meant to sharpen them – or grind them into dust.

Danu felt a soft hand upon her arm. She looked down – far down – at the tiny old woman, who had shuffled over to her side.

"I suppose you might as well come sit with us, then," the woman said. She glanced at the body on the floor with a look of mild distaste, but patted Danu gently, kindly. "I hope at least they remember how to tell a story. We could use some new ones."

Danu let herself be led to the floor where the others sat, on the far side of the cairn.

"Stories?" she repeated.

"Why yes, love," the old woman replied. "The nights can be very, very long."

ONE MAN'S FOLLY

Pauline E Dungate

JOHN PERROTT SMOOTHED out the plans on the surface of the trestle table, anchoring the corners with quarters of red brick. He placed a compass in the centre and checked the alignment of the drawings with the poles and string set out in the field before him. He nodded to the architect who was standing beside him and asked, "How long before you've dug deep enough for a firm foundation. I don't want it falling down after the first winter gale."

"Bout five days more, squire," was the reply.

A boy, no more than ten, came belting across the grass towards them from the direction of the excavation. He stopped breathless on the other side of the table. Perrott gave him a few moments to recover before asking, "Your message, Tom?"

"Mr Bathgate. He says can you come look. They've dug into summat."

"Very well. Tell him I'm on my way." Perrott carefully rolled up the plans and stowed them back into the metal carrying tube before handing them to the architect. He picked his way across the field, carefully avoiding the larger tussocks and mole hills. He came to stand beside Bathgate, the man in charge of the crew doing the actual construction.

"What is it, man?" he asked.

Bathgate tugged his cap further down over his face. "It's the 'ole, squire. There's a ruddy great rock in the bottom of it. We won't shift it short of gunpowder."

"Hmm. How far down does it go?"

"We dug down next to the bugger. Ain't found the bottom yet."

"I'll look at it." Perrott walked round the edge of the excavation until he reached the wooden ladder that was the only easy way to the bottom. He tested it for security before trusting his weight to it. The distance to fall wasn't great; the risk of loss of dignity was greater.

From above, Bathgate shouted, "Barker, 'old the ladder fer the squire."

One of the men, liberally smeared with mud from the digging, dropped his spade and trudged the few paces to grip the uprights of the ladder and prevent it slipping. These men might be uncouth but they were compliant and hardworking. He couldn't fault Bathgate's choice of workforce.

The clay soil quickly adhered to the soles of Perrott's boots as he picked his way across to the large boulder. Bathgate was right. It would be a devil to move. He knew of others in the area and one theory was that they had been dropped by ice rivers such as he had seen in the Alps. He put his hand on it, feeling the rough surface. The minerals sent a slight tingling through his fingers similar to brushing against nettles. He rubbed the tips of his fingers together, the sensation passing once he no longer touched the surface.

The overseer clumped up beside him.

"What do you say, Bathgate?" Perrott said, "Can you bury it as part of the foundations?"

"I could that. Save digging it out."

"Do that then. Now, did you say you'd found other pieces of a similar rock scattered around the site?"

"That I did."

"Show me."

Perrott and Bathgate climbed back out of the diggings and crossed to where the boulders had been piled up. "Seems a shame to waste them," Perrott said. "Could they be dressed and used in the construction?"

"Don't see why not, squire."

"Good. They should do well as the corner posts for the top floor. How many are there?"

"Eight."

"Perfect. See the architect for the dimensions and get the masons working on them."

"As you wish, squire."

"I do." Perrott clasped his hands behind his back and allowed himself to smile as he imagined his tower rising above the countryside, a perfect place from which the ladies who did not wish to ride to the hunt could watch their men-folk enjoying the chase in the fields and woods that made up his estate. And afterwards, somewhere to relax away from the concerns of the conflict with the pesky French.

ROSE DROPPED HER bag on the floor just inside the kitchen. "What you doing?" she asked eying the large map her house-mate, Saira, had unfolded across the table. She had laid sheets of tracing paper over it and was marking lines on it.

Saira unbent with a sigh, tucking a strand of dark hair behind one ear as she did so. "I've been given a project on canals to develop with the geography group and I know almost nothing about them."

"Aren't there supposed to be more canals in Birmingham than Venice?"

"My tutor says that's just a rumour and challenged us to prove it."

Both girls were Education students at Newman College; both were preparing to embark on their final teaching practice. "At least you have a map as a starting point," Rose said, "I've been given an AS level group and I've got to explore Birmingham as a source of literature."

"Are there any Birmingham writers?"

"Lots, apparently. But none of them seem to have made much of a mark on the establishment – with one exception."

Saira leant over her map and began to trace lines across it. "Who?"

"J J R Tolkien."

"The *Lord of the Rings* guy? I thought he was an Oxford man."

"Seems not. Went to school here or something. Tell you what. I'll help you with your canals and you help me with my Hobbit man."

"Deal," Saira said. "Just give me a moment to fix these sheets together."

"I'M NOT SURE I'm making much sense of this," Saira said, once they had laid out the map on the floor of the kitchen, the only hard surface big enough to take the full size flat out. "None of these bits seem to join up."

"Except in this area," Rose said. "I think that's the Worcester Canal where the tourist boats go through the City Centre."

"There's nothing I can see that would rival Venice. I wish I'd been assigned the railways instead."

"Why? Half of those got closed down years ago. My granddad still moans about it."

Saira sat back on her heels. "That's it. They don't show up

because they've been closed."

"Or filled in."

"And built over. We need an older map. Do you think they'll have one at the Central Library?"

"Hope so. I want to be able to get an idea of what the place was like when Tolkien lived here. What places he might have seen." Rose looked at her friend thoughtfully. "I've got some free time tomorrow. I'll go into town and see what I can dig up."

IT COST ROSE a fair amount to get the whole of the Ordnance Survey map from 1901 copied. She and Saira spread it out and carefully joined the sheets together. The black and white patchwork looked very different from the coloured version Saira had been using.

"Where are all the houses?" Saira asked. "It's mostly fields."

"I suppose they hadn't been built. They didn't have a colour one I could copy."

"Might be tricky deciding which are the canals. Isn't that that Sarehole Mill, one of your places?" Saira pointed at the tiny group of squares.

"Yeah. They do bus tours to all the important places." Rose dropped a leaflet onto the map. "How about we go Saturday? We get entrance to some of the places on the tour as part of the price."

"Only if you walk some of these canals with me Sunday."

"Deal." Rose squinted at the map. "I'd guess that the wriggly lines are more likely to be the rivers and the straight ones are the canals. Do you want me to help you plot them?"

"Yes please. You start on that side, I'll start here and we'll work towards the middle."

An hour or so later, the girls sat back to survey their work. "It makes an interesting pattern," Rose said. "All these lines seem to converge towards one point. A bit like ley lines."

"What are those?"

"They were supposed to be lines of power running through the earth."

"Well, these are," Saira said. "Lines of commercial and industrial power running in and out of the city. Look at all the factories they had lining them."

"What's this then?" Rose pointed to a spot where many of the canals seemed to merge.

"The reservoir. They used it to top up the canals when idiots left the lock gates open. Hey, what's this place near it? I can't quite read the funny script."

Rose peered at the octagonal square, turning her head to read the tiny gothic writing. "It looks like *Folly*. Hang on." She reached for the leaflet. "That's one of the places the bus will take us on Saturday. And it's one of the few days it's open so you might be able to see the reservoir and some of the canals from the top. Don't forget to take your camera."

THE BUS, A vintage model from the 1950s, drew up at the curb side in a narrow Edgbaston street. The woman who was controlling the Tannoy told the passengers that there would be a short walk from the bus along Monument and Waterworks Roads and that they would be able to ascend the tower of Perrott's Folly in small groups. It was not safe for too many people to be trying the steps at one time, but would everyone stay together and not wander off. Rose nudged Saira and whispered, "Should we ask to see her risk assessment?"

Saira giggled and tucked a stray lock of hair back under her head-scarf. She found the *niqab* restricting and only wore it out of doors because she had promised her father she would. That promise was one reason he had let her move out of the family home and into the student house when she began her teacher training course three years before. Since then she had gradually been finding ways of stretching the restriction. He had also persuaded her to agree to consider potential husbands. Her period of freedom was rapidly coming to an end – he had even started sending her CVs of suitable *boys* (anyone younger than him was a boy). Her response was to be picky. She had no objection to him matchmaking but she wasn't interested unless the candidate was under thirty, childless, British born and university educated. And she had to like him. Father had, literally, muttered into his beard. If she was honest, Saira didn't really want to settle down with a family yet. There was a lot of world she would like to experience first.

Following the rest of the visitors, she wondered if inside the Folly would count as being *indoors*. She took stock of the others in the group and thought that she might take the risk as long as the Muslim family striding along at the head of the column were not in her group. Rose said she should make up her mind either to follow her father's instructions as he had intended, or renounce them altogether; to stop trying to reconcile tradition with her own instincts.

"Do you want to go up in the first group?" Rose asked as they passed the gate and started up the narrow path.

Saira shook her head. "I'd rather look around outside first."

"Okay. I'm going to get pictures." Rose headed off into the garden surrounding the base of the tower.

Saira let her gaze drift slowly upwards. The base of the red-brick tower seemed to grow from the cluster of buildings huddled against its base. She counted four sets of arched windows before a ring of small round ones circled the structure. Above that another set of recessed windows was separated by grey stone pillars. At the sight of those she felt a tingle of anticipation.

Something made her want to touch them, despite their height above the ground. She couldn't walk all the way round as the city had encroached on some of the original grounds but she could see the octagonal structure with its abutting circular tower would have looked spectacular when first built – a monument in green fields. She smiled suddenly. Monument Road had been the track that led to this tower. For a moment she wondered why it had the strange column attached to the side, spoiling its symmetry, then realised that this was where the staircase was. Now, she was eager to climb the steps to see the view from the top, to try to imagine what it was like when it had first been built.

She found Rose taking snaps, trying to get Perrott's Folly and the other brick tower in the distance in the same picture. "What is that?" Saira asked.

"The Waterworks. Some reckon they gave Tolkien the idea for his Two Towers. Are they the same age?" Rose consulted her notes. "No. The Waterworks is Victorian. I think it pumped water from the Reservoir and the canals."

"Then I want to go up and see the view. Let's try for the next batch."

The inside of the tower was a little disappointing. Empty, white painted rooms opened off from the spiral staircase at intervals on the way up. Saira stopped in the first one to peer through the grimy windows at the surrounding houses. It was not particularly inspiring. She missed out the others, hurrying upwards, feeling the pull on her calf muscles at the unaccustomed number of steps. She ducked into the top room. The ornamentation around the windows was a little more adventurous but the white paint hid most of the detail. In several places it was flaking away, especially on the corner pieces, exposing the bare stone beneath. The view was better now that she was looking down on the roofs. She rested her hand on the wall as she tried to peer around the side of the building. For a moment it appeared as if the houses below were a tented encampment. She giggled at the illusion caused by grimed windows, light-headedness from the climb and imagination, after watching all three *Lord of The Rings* films with Rose during the past week.

"You coming onto the roof?" Rose asked, startling her. When she looked back, the scene was normal, just a cityscape viewed through smudged glass.

They had to walk carefully, not venturing into the centre of the lead-covered space. Saira walked round peering between the crenellations before taking the map from her shoulder-bag and trying to make sense of what she was seeing. The perspectives were very different from this elevated position. Rose was busy photographing everything from every angle.

Saira glanced around at the other people up here. What she wanted to do was take off her headscarf and allow the breeze to ruffle her hair. These were times that she envied Rose her freedom from parental strictures. Saira didn't quite have enough courage to flaunt them. She sighed and left her hair covered. It would be too much of a hassle to try putting it back on neatly at the bottom of the tower. Too soon, the guide was hustling them back down, to let the next group have their turn.

As she stood in the garden, half listening to Rose's enthusiasm, Saira's gaze was drawn upwards again to the highest windows. Someone peeped over the top but she scarcely noticed. "Why are the pillars between the high windows stone instead of brick?" she asked.

Rose shrugged. "Decoration I suppose."

Saira shivered as if a cloud had momentarily obscured the sun. A glance showed her that the sky was clear. "I'm going up again," she said.

"Our guide won't like it. It's bad manners."

"Who cares? I'll just tag onto the last group. Coming?"

"No. I want to get a few more pictures from ground level."

Saira deliberately lagged behind as the tourists climbed the stairs. She found it easier this time, perhaps because she was going more slowly. She stayed in the top room when the others went onto the roof. Initially, she did a swift tour, glancing out of the seven windows in turn – the doorway occupied the eighth wall of the room. She saw only Birmingham. She put her hand on the stone upright and closed her eyes. What she had seen before was undoubtedly an illusion.

She opened her eyes, intending to make her way down. The view had changed. The window panes were out of focus and beyond she could see the tented encampment. It appeared to be only a little lower than her viewpoint. Leaning forward to look closer, her fingers lost contact with the stone. Instantly the window, and Birmingham, was back. When she touched stone again, the tents reappeared.

Saira trailed her fingers along the window sill to the next aperture and touched the stone where the point had flaked away. There was a different scene. She was looking into a farmyard, the space filled with milling sheep. She glanced behind her and above the doorway, expecting to see a video projector triggered by her touching the stone. The wall above the architrave was bare. As she looked back, a skinny black-skinned child turned and waved to her. Saira took a step back and the vision disappeared.

Fascinated, Saira stepped to each embrasure in turn. Each gave her a different image, except for the fifth which remained window – or it did until she realised the paint still covered all of it. She glanced around, listening to the muted sounds of people on the roof before taking a nail-file from her bag and using to scrape away some of the paint. Then she saw a place of slender towers linked by walkways. Sleek, futuristic vehicles zipped between them. She leaned forward to get a better look, one hand reaching out to steady herself against the glass. It wasn't there. She stumbled forward panic rising in her throat, expecting to fall. She didn't. Her feet touched grass.

She turned quickly. Behind her rose a small grassy knoll capped with a ring of standing stones. Terrified, she reached out to touch the pillar. It was rough beneath her hands. Her momentum carried her forward. She stood in the centre, grass beneath her shoes. Frustrated and wondering how she could get back, she clenched her fists and closed her eyes. Then she deliberately calmed herself down. Panic was not going to help. Slowing her breathing she reviewed the events that had got her into this place. Then she touched one of the stones and just looked, going round the circle, inspecting the views between each pair. Some she recognised. One was the interior of the tower. She took a deep breath and stepped past the stone into the upper room of Perrott's Folly.

"Wow!" she stood in the centre of the room, hands covering her mouth. No wonder they only opened the tower a few days each year. It wouldn't do to have people wandering in from these other places. Rose would love this, she thought. Pity there wouldn't be time to get up here again before they were moved on to the next stop on the tour.

Much as she would have loved to explore these alien worlds, Saira was conscious not only of her own ambitions – to be a good teacher – but also of the expectations of others, including her parents. As she reluctantly turned away from her discovery, she realised that the tower was very quiet. She couldn't hear the echoes of steps on the roof above or the clatter of feet on the stairs. For a moment she thought she was in the wrong place, then realised that the tour had gone on without her. She hastened down the stairs as fast as she could but still placing her feet so she didn't trip on the uneven stones.

The door, when she reached it was locked. No matter how she twisted the handle, it wouldn't budge. She tried hammering on it then gave up with a final, disgruntled kick as she realised that the wood was too thick for anyone outside to hear her.

She raced up to the first floor and peered out of the window. Over the hedge she could see the heads of the party as they traipsed back to the bus. She banged on the window and shouted. No-one gave any sign of noticing her.

Saira slid to the floor, dispirited and leaned her back against the wall. Someone would notice she was missing. Then she grinned. She could phone Rose. She dived into her bag and pulled out her mobile. She pressed the on button and waited for the screen to light up. It didn't.

"I don't believe this," she muttered. She was sure she had recharged the battery. She often forgot. Here it was, dead. At a time when she really needed it. All she could do was wait.

ROSE SCANNED THROUGH her pictures as she ambled along behind the group heading back towards the bus. She was pleased with the results. In her head, she was already planning the lesson that would impress her tutors. She climbed onto the bus and was part way to her seat when she stopped.

"Where's Saira?" she said to no-one in particular as she looked round at the passengers.

"Please sit down," the guide said irritably. "We are already behind schedule."

"Saira's not here."

"Who?"

"The girl I was with. She's not on the bus."

"There was no-one else. When did you last see her?"

"She went up the tower with the last group. You must have noticed her. She was wearing a bright blue headscarf."

"I checked. No-one was left in the tower. I was last down."

"But..."

"She probably made her own way home. Though she should have had the courtesy to say so."

Reluctantly, Rose took her seat. She pulled her phone from her pocket and dialled Saira's number. It went straight to her voice mail. Frustrated, Rose left a message. Her friend tended not to turn her phone on unless she actually wanted to use it or she had forgotten to charge it – again.

Maybe the woman was right and Saira had gone home. She wasn't going to worry until she'd checked it out.

AS IT BEGAN to get dark, Saira started to worry that no-one was coming back for her. Rose, surely, would have realised she was missing. What if they didn't think to look in the tower? After all, she hadn't actually been in it when the last group had made their way out. She felt panic bubbling up inside. She could starve to death here. When they next had a public opening, all they would find was her skeleton. Firmly she suppressed the fear. She wouldn't starve. She had seven other places she could go.

Slowly, Saira made her way back up to the top room.

Which one? She closed her eyes and pictured each of the scenes. Then she took off the *niqab* and stuffed into her bag. With one hand pressed firmly against the stone Saira stepped forwards between the standing stones and walked down the slope to the farm, the flock of sheep and the little girl who had waved to her.

DRAGONSBRIDGE

Anne Nicholls

MY SHOULDER'S ITCHING unbearably. There, right on the top of the shoulder-blade. I'd give a bloody fortune to be able scratch it. Trouble is, I can't reach it. The only bit I can really move is my eyes. I look around for something I could use: a bit of bracken, a twig, anything. Everywhere's so hot, so bright, than I can't make out anything much against the glare.

I can feel the sun beating down, though. My brain feels like it's being fried. Down below, there's the stream, burbling merrily away through ferny dell and mossy bridge, I think sourly. Valley of No Return, for Chrissake. I thought they were joking.

You wouldn't think you could get lost in a poxy valley, would you? You just walk downhill till you get to where you're going. Or follow the hum of tourist traffic to the castle.

But what happens when you can't walk? When you're stuck at the edge of the bog, can't go forward, can't go back, your head's thumping like a jackhammer bashing the inside of your skull, and the rocks and trees don't give a damn? That, and the endless bloody crickets screeching away. The ancient oaks are alive with squirrels and woodpeckers and all that rustic shit, the leaves are that special green you only get in May when they're opening up, and I'm stuck here with my shoulder on fire.

Yep, there goes the other one. It's worst when the top layer of skin suddenly unglues itself from the flesh: pop! Well, how would you like it if someone ripped off a layer of your skin?

I wish I'd listened to Maddie. I know what's going to happen when the sun goes down.

IT WAS SEVEN years ago, in the middle of the building site. He ripped up his returned proposal and scattered it. Then he trampled it underfoot, his Totectors slithering in the mud.

"Got a medical appointment, Billy," he said as he passed the foreman. "Urgent."

Billy hid a smile. It was code for pissed off and going to the pub. "Is that right, James Elliott, Dip. Arch.?"

"Stuff the bloody Dip. Arch. Ever since I qualified I've sweated my knackers off drawing brilliant proposals and every sodding time the funding's cut off. If I had that bastard Osborne here I'd teach him to play Ludo with the economy."

Billy slung an arm round his shoulders and whispered in his soft Irish brogue. "So you going to quit playin' at bein' a professor and start being a bloody builder? 'Cause you've got it in you, you know. If me 'n' you put our minds together, Jimmy my lad, we can make a bloody mint. I've got this contact up the council..."

Jimmy – formerly James – Swanwick, builder *né* architect, gratefully let his boss's promise of tax-free wealth hide the size of his debts. Gas and electric. Bastard student loan. Credit card bills...

He thought it all through during his appointment with thirteen medicinal brandies. He'd do it, go in with Billy. Sod the Royal Institute of *Bloody* Architecture. His wife Maddie wouldn't like it but then again, she didn't have to know.

THE SUN'S GOING down behind the brambles now, thank fuck. It's gilding the trees, bringing out the scent of sap, bringing the end of the relentless sun. For a while it won't be adding to my third-degree burns. But later, when the bats fly through the dusk and the moon rises, what happens will be maybe worse.

Although the waiting's torment enough as it is...

HE WAS RIGHT, Maddie hadn't liked it when she found out, not the fear of the taxman nor the endless 'foreigners' he did, the jobs on the sly, but she was just being a snob. Didn't like him working down the sharp end of the building trade. Her and her bloody Bachelor of Fine Arts. What use was that, for fuck's sake? There was sod all she could do about it and anyway, the money came in handy. He liked to get his round in for his gang at the end of the day. A little kindness always helps keep their mouths closed, Billy used to say, and a little threat or two don't go amiss. You stick with me, Billy had said. I'll see you right. But for fuck's sake, stop going round talking like Little Lord Fauntleroy. Jimmy didn't point out that the boy in the novel had been American. People don't trust poncy gits 'cause they're all on the take. Be Jimmy, my lad Billy had said, and Jimmy he'd become.

IT HURTS LIKE buggery. Not long to go now. Something's changed in the air: the light. I can't see colours any more, just black and grey and silver. Here in the Valley of No Return, only two or three hundred metres from the Castle of Brocéliande, I shiver. I feel another blister pop, and then the sting as the sweat rolls into it. But I can't move. I'd give anything to be able to move. The stars are bright, owls are making spooky noises in the forest, there's a sniffing noise and the stink of a fox as it trots closer. It sniffs again, pricks its ears to listen, then starts licking my blood. If only I could scream. If only I could scream – but I daren't open my mouth.

MADDIE LOST THE baby. It was her own stupid fault, he told her. He'd *said* he was working all the hours God sends so she didn't need to. OK, half the time he was out with his mates, doing a line of coke, going to the casino; there was nothing like it. But she was so stubborn! Paying her stupid bloody student loan instead of getting his accountant to get her out of it. And he'd *needed* that Range Rover, for Chrissake. It'd help him get home earlier, wouldn't it? So why she had to go and act the martyr, he didn't know. She only had two airy-fairy office jobs and neither of 'em was anything like as demanding as his was. Well, one proper one at the factory and some twilight shift messing about that meant half the time she hadn't cooked his dinner so he'd go up the Dog and Duck. They did a decent steak and chips. He might see Lee and Jason and they could have a game of darts. Leave the old girl to have her cry in peace. She'd be better for it and then they could get back to normal.

NOW THE NIGHT wind's rustling these sodding reeds. I never knew the countryside was so bloody noisy! There could be anything out there creeping up on me. After this, rush-hour in London's going to seem really peaceful. That's what I tell myself but fear's bursting through me.

Any minute. Any minute. I can feel it coming. It'll start soft as moth's wings on the raw skin of my burns. The itch'll start to burn like someone's stabbing me with a lighted cigarette. Pain'll sing through me, a vibration of agony so shrill it's above the range of bats. Like last night. And tomorrow night. And all the nights that have ever come.

It's the healing, you see. People say itching's a good sign, don't they? It means things are healing. Bit by bit, day by day, the new skin and tissue grow. A few weeks and Bob's your uncle, good as new.

That's what they say. Or that's what they used to say before I stepped through the Dragonsbridge. It'll take time.

But now it doesn't take time, or not enough. Like fire leaping in darkness the cure goes *Slam!* My heart-rate drops from a hundred-and-twenty-six to eighty-four, just like that. I almost pass out. Healing swarms up the capillaries, stampedes through my muscles. You know when your leg's been asleep and you get killer pins and needles as it wakes up? That's nothing. The edges of my skin crash together like continental plates. It sets up volcanoes of agony.

God, that bitch Maddie! Why'd she have to drag me to fucking France? Leaving me to suffer alone for bloody ever. Just wait till I see her.

"BLOODY BELLA! I never s*ee* you, Maddie! She's got you like a bitch in heat," he sneered, sure in his rightness as he faced her over the bills on their Saturday breakfast table. He was *entitled* to a new car, wasn't he? He worked hard enough. He'd earned it! How *dare* she moan?

"Oh, grow up!" Maddie clamped her hands round her mug of tea, otherwise she'd have thrown it at him. Only she wouldn't, not really. She always said she wouldn't stoop to his level and start any aggro but she fought back right enough, didn't she? She gazed out at the mothers with their pushchairs going down to the village stores, the families with children taking kites and model aeroplanes to the field at the back of the parish church. She couldn't see the trees at the side. His scarlet and silver Range Rover and now his Porsche got in the way.

She counted to ten, slowly, then said in a voice of saccharine calm, "Did you expect me to stick around twiddling my thumbs at home when you were five, count them, *five* hours late home? I left you a note where I was, didn't I? Seeing as you'd switched your phone off."

Oh, she had to get the dig in, didn't she? Bloody dragon. That's what Billy called her. "How's the old dragon this morning?" he'd ask when Jimmy came to work grumpy.

He tried to say something but she rushed on, "I didn't *ask* you to wait up. I didn't do anything to deserve this." Gingerly she felt the swelling that ran half-way up her arm.

"What d'you mean, *this?* It's only a little bruise and you did it to yourself. You're just trying to make me feel guilty, you manipulative cow. All I did was give you a push 'cause you'd gone mental! How was I to know you were going to go and trip into the wardrobe? I got home before you, didn't I? And *you* have the cheek to yell at *me!"*

At least she didn't try to pretend he'd started it. OK, so he'd moaned a bit, but it was her own fault, anyway. He got back to the thing that was really narking him. "You and that bloody Bella. Fat Lesbian whore! I've *told* you." His blood boiled when he thought of all the times he'd come back late and she wasn't there 'cause she'd gone to bloody Bella's. Jimmy's expression could have stripped paint. "She's only got to snap her fingers and you go running after her like a baby. Go on, just give her a great big wodge of cash and she'll be your mummy."

Usually the baby thing shut her up because she felt so guilty about losing the sprog, but not this time. "It's *work*, Jimmy. It's an investment of *my* time and *my* money. She's a nice woman and she's got a wife anyway. We just work together."

"That's what you say. You come back sometimes all covered in sweat and I wonder what the two of you have been up to."

"What we've been up to, Jimmy, is designing a computerised weaving machine. Which means screwing bits of loom together and that's heavy."

"So long as that's all you're screwing."

She shot him a glare.

He had to get her off-balance. A guilt-trip would do it. "On which you spend *our* money."

"On which I spend *my* money that *I've* earned with *my* dragon designs in *my* spare time. And which the Chamber of Commerce in our twin town in Brittany has now started importing so I can pay off our debts. You *know* the money I earn from the factory all goes into our joint account. Which is more than can be said for your bonus. Why you had to squander it on a sports car I can't image. You've already got the Range Rover. Don't you *know* our mortgage is three months in arrears? I can't do it all on my own. And your student loan's piling up the interest, and I bet you've got more credit cards than you're letting on. So no, I am *not* running after her. And besides which, I only go over to her when you're off with your mates."

He stalked over to the sofa and left it up to her. Put the football on, even. He could see her bottling down her rage. She'd crack soon. She'd come crawling back like she always did. And he'd get something out of it, see if he didn't. Teach her to try and stop him enjoying the Porsche he'd bought with his own money.

She paced up and down the living-room, keeping well clear of the line of sight between him and the telly. He'd taught her well.

At last she sighed, plonked down beside him and slid her arm across his chest. "Come here, you big silly. It's daft you being jealous. It's you I love, isn't it? It's you I'm married to. Don't be cross. We'll just get through this quicker if we work together, that's all." She threw her arms round his neck.

So he'd won. Automatically he hugged her to him, glad of the warmth of her body touching his skin. Sometimes he didn't understand why a woman like her loved a man like him. But no other bastard was going to have her, especially not some cowing Lizzie. He gave her a long, deep kiss that plunged inside and twisted her mind. Her breathing shifted up a gear with the longing he'd learned to cause her.

"Wish I wasn't going to my darts tournament, gorgeous," he whispered, gave her a peck on the cheek. He was half-way out the door when he said, "Don't wait up."

THE MOON'S SINKING now. It's odd when the moon and the sun are in the sky at the same time. At the edge of my vision the fat white disc glows, sheer and pale. On the other side of the valley the blue of dawn flies up like a sodding skylark, heading for the new day's torture. What will They choose for me this time? If only I could have a drink.

The healing's almost finished but my tortured muscles won't stop twitching. Every time I do, the new skin stings as though glaciers are grating over it. I can't even call for help. Surely they've missed me? Surely Maddie'll have *le* PC Plod combing the woods for me after. Christ! I can't even work out how many days I've been stuck here. Day after day, all the same, except that They vary the tortures.

And soon They'll be here. I never know which one it's going to be. They kind of blend into each other. When it's really bad I can't tell them apart, and that scares the pants off me 'cause it makes me scared I'm going doolally. One's a beauty with some kind of pendant glowing on her forehead. The other's a right old bag, her bare arms all stringy and wasted with age.

The beauty's fierce, a proud warrior, wild hair fanning out like a lion's mane, the same colour as Maddie's. The first night I found her irresistible. I was drawn to the passion that flashed out sometimes when we had sex, or when we stayed up all night talking. She seemed, I don't know, all golden and lit up from inside. She made me laugh and taught me glory.

Until that time everything changed. She just couldn't stop rubbing it in when my dreams died but hers didn't. She was so bloody arrogant! Ringing me at work as though I cared a toss that someone wanted to buy her tuppenny-ha'penny doilies. I swear she only wanted to show everyone she was better than me. I *heard* her brother talking about her builder's-bum husband. But he's a posh twat. So what if I like to wear low-riders like Billy and the lads? It's cool isn't it? If she hadn't been such a show-off I'd never have nipped up West with the lads and then I wouldn't have started gambling.

Then she was a fury. Rage sparked from her hair, glittered with the sharpness of her remarks until she seemed armoured in scales. Or she'd cry, a keening that was so bereft, it stabs guilt up right below my ribs.

It might be a relief if it's the old woman who comes. She's got the same delicate architecture to her face though her wrinkles soften the curves. She'll flow towards me through the darkness, lovingly salve my wounds.

Bugger! The pain's so bad I've bitten through my lip and ants are crawling onto my mouth.

Maybe – God! I hate myself! I'm longing to drown in her pity! Maybe she'll brush them away. Set me free. Tell me what's bloody going on!

But as the sun rises up, she hunches beside me, her pity all kept for herself, weeping bitter, bitter tears and wishing she'd never been born.

And I've made her into this pitiful thing.

By the third aeon of torture, I knew They were all one.

THE SUN PEEPS through the leaves and lances into my new pink skin. It's like it's writhing over me, crawling over my scraped nerves, stinging like acid.

No! I crane my neck and shudder. There're all these leeches slithering over me, taking a bite. I thought they weren't supposed to hurt? On my arms they are, and on my chest. One's wriggling into my ear. I shake my head – fuck me that hurts! – but I can't get rid of it. The bloody dragons are playing their daylight games.

MADDIE TEXTED HIM a month ago to say she'd won them a free holiday, and wasn't it great? She couldn't have made it Agia Napa or Ibiza or somewhere good though, not goody-goody Madeleine. A load of councillors on a minibus to some grotty little town in the arse-end of France? He wouldn't have gone at all except she'd have asked Bella to take his place, the heartless cow.

So here they were, around twenty kilometres west of Rennes. And everywhere they went, they got introduced in mangled English to another load of old fuds or dragged round another bloody chateau. And some old tart would tell them a load of stupid stories about magic and King Arthur and Merlin and that. That first day when they got back to their room and he started taking the piss out of all that New Agey bollocks, she'd practically broken the sound barrier to hiss in his ear, "Not with the window open! They'll hear."

"What do I care? It's your bloody jolly, not mine. I'm missing the big match for this so shut the fuck up. Just because they've all been fawning over you and your bloody lizard doilies all day, it doesn't mean I like the sound of your voice as much as you do. They can all go fuck themselves. Where's that bottle of wine?"

MY SKIN IS like one of those delta maps they got me drawing back in geography, only the rivers are all my blood. It makes me sick just thinking about it. My stomach heaves but there's nothing left in there to come out. The stink of my puke rises up on the hot winds that always blow through this sodding forest but I can't get away from it. All I can do is lie here – hang here? – and bleed.

Maybe she isn't looking for me at all. Maybe she just thinks I'm sulking. Maybe she's had enough, gone swanning off to the standing stones at Karnak with the Chamber of Commerce. I shouldn't have yelled at her last night.

I so, so, so want to call her. Maddie would listen to me. She'd talk me out of these terrible imaginings. Or – or if I *am* going mad, she'd take care of me. She always has. I bet she's giving the local rozzers gyp.

But what if that mayor won't let 'em search for me? It was his bloody wife giving me the eye that made me nip down the Valley out of her way. She looked like an elephant wearing face-powder. Mind, if it had been that receptionist in that last hotel I wouldn't have minded getting my end away. Besides, I couldn't stand listening to any more of that bollocks about the gateway to the Otherworld. The tour-guide might have Maddie fooled with all that choosing our fate in the Otherworld shit. I mean, if you crawl under the bridge you face your own dragons or come out into the Summerland. Tir na bloody nÓg. Your own choice, the sodding guide had said. I only wanted a quiet fag.

But slugs are swarming up my nose. I'm choking! I can't breathe. I've got to open my mouth.

And a wasp stings my tongue.

IN THE ENDLESS noon of the Otherworld, Maddie pleaded through her tears. All around was paradise: friendly beings in lush green meadows, and the sea sparkling under the bluest of skies. And she couldn't touch any of it. She stood in a crystal bubble.

"It's not his fault," she wept. "He tried so hard but nobody would give him a chance at a project that might actually get off the ground. And it seems so unfair, now Bella and I've got this fabulous new contract thanks to the Chamber of Commerce. Let me go and rescue him, please! I can't leave him there."

"It's your life," said the ageless queen in the beautiful gown. "You're the only one who can decide what path you will take."

"HELP ME!" I keep trying to croak but the words can't struggle past my agonised tongue. What air I can get whistles round the swelling.

Again that creepy whispering in the grass. I strain to see what's making it. It looks like the earth's walking beneath the grass, and suddenly I realise it's the leeches, red and leaking my blood. All those ones that were piercing my body, she's sent them all away with just a thought. The end of the torture. I'm so grateful to her for just being there. My Madeleine.

She kisses the hollow of my neck. Instantly my breath comes easier. The pain's going, leaving hardly a memory, only snap-shots, not the feel of it. Suddenly green leaves shade my skin.

"Are you all right, Jimmy?" I can see the concern in her eyes. Maddie gestures, and all at once I'm free. I didn't think I'd be able to walk after all this time but I float effortlessly towards her. We hug for the longest time, and nothing hurts at all.

Then I remembered how long she'd left me there, tortured day and night. A wave of anger scalds out from my heart. "Don't you care about me at all, you daft cow? Fuck knows how long I've been stuck here yelling my head off." A little dig to make her guilty, not too much, just a cocktail-stickful, but nice and vinegary so she'll know her place. "Where the hell have you been?"

She backs up, shocked, almost tripping on a tuft of grass. The sun's behind her now, right in my eyes. "What's the matter,

Jimmy? Have you bumped your head? You've only just stepped under the bridge."

I give her my best glare. "Don't you fucking lie to me!"

"You did, Jimmy, no more than a second ago. I was right behind you."

A ghostly silhouette floats onto her. Into her. It makes her denser, somehow. Gives her – what's the word? Gravitas. The warrior maiden's anger forms a shield. Suddenly, my Maddie's more real than I've ever seen her.

Another phantom bursts through her, the old one, kindly arms wrapping her in comfort and protection. She begins very gently to shine.

I'm so stunned I can't move.

"They're not lizard doilies, Jimmy. They're tapestries of dragons and Merlin and the Celtic Triple Goddess, and they're beautiful. They're made with love and pride, not like you and your corner-cutting crook of a boss with your substandard buildings. Bella's a friend, not someone who uses you like Billy uses you, or you used to use me. But no more. Our first order's more than paid our overheads. I know you're in debt so I'll buy the house off your hands." She twinkles her fingers in mockery, and the light seems to swallow her. The last thing I hear is a derisive, "Ta-ta."

GOD KNOWS WHY they thought they'd bring me a newspaper with *that* in it. For one thing I can't read it 'cause it's in French, and for another, that's a photo of my wife – my ex-wife – with a giant cheque with lots of noughts on it. It drives me nuts.

All three of them come back to haunt me: the three dragons. Woman the warrior, woman the caregiver, woman the wise. They tried to feed me this bollocks, that I'd brought it all on myself.

True, at some time, some age that felt long enough for the

whole galaxy to revolve on its axis, Madeleine the mother came to let me go. "Ta-ta!" Cheeky bloody cow. I swear one of these nights I'm going to go round there and bash her face in just to teach her that if I can't have her, no one else will. I'll read her the riot act right enough.

But not just yet. I'm in some kind of a hospital with some Frog copper standing guard when I have visitors, but Billy says he knows this lawyer.

THE SATAN STONES

Misha Herwin

THE SATAN STONES loom up out of the twilight. The King Stone is tall and proud against the lowering sky; at its side lies the Queen Stone. A perfect circle hollowed out over the millennia, it frames a glimpse of the rising moon. Darkness steals up from the ground, the Stones grow dark, their shapes silhouetted against the brightness of the moon.

Backlit by this silvery light a girl comes across the field. Dressed in a white robe, her hair flowing freely down her back she is crowned with a wreath of flowers. Her feet are bare, her eyes blank. As she nears the sacred site she is joined by others. Cloaked and masked, they merge into shadow, watching as she moves up the slight incline. When she reaches the Queen Stone, she bows her head and kneels before it and their voices rise in a chant of welcome. The girl lifts her arms. Her wrists are seized and bound. There is a sudden flash of steel. Blood drips on stone, seeps thick and warm into the waiting earth.

Music sounds. Low, threatening. Credits roll. Written in script jagged as lightening, they are smeared by stains of scarlet like a dying hand clawing at glass.

But the girl goes willingly. She does not fight her destiny.

Remote in hand, Alexa stares at the screen. The curtains in the lodge house are drawn against the dark. A log fire burns in the hearth, the lamps cast a warm glow around the sitting room and yet long cold shudders slither up her spine. Out there in the darkness there is something otherworldly, unknown. It comes with the night and the impenetrable silence that presses against the house.

Her phone lies on the coffee table in front of her. She has only to pick it up and she will hear Sam's voice, but she doesn't want to talk to him. He will try to rationalize away her fear, but if it wasn't for him, she wouldn't be feeling like this. He was the one who pressurized her into coming this weekend. He should be here, not a time zone away in New York.

This cottage was his idea. As soon as it had come on the market he had to have it, worrying at her until she agreed. He'd wanted it since he was a boy living in the village and going up to the Hall to see his cousin Kit.

She'd love it, he told her. It would be their own weekend retreat, the magical place where they would escape from the rush and bustle of their lives, hers as a top divorce lawyer, his as a media consultant.

Alexa catches her lip with her teeth, breathes in an angry sob. They had such plans, but once the lodge was theirs Sam seemed to have lost interest. The week before they took possession he told her he would have to be away on business, but he still made her promise to go ahead without him.

Which is why she is here. Alone in the dark watching Kit's latest film, his most recent foray into the horror that has made his name. Alexa chews at her lip. She should have known better. Kit's films are always disturbing, but this one is based on the ancient stones that stand somewhere out there in the fields, not too far from the lodge, which makes it more relevant, more personal, somehow. Is this why she is reacting so strongly? Alexa shakes her head and reminds herself that she is a rational being and there is a perfectly good explanation for her sudden burst of fear. She's tired after a long week and so has fallen for the age-old cliché of Neolithic stones and sacrificial maidens. Damn Kit for making such a good job of it. Her nails dig into flesh as she shakes her head to clear her thoughts.

In the oak tree opposite the lodge, an owl hoots. Car headlights sweep round the corner. Is it Kit coming home to the Hall? If it is then he should bloody well stop and come and see if she's all right. Leaving that DVD like a calling card, for her to watch was a pretty mean trick.

The car drives past at speed. Alexa grits her teeth. If that is Kit, then she'll go up there tomorrow and tell him that she wasn't impressed by being abandoned on her first night. She might even, after a glass of wine or two, confess that for a moment his film scared her. They'll laugh about it and she'll tease him for using every corny trick in the book to curdle the blood. As Kit likes to think of himself as sophisticated and radical, that will really get to him.

Alexa rubs the tops of her arms where her grip has bruised the skin; she stretches her legs and wriggles her toes, wincing as the blood flows back into her feet. Smiling wryly at her childish reaction to what is *only* a film, she walks into the kitchen and pours a large glass of wine. She does not, however, let herself look out through the un-curtained window, where two fields away she knows the Satan Stones stand.

She sleeps with the light on, but she does not dream.

In the morning the January sky is blue and the shrubs in her tiny garden glisten with frost. There is no message or text from Sam. Sitting at the kitchen table, drinking coffee and nibbling toast, Alexa watches a robin pecking at the bare earth then draws in her breath as a small black and white cat appears. Holding its tail like a question mark the cat strolls down the path towards the unsuspecting bird. Fearing for the robin's safety, Alexa jumps up and taps on the window. The cat turns its head in her direction. Its green unblinking eyes hold her gaze. She is the first to look away and when she does she sees that the robin has flown.

Baulked of its prey, the cat turns its attention to the grey haired woman coming down the drive towards the lodge house. She is wearing a long flowing skirt and battered coat and carrying a basket over her arm. Thinking it must be one of Kit's odd friends Alexa raps on the glass and waves. The cat, as if preparing itself for a visit, sits down on the path. Alexa knocks again, but there is no sign that the woman has heard her. She has reached the stile and is climbing over it into the field that stretches out in front of the cottage.

Where is she going? What is she doing? And what gives her the right to ignore a friendly greeting?

Fuelled by a sudden flash of anger, Alexa goes to the back door, takes her jacket off its peg, shoves her feet into her boots and strides out into the crisp cold. The cat gets up and twines itself around her legs, but of the woman there is no sign.

"Great," Alexa says to the cat. "And I thought people in the country were supposed to be friendly." The cat gives her an inscrutable look and stalks off towards the house across the road. Once the mirror image of their lodge it now looks slightly shabby, the windows small and secretive, the garden over-shadowed by the oak tree where the owl roosts.

"Is that where you live?" Alexa says as the cat sits down by the front door. "Grief, I'm talking to a cat. One day out here in the wilds and I've lost it." Hastily she goes back into the house. Glad that she had not opted for a Sainsbury's home delivery, she makes a note of what she needs and sets off for the local supermarket.

After the stillness and emptiness of Oakley, the small country town is bustling with Saturday shoppers. Walking down the aisles of the supermarket, Alexa is soothed by the familiar routine and when the shopping's been done she feels calm and in control. She drives back along the narrow lanes and as she reaches the lodge she has to slow to avoid the figure coming towards her. Although the sun is at her back, the woman's hand is shielding her eyes as if she is looking out for someone. Alexa brakes and the woman walks over.

"Hello. I'm your new neighbour," Alexa says lowering window. She thinks her voice sounds foolish in the still winter air.

The woman looks at her with eyes as green as the cat's. She says nothing. Alexa opens the door and scrambles out. She feels cross, flustered, wrong footed somehow although she has done nothing but be perfectly pleasant. "I'm down for the weekend. My first night in the cottage. Alone." She tries a smile but her mouth won't quite obey. "I've been watching Kit's film. Apparently it was all based round the Stones."

"The Devil's Ring and Finger." The woman's voice is low and husky.

"Oh yes, that's what they're really called. I forgot. Sam, my partner, showed me them on the map." She's gabbling. "He's from round here you know and he thinks it's really exciting to be living so close to an ancient site." Again the disconcerting silence. "Oh well must get on." Alexa moves towards the boot. "Shopping." She gives an apologetic shrug.

"Have you seen them?"

For a moment Alexa is confused. She has the strangest feeling that this woman knows all there is to know about her and yet she is sure that she has told her nothing.

"No. I told you. Didn't I?"

"You should." The woman is holding out her hand.

"I don't think," Alexa begins, but already she is letting the boot lid drop. The woman's grip is warm and firm; her fingers close round Alexa's, tight as manacles. As she is led across the field, images of blood dripping onto stone cross Alexa's mind and she drags her feet, glancing behind her, half hoping for rescue.

"Don't be afraid. There's no moon," the woman says and Alexa takes comfort in the hard bright sunlight, the rough tufts of grass, the splodges of cow pat that seem so safe and ordinary.

The Stones stand on a slight hillock. They seem smaller, less powerful than in the film, but as the two women approach, something passes between them, like the pulse of an electric current. Alexa's hand grips the woman's.

"You feel it." The woman is smiling.

"Feel what?" Alex's mouth is dry, her throat tight. "The evil?" she manages.

The woman stops, her eyes crinkle, she is laughing. "The Stones are not evil."

Alexa swallows. "Then why are they called the Devil's Ring and Finger?"

"Because they are powerful."

"You mean because people were sacrificed on them."

"Oh no." Once again there is a trace of laughter in the woman's voice. "They bear the name of the horned god because within them they hold the gift of life. The ebb and flow of the seasons, the sowing and the ripening and the harvesting of crops. What sacrifices there are, are the ones we women make for our people and our land. See, feel." She stretches out her hand and Alexa finds that she is touching the rough surface of the upright stone. Her fingers explore the uneven planes, dig into clefts and crevices gouged out by the centuries. And then she is at the Queen Stone where the hollowed out centre is smooth and sensuous as marble. She half closes her eyes, her breath slows, and she is seized by the desire to slip within that circle, to slide back into some primeval time when everything was simple and clear cut, when all that mattered was the giving and taking of life.

A cloud veils the sun bringing with it a chill breeze, then it moves away and the warmth returns. Alexa blinks hard in the harsh light. Turning her head sees she is alone.

She walks slowly back to the lodge trying to make sense of what has just happened. Part of her feels that she has been given some sort of message, a message she does not understand. Logic however tells her that the woman is one of Kit's crazy, drugged up hangers on, who has somehow managed to involve her in her fantasy.

"I'll get you for this Kit," she promises, sending him a text. Then she unpacks the shopping and makes coffee. Checking her phone she finds no message from Sam. She swears briefly then settles down to work. The divorce she is working on absorbs all her attention. Celebrity parents fighting over the custody of their children; it is high profile and very acrimonious.

After hours of work, eyes aching, she rests her head in her hands, raking fingers through her hair. Cases such as these make her glad that she and Sam have decided not to have a family. Children are nothing but a distraction. She has her career, he has his, plus a couple of kids from his last but one marriage. The eldest boy he hopes will one day inherit the Hall, for Kit is unlikely to provide an heir; after all, the house and estate has passed through the family for centuries.

Alexa stretches and leans back in her chair. It is later than she thought and the house is still and silent.

The sudden sharp cry takes her by surprise. Her hands fall protectively to her stomach. Senses alert she turns her head. Nothing. Not a whimper.

Then it comes again. A faint gasp followed by the desperate sobbing of a baby left alone in its cradle.

She is on her feet and opening the bedroom door before she remembers that there is no child in this house. And there never will be, she tells herself with grim determination as she checks the TV, radio and laptop. She throws open the door and steps out into a clear star-splintered night. Silence. She stands and listens, frowning in concentration, hands balled into fists, straining to hear from which direction the cries are coming. Nothing. The icy air sears her throat. Behind, the lodge house windows blaze with light, the kitchen door stands open tempting her back. Alexa hesitates.

A small black shape charges across the flagstones. The cat butts against her legs purring and fussing, until she lets it guide her out of the garden. The stile is slippery with frost; the rough grass crunches under her feet. The moon hangs low over the tops of the trees lighting her way towards the dark outline of the Devil's Ring and Finger.

There is no way back. All thought of the child is gone. She is conscious of nothing but the smooth roundness of the Queen Stone, drawing her as inexorably as the moon draws the tide. She has to touch, she has to feel, she has to lie in the centre of the Stone.

Enfolded in its power she has no idea of time. All she knows when she crawls out on the other side is that she is sated. She yawns and raises her arms to the moon and as she does so a dark figure steps out from behind the King Stone. In the eldritch light she sees horns, breathes in the scent of musk and brine.

"Alexa." Kit's eyes gleam through the darkness. They slant a little giving him an ethereal faun like air. "You're here." She takes his hand and somehow he and the horned god are one.

"Yes, I was here earlier too, but… " Alexa stops, too sleepy, too content to say more.

"She showed you. She always knows," Kit sighs and grins, teeth white and sharp. "Come on let me take you home." He puts his arm around her shoulders. When they get to the lodge, he kisses her and she kisses him. It seems right.

In the morning there is a message from Sam. "Happy?"

She stares at it perplexed. "What does he mean?" she asks.

Kit grins. "What do you think? You're here where he wanted you to be. Where we all want you."

Alexa nods. There is nothing more to say. No questions to ask. It is as if everything that happened at the Stones has led up to this moment. Her previous life is over. She feels nothing when Kit tells her that Sam won't be coming back, that he's met someone else and will be staying in the States for the foreseeable future.

It's my destiny, Alexa thinks, her mind flickering back to Kit's film. It's where I'm meant to be.

She rings the office and tells them that she won't be going back to work.

She moves into the Hall for the nine months until her child is born. He comes swiftly and painlessly one midnight, delivered by the woman with the long grey hair. As her son is handed to her Alexa is not perturbed by his appearance. She knows that by the time he is walking his feet will be perfect, that he will be a wild and handsome child, the true heir.

GANDALPH COHEN AND THE LAND AT THE END OF THE WORKING DAY

Peter Crowther

WAITING FOR HIS drink, thinking about Tom 'Ankles' Talese – an epithet (of sorts) earned over many years as a result of the fact that Tom spends so much time so far up the Chairman's ass that his ankles are usually the only parts of his anatomy visible – McCoy Brewer watches himself in the large mirror propped up behind the bottles on the back counter at The Land at the End of the Working Day, playing back the events of the past few hours.

The Working Day is a two-flight walk-down bar on the corner of 23rd and Fifth that not many people know about, even though it's been here for almost eight years and is just a block away from 'The Dowager of 23rd Street', the Chelsea Hotel. It's there that the tourists go with their Nikons and their Pentaxes, capturing each other's vacuous smiling face on cheap film – a strangely talismanic process that somehow imbues their empty lives with a little art and, maybe, just a little history – to take the shaky and badly-cropped results home to bore their friends at the end of interminable dinner parties for which the level (not to mention the sheer invention) of last-minute cancellations never ceases to surprise them ... strange illnesses and bizarre accidents, such as obscure relatives (from equally obscure out-of-state towns) who have cut off their feet with a lawnmower.

In the early hours of a clear morning – spring or fall, summer or winter – when Jack Fedogan's booze has been flowing and the conversation has been just right, you can walk up the Working Day's steps and out onto the waiting street, and you can maybe hear Dylan Thomas eternally whispering to Caitlin that he's happier here than anywhere else, and her telling him she feels that way too, their voices drifting on the Manhattan breeze the way only voices can drift, moving away for a while and then moving back, saying the same things over and over like cassette ribbons, proving that no sound ever dies but only waits to be heard again.

So, too, do the voices of James Farrell – who really *was* the hero of his own book, *Studs Lonigan* ... and don't let anyone tell you different – and Arthur B. Davies, Robert Flaherty, O. Henry, John Sloan, Thomas Wolfe and Edgar Lee Masters, all of whose names are recorded forever on a plaque fixed to the red brick wall of the Chelsea, the ancient echoes of their soft words wafting up the ten storeys past ten little cast-iron balconies, there to drift around the gabled roof and maybe roost a while, watching the sun come up across the East River and the distant smoky towers of fabled Brooklyn.

There are other voices, of course, and if you strain real hard maybe you'll even pick up Martha Fishburn, a native of Des Moines, telling her husband Garry he drinks too much as he stumbles up onto the sidewalk of many months past ... or Nick Hassam, a British would-be writer of American detective fiction, telling both the street and his wife of one week, Nicky, that he's having the greatest honeymoon anyone could ever have, that this is the most magnificent city and she the most wonderful wife.

The people who come to The Land at the End of the Working

Day are no strangers to the voices that ride the currents around 23rd Street. Just as they're no strangers to the voices *inside* Jack Fedogan's fabled bar.

Most nights, the ambiance in the Working Day is just about right: not too many people so that it's crowded but enough so you don't feel like a single coin shuffling in a lint-lined pocket, bereft of old friends and realising you're the next one to go. But no matter how many people, there's always laughter in the air, and talk, and company.

Tonight is different somehow.

It's different because the place is just about empty and it's different because the night itself is different ... hesitant and expectant, its cosmically existential heart as alive to the myriad possibilities that confront it as a light bulb is to the eternal promise of a daily dose of electric current.

McCoy Brewer watches the reflected world through the big mirror, accepts his dry martini and nods to Jack Fedogan, who grunts obligingly and then shuffles along the bar trailing his towel down the polished surface while McCoy takes a slug of almost pure gin. Almost pure because Jack Fedogan's dry martini means he simply immerses a glass pipette into the vermouth, waits until most of the liquor has evaporated or dripped off onto the waiting tissue, and then briefly submerges the now little-more-than-scented implement into the waiting highball glass of iced gin. Strong but good.

It's a little after six p.m. and McCoy feels the winter in his bones.

The drink helps some, but only some, managing to dispel the memory of the darkness of the early evening streets but failing to touch the greater ebony gloom in McCoy Brewer's soul. He feels it course down his throat and he slides sideways onto a barstool, already thinking of the next martini and the one after that one.

While he thinks, he watches the people in the mirror-world behind the bar.

Over in back, in one of the booths, a woman sits against the wall, a lady lifted straight from the musty dog-eared pages of a Jim Thompson paperback original, her nylon-stockinged right leg propped up along the length of the mock-plastic cushioned seat, the high-heeled shoe hanging from her foot and swinging to and fro in the narrow aisle that gives onto the ornately carved three-foot-high balustrades separating the booths from the tables. She's sipping a cocktail, her fourth since five o'clock, and she looks as though she's nowhere near finished yet. Almost as though she can feel him watching her, the woman glances up and looks across the tables into the big mirror, sees McCoy looking at her through the glass, sees his eyes, and smiles briefly.

McCoy nods, lifts his own drink and raises it in salute, watching his own reflection and that of the woman lift *their* own glasses in response and in the silent camaraderie of drinkers, two characters in a lost Edward Hopper painting, swimming the dark seas of night-time and solitude.

The woman's name is Rosemary Fenwick – a fact which McCoy will learn later – and she is drinking Manhattans to the memory of a husband and son she left behind in Wells, on the New England Atlantic coast, almost a year ago, seeing their faces in her mind's eye superimposed on the face of the man in the barroom mirror, never having heard from them in all that time, silently wondering, now, this night, what they're doing.

Only one of the tables has people sitting at it. It's a quiet night in the Working Day, unusually quiet. But maybe it has something to do with the mood of the streets outside. Sometimes the streets have a frenetic quality, a nervousness that splashes up unseen from the pavement and the sidewalks and seeps into the people of Manhattan like radiation, giving birth to uncertainty and a need to consolidate and re-group, maybe around a cocktail or two or a couple pitchers of beer.

The streets disguise this activity under a cloak of subterfuge ... worries about money, about health, about work and about the faithfulness of partners. But it's the City and, deep down, most people recognise this, though only a few acknowledge it. For nothing that ever happens in the City happens without both its knowledge and its approval.

At the table midway between Rosemary Fenwick and McCoy Brewer, two men sit hunched around a pitcher of beer. They're exchanging stories, telling jokes. Telling them in the slurred tone that comes with the temporary abandonment only liquor can give, laughing as they recount and sometimes even before they hear the punch line.

Jim Leafman works by day in the City's Refuse Department, collecting garbage ... sometimes picking up broken and discarded memories thrown out along with the ends of greening cheese and bacon rinds. His wife, Clarice, is having an affair with a salesman who sells office furniture, wood-veneered desks with pull-out work surfaces, and who lives one block away from their 23rd Street apartment. She thinks Jim doesn't know about it, but Jim knows. He's smelled the cologne that isn't his and he's imagined the hands that aren't his travelling around his wife's body, imagined Clarice whispering *No ... no*, but really meaning *yes ... oh, yes!* ... something Clarice hasn't said to her husband in a long time, a time that Jim has measured only in gained pounds, thinning hair and punishing credit card bills.

Jim has parked up outside the man's apartment building, sitting out on the street in a '74 Oldsmobile that's two parts yellow and eight parts rust, its muffler held in place with hope and Scotch tape, watching the doorway, nursing his old .38 in his lap like it was a baby, waiting for the travelling salesman to show. Jim has seen this guy, seen him a couple times now, watched him strolling along the sidewalk like he didn't have a care in the world, strolling along in his Gucci loafers and his soft-woven plaid jacket, pants with front creases that could cut meat, immaculate hair swept back and held in place like Cary Grant or an underworld hoodlum out of a Scorsese movie. Then, on these occasions, Jim has glanced in the rear-view, seen his own jowly face and pasty complexion, and he's decided that a guy doesn't deserve to die simply because he looks good any more than a guy deserves to die simply because he looks like a small-town department-store-window mannequin, its plastic skin worn and dented by the years and the constant magnified sunlight.

After some thought, on one of these occasions, Jim has also decided a woman doesn't deserve to die simply because she wants to do better. But these decisions have taken their toll and Jim Leafman is now in need of a joke.

So, too, is Edgar Nornhoevan, one-time-big but now slimmed off some, slimmed off a little too much some ... like the guy in the Stephen King book who just keeps on losing weight and can't do anything about it no matter how much chow he puts away. Edgar Nornhoevan, bearded and full of bluster, even though it feels like he's passing broken glass when he pees, a thin trickle that falls from his penis in drops instead of powering against the back of the stall the way he hears other men pee when he's standing there, concentrating on his flow the way his doctor has told him. This same doctor has told Edgar it's a problem with the prostate and he's having Edgar take pills that seem to help a little. But Edgar has also had some tests, one of which involved the doctor running a tiny seeing-eye down his penis and then staring, one eye closed, into the end as he twisted the thing around inside Edgar.

Lying there with his dick feeling like it was on fire, feeling like he needed to pee worse than ever before in his whole life, all fifty-three years of it, Edgar watched the doctor, saw him frown, twisting the tiny seeing-eye back and forth in his belly, heard him let out a tiny groan, an *Oh, dear, oh dear* groan, like the doc was seeing something that he didn't want to see, something that didn't ought to be there in Edgar Nornhoevan's stomach, something maybe like the thing that burst from John Hurt's guts in that *Alien* movie a few years back.

The doctor told Edgar, as he was pulling his pants on – Edgar, not the doctor – still feeling like his dick was on fire, that he was going to send off a swab for analysis but that, certainly – that's the word he used: *certainly* – the prostate seems unusually large. The results came back two days ago, since which time Edgar has been hitting the juice ... drinking for two, is how he tells Jim Leafman.

So, yes, Edgar needs to laugh right now.

"Hey Mac," Jim Leafman shouts across to McCoy Brewer, "you too good to sit with us these days?" Jim has just been told a joke about a guy with a bad flatulence problem which ends with the line 'You're wrong about the smell' and he's still laughing. Jim laughs a little louder and harder than he needs to do mainly because he's covering up the fact that until a few minutes ago he didn't know 'flatulence' was just a two-dollar word for 'farting'.

McCoy turns around and beams a big smile, raises his glass and moves away from the bar, moves a little reluctantly, reluctant because he doesn't really want to talk to anyone right now. He doesn't want to talk to anyone because he's just lost his job, this very day, his job with the Midtown & Western Trust & Loan, the only company in the city with two ampersands in its name. Right now, staring in the big mirror, McCoy Brewer doesn't care squat about ampersands – he just wants to come to terms with corporate speak, words like 'downsizing' and 'outsourcing', words he doesn't know, whether they're hyphenated or not.

As he walks across, McCoy hears Jim Leafman keeping the fart joke rolling with a few one-liners, schoolyard rhymers like, "He who smelt it dealt it," to which Edgar Nornhoevan says, pointing his finger in mock accusation, "Hey, you do the crime, you do the time!"

McCoy pulls up a chair, says, "Hey."

Jim waves him and carries on chuckling, shaking his head as he pours another glass of beer from the pitcher.

"Hey, listen up now," Edgar says, leaning across the table, resting a hand on McCoy's arm by way of greeting. "You ever wondered why a man's dick is shaped the way it is?" He looks at Jim, sees he's not about to get anything reasonable by way of a reply and turns to McCoy. "Mac?"

"Uh uh," McCoy says, truthfully.

"I mean," Edgar goes on, looking around to see if anyone is listening, forgetting that, apart from the woman, the woman who always seems to be in here, so regular she's almost like one of the chairs or a pile of beer coasters, "you know—" he draws the shape of a penis in the air in front of him, accentuating the large end of the shaft. "—why it's wider at the end than it is on the shaft?"

"Uh uh," McCoy says again, just as truthfully.

This time Jim Leafman shakes his head, too, getting into the yarn.

"Well," Edgar confides, twirling his fingers around the rim of his glass, "it's something that's been bothering folks in the medical profession for a number of years." He pronounces it 'perfession', slurring the first syllable and pulling it out it so it comes out kind of like a belch, waving his left arm with a flourish. "Particularly the French, the British and ... the Poles."

"Yeah?" The way Jim says that, he could almost be believing

it and, just for a moment, both Edgar and McCoy consider telling him, '*Hey, Jim ... it's a story, right? It ain't real*', but neither of them does. Instead, Edgar goes on.

"Yeah," he says. "See, the French, they conducted their own research ... took 'em eight months and a couple million francs and, at the end of it all, they come up with this: the reason a dick is shaped the way it is, is to give maximum pleasure when the guy's dipping his biscuit in the gravy. You know what I mean?" Edgar pushes his finger in and out of the hole made by the thumb and forefinger of his other hand.

McCoy smiles and leans forward on the table, reaches for the pretzel dish and lifts a couple to his mouth, crunching them.

"Okay," says Edgar. "So, the British ... they been wondering about the same thing and they conduct their own research. They are not convinced by the French, no siree. You know what I mean?" McCoy and Jim decide they do know and they nod. "Hey," Edgar says, "fuck the common market, you know what I mean?" He laughs and watches them both nod and smile before continuing.

"So," says Edgar, "they spend ... oh, a half a million pounds, something like that, and after another six months they agree that it's to improve, you know—"

"Dipping the biscuit?" Jim ventures.

"Yeah," says Edgar, repeating the stunt with the finger going in and out of the hand-hole, "only this time, they decide that it's for the woman's pleasure. That's why, you know, why the dick is shaped that way ... it's so it gives a little flick on the vulva as it goes in and out. You know what I mean?"

McCoy frowns. "The vulva?"

"Yeah. *Is* it a vulva?" Edgar says, suddenly unsure.

Jim Leafman shrugs, looks first to one of the men and then the other.

McCoy says, "Vagina. I think it's called a vagina."

Now Edgar shrugs. "Vulva, vagina ... who the hell cares?"

"Right," agrees Jim, taking a hit of beer.

"Yeah, right," echoes Edgar, the debate over anatomical correctness clearly having put him off his stride ... and he also now feels like he needs to pee. "What are you," he asks McCoy Brewer, "some kind of optometrist?"

"Uh uh," says McCoy, "I'm a mortgage clerk, you know that. Only, I lost my job today ... so now I'm nothing."

"You lost your job?" says Jim, his face slack and concerned.

As McCoy starts to respond, Edgar bangs the table with his right hand. "Hey, we telling stories here or what?"

"Sorry," says McCoy.

"Sorry," says Jim Leafman.

"Can you believe this guy?" Edgar asks McCoy, nodding in Jim's direction.

"Just tell the story already."

"Okay. So, where was I? See, I can't even remember where the fuck—"

"The British," Jim says softly. "They decided it was for the woman's pleasure." He looks like he's about to do the trick with the fingers and the hand-hole but instead he reaches for his glass.

"Yeah, right," Edgar says, and he chuckles. "So, the Poles..." Now he gives a real snort. "They decide they want to do their own research, cos, you know, they don't agree with either of the other two.

"So, they start their own survey study, you know ... and they spend ... they spend a couple of days and a few..." He pauses and looks across to the bar, sees Jack Fedogan polishing a glass while he watches them.

"Jack," Edgar shouts across, "Poles. What do they spend?"

Jack Fedogan squints and shifts his weight from one foot to

the other. "What do they spend?" For a second he wonders if Edgar is having him on, asking him something so he can make him look dumb. He rubs one callused hand across his chin and, with the other, carefully sets the glass down on the bar counter.

"Yeah, what do they use for money?"

Jack shrugs, says, "They use the same as everybody else does, leastways they do in *my* bar."

Edgar waves his arm. "No," he says, "in *Poland* for Chrissakes. What do they use when they're at home in *Poland*?"

"Pesetas?" Jack suggests.

McCoy sniggers.

"Is it drachma?" Jim ventures, looking first at McCoy and then at Edgar. "I think I heard something about drachma. I thought maybe it was rubics but that was the guy that made the cube. Did you ever have one of those?" Jim Leafman says to McCoy.

McCoy nods. "When they first came out I bought one."

"Me too," says Jim. "Almost did it one time. Two squares out."

"Okay," Edgar says, impatiently, "we'll go for drachma. So, they do this research, right, takes about two days and costs around fifty drachma—" He shrugs and raises his eyebrows. "In other words, not very much, you know what I'm saying here? Anyway, they come up with the answer." He leans forward and lowers his voice a little.

"The Poles, they figure a guy's dick is shaped the way it is so that your hand doesn't fly off and hit you in the face." He slaps the table in tune with the word 'face' and leans back in his chair guffawing.

McCoy laughs in spite of himself, feels some of the pressure lifting from the back of his head, unsure whether he's laughing at the joke or whether he's just starting to feel the effects of the martini.

Jim Leafman has a big dumb smile on his face, wants to laugh but just can't quite tie everything up to allow him to do so.

Edgar repeats the last line, making a jerking-off movement with his right hand and then hitting himself in his face with it.

"Oh, right," Jim says, laughing now but the laughter sounding a little forced and unreal, echoing around the empty room.

Outside on the street the sound of this merriment distils the intensity in the air and wafts along with occasional exhaust fumes and the smells of roasting chestnuts and hot dogs and catsup, wafting and diminishing with each foot and each yard it travels until, a few steps either side of The Land of the Working Day, it fades completely as far as normal people are concerned, normal folks hurrying home or rushing out on dates or to dinner parties, moving through the drift of silent laughter like it wasn't there, arguing about this and that or lost in thought cultivated and even approved by the City.

But though it is now silent, this laughter, still it exists and still it moves, drifting in all directions ... up towards the Empire State, down to Washington Square and Greenwich Village, and east across Madison Square and on to Gramercy Park. It will continue, this sound, moving across all barriers, fading and fading until it is the ghost of a ghost of bygone laughter, but it will continue to retain some residue of itself and of why it came about. For though there is always something special about any laughter, there is something doubly special – almost divine – about laughter that *needs* to be, laughter that, through the simple process of coming into being, releases and repairs.

And out in the night-time City, out there amidst the trees and the trashcans and the lonely alleyways, beneath the ever-present hum of siren, engines and human breathing, there are people closer to the Heart of the City than everyday normal folks. And one of these, a man, hears the sound on the breeze like tinkling bells, wind-chimes fashioned out of coral shells and plastic cord. This man on this night is closest of all to the Heart of the City. He is the custodian of its welfare, though this is not a post he has sought.

On other nights and at other times there will be others, men and women, boys and girls, whose unsought and un-asked-for responsibility will be to restore the balance of the streets. But for some nights past and for some nights still to come, it is this man's responsibility and his alone.

As he hears the sound he chuckles to himself, sitting on a bench in Gramercy eating the remains of a tuna niçoise sandwich that someone has discarded earlier in the day, cocking his dirty head to one side and lifting the earflap of his conical hat, he discerns the direction from which the sound has come to him, then turning, almost as though he can see it travelling on away from him, away to Stuyvesant Square and then to the East River and then across to Brooklyn ... which some might say is in most urgent need of the ministrations of laughter (but only those who do not live there).

He wraps the remains of the sandwich in the dirty greaseproof paper and thrusts it deep into an old coat tied colourfully around his waist. Then he lifts from the floor by the bench an old satchel fashioned out of soft leather and upon which are strange runic symbols that he has carved over the years, and he faces diagonally across Park Avenue South, sniffing the air and smiling.

Then he starts to walk.

Back in The Land at the End of the Working Day, the jokes and the stories are coming thick and fast, thicker and faster as the drinks are replenished. And, strangely – strangely because Jack Fedogan's bar is a popular establishment – no more people have come in on this particular night and no one who was already in the bar has left, as though the single room, with its softly whirring air conditioning and a steady stream of faint piped jazz music put out from Jack's CD player, had become the room in the old Bunuel movie where people simply *cannot* leave, though for what reason they are never sure.

"Okay," says McCoy Brewer, sensing that it is his turn and taking advantage of the natural lull in story-telling, "so, the Pope comes to New York, right? Pays the Apple a visit."

Edgar Nornhoevan nods, playing the table-top like it's a piano, joining in with the sound of Bill Evans playing 'My Melancholy Baby' out of the old speakers on either side of the bar, shaking his head like he's living the notes and the chords, forgetting for a while that he needs to pee.

Jim Leafman nods too, and takes a drink, whispering the punch line from Edgar's last joke, "No thanks I'll smoke my own,'... heh, heh ... I like that, I really like that ... heh, heh..." He dribbles beer down the front of his shirt because he's still talking as he drinks.

"So," McCoy continues, "the Pope, he's finished his visit – he's done all the touristy things, you know, been up the Empire State, got mugged in Central Park, bought a slice to go from Ssbarro ... the full works – and now he's about to head home for Rome and the Vatican. Anyways, this huge limo picks him up from the hotel – he's staying at the Waldorf, right?"

Edgar nods his head, half-closing his eyes in agreement and momentarily giving in to an increasing feeling of disorientation and general drunkenness. "So where else would the Pope stay?" he says, pronouncing it 'elsh' and 'shtay'.

"Right," says McCoy. "So, the limo picks him up and they set off for the airport." He takes a sip of martini, savouring the taste, and then continues.

"So, as they're driving, the Pope picks up the intercom to the driver. 'Hello driver,' he says," says McCoy, holding his empty right hand up to his mouth like he's talking into something. "'This is my first time in the United States and I have *never*, I mean *ever*, been in a car like this before. Do you think it would be okay if I drive it for a while?' Well, the driver, he's a little taken aback. I mean, nobody has asked him this before, right?"

Nods from Jim and Edgar. Glancing to the side, McCoy sees that Jack Fedogan is leaning across the bar trying to listen, having shuffled closer and closer during the last couple of stories. "You with it so far, Jack?" McCoy asks.

Jack stands up and, for a second, looks a little hurt.

"Whyn't you come over, Jack," Edgar shouts.

"How about me, too?" shouts Rosemary Fenwick, the lady from the Jim Thompson book, who, McCoy thinks as he turns around to see who's asking, looks like Barbara Stanwick from the old movie with Fred McMurray where the two of them get together and throw Barbara Stanwick's husband from a train. "I could use a little laughter tonight," she says, the words blending in with the *click-clack* of her heels as she walks to the table without waiting for an answer.

"Sure," says McCoy Brewer, "let's all of us gather around this table."

"I'll bring some more drinks," Jack Fedogan shouts, looking happy now, like a child who's just been allowed to play with the big boys. "On the house," Jack says.

"Then I'll have a double," says McCoy.

"Make mine a double Bud, bud," shouts Jim.

And everyone laughs while Jim Leafman pulls over another couple of chairs, and stands while Rosemary Fenwick joins them.

Pretty soon, they're all at the table, fresh drinks lined up in front of them, five lost people in the greatest city in the world, enjoying life unexpectedly.

"So, where was I?"

"Hey," says Jack Fedogan, "this table feel strange to you?"

"How's come strange?" asks Jim Leafman.

Jack places his hands palm down on the table. "I dunno ... strange like ... like there's some kinda current going through it."

"Current like in electricity-type current?" says Jim, pushing his chair back a ways.

Rosemary Fenwick places a hand on the table and lifts it quickly, then places it down again, leaving it there this time. "I can feel something," she says. "Like some kind of vibration."

McCoy Brewer says, "Didn't feel anything before," saying it carefully, considering the validity of the statement.

"Until there were five of us," Edgar says around a hiccup, pronouncing it 'ush'.

"Until there were five of us? What the hell' – pardon my French," Jack says, glancing across at Rosemary Fenwick, who has now introduced herself to the others who have, in turn, introduced themselves to her. Rosemary shakes her head, and Jack continues while Rosemary smiles and uses two slender fingers to pull a cigarette from a crumpled and sorry-looking pack of Marlboro Lights.

"What's *that* got to do with the price of beans?" Jack asks, feeling like it's his fault that the table is shuddering ... because, dammit to hell, it *is* shuddering.

"Must be the subway," Jim says, nodding slowly at his own wisdom.

"Right!" says Jack Fedogan, relieved.

McCoy places his hands gingerly on the edge of the table. "Doesn't seem so bad now," he says.

"Prob'ly a train passing," says Edgar.

"Okay." McCoy takes a long slug of beer and then a sip of his martini. "So back to the story."

"The Pope just asked if he could drive the limo," Rosemary says, lifting her Manhattan in salute to Jack, who nods like it was nothing but who flushes kind of pink around the gills.

"Right," says McCoy. "So the driver considers who's asking and he decides, hey, what could be the problem, right? The car will be safe enough and so he agrees. The Pope jumps into the driver's seat and straight away floors the acceleration pedal throwing the driver onto the floor at the back.

"The limo screeches up Broadway like you wouldn't believe, running red lights, scaring the bag ladies and the muggers and the pimps, doing nearly one hundred miles an hour. Anyway, pretty soon this prowl car sees them come by and pulls out in pursuit. After a lengthy chase that takes them almost up into Harlem, the prowl car flags the limo down."

"One hundred miles an hour up Broadway! Shee," says Jim Leafman. "Can you imagine that?"

"That's fast," says Rosemary Fenwick.

"That *is* fast," agrees Edgar, saying 'fasht'.

"So," says McCoy, "the cop gets out of the car – there's only one cop in there – and he knocks on the driver's window. The Pope sheepishly lowers the window ... at which point the cop takes one look and then goes back to his own car and radios the precinct. 'Er, this is Car Sixteen,' the cop says, 'I think I've got a problem.'

"'Problem?' says the guy at the precinct. 'Yeah,' says the cop. 'I've pulled over a VIP.' 'Who is it?' comes the reply, 'not the Mayor again?'

"'Nope,' says the cop. 'More important than him.'

"'Not the Senator?' says the precinct house.

"'Nope, more important than *him*,' says the cop.

"'The President? Tell me you haven't pulled over the President,' says the precinct.

"'Nope,' says the cop. 'It's even more important than *him*.'

"'More important than the President of the United States?' comes the reply. 'Who could be more important than that?'

"The cop says, 'I dunno, but he's got the Pope as his chauffeur.'"

The laughter mixed in with Herbie Hancock's 'Maiden Voyage' and the hybrid sound of cymbals and piano and pure good times rings out in the dimly lit barroom and washes against the walls and over to the steps leading up onto the street, spilling out into the night air like a beacon.

And it *is* a beacon, of sorts anyways.

And it *has* been noticed.

For out in the wintry night sidewalks of New York City there is one more soul adrift in the night. And he is following the sound like it's a clarion call and, staring into the dark skies awash with reflected colours, he senses the direction of the sound and adjusts his own path – not by much ... maybe by only a few feet – and he crosses over the street.

"Yeah," says Jim Leafman, "I love a good joke."

Jack Fedogan nods and glances towards the stairs.

"Jack?" Edgar Nornhoevan follows Jack's stare. "Something wrong?"

Jack shakes his head like he's coming round from a punch to the face. "No, just thought ... just thought I heard something."

McCoy looks around at the stairs and sees the darkness of the streets lying at the top, curled up away from the overhead lights on the stairs and, for a second, it reminds him that the world is waiting for him. Reminds him that the funny stories are only down here, down here in Jack Fedogan's bar, and that up there he doesn't have a job. Up there, funny stories are strictly for people who are in work. "Can't see anything," he says and looks back down at his beer and his highball.

"Hey, you're thinning down, Ed," Jack says, changing the subject. "I hadn't noticed that before," he adds, patting his own stomach and nodding to Edgar Nornhoevan's. "You lost a little weight. Looks good on you." He nods and takes a slug of beer. "You working out?"

Edgar pulls in a long sigh. "Tumour," he says, letting out the air.

"Tumour?" says Jim Leafman. "That some kind of diet?"

Grimacing, Jack says, "It's cancer, you dumb fuck," hissing it. He turns to Rosemary Fenwick and adds, "Pardon my—"

"I know," Rosemary says, "pardon your fucking French."

McCoy Brewer reaches across and pats Edgar's arm. "Where?" he asks.

"Prostate. Me and Timothy Leary."

"Turn on, *tume* in and drop out," says Jack.

"Oh, that was awful," says Rosemary.

"Leave him be," says Edgar. "He's just trying to make me feel better."

"He's just a comedian, he don't mean nothing," says Jim Leafman, filling his glass from the pitcher, filling it right to the brim and watching the froth turn into beer and slop down the sides onto the table.

"I guess we're all comedians tonight," says McCoy.

"Yeah," Rosemary says, "it feels special alright. You feel that? Can you feel something special about everything?"

"How special?" Jack slides his hand across the table and shakes one of Rosemary's cigarettes out of the pack, then lights it.

"I thought you quit?" says Edgar.

"I did." Jack takes a pull on the cigarette and blows smoke, smiling.

Rosemary shrugs. "Dunno. Just special."

"It's cos we're telling jokes," says Jim, "cos we're comedians, like Mac said."

Jack Fedogan says, "What was it Lenny Bruce said about comedians?"

Grunts from everyone. Nobody knows what Lenny Bruce said about anything.

"He said something like a comedian is someone who makes up his own material, not someone who just repeats other folks' stuff," says Jack, remembering hearing Lenny interviewed by Studs Terkel on WFMT back in '59, when he lived in Chicago. "They're just echoes."

McCoy turned to him. "Lenny Bruce said that? Echoes?"

"No ... well, I don't recall him actually *saying* that, but that's what he *meant*," says Jack. "He meant they're not the real thing."

The sound on the stairs happens right then. McCoy, Rosemary, Jim, Jack and Edgar pulling themselves back from the table like they're resting on an oven surface or a barbecue grill, staring at the table, feeling those same vibrations again, like the granddaddy of all trains is moving right under where they're sitting, but they're unable to take their hands away, each of them holding their hands flat on the table's surface like they're trying to stop it rising into the air. And then they all glance across at the stairs, from where the unmistakable sound of feet descending can be heard.

"Now *that's* the real thing," says Edgar, saying it quietly, like he's saying it only to himself.

Coming down the stairs, looking around the room like it was an Aladdin's cave of treasures, is a man. At first glance the man looks to be old, but then the assembled patrons of The Land at the End of the Working Day see that the man's long hair and beard are probably only discoloured by the city, made grey by the traffic exhausts and the cooking smells, and that they don't actually relate to his age. For his face is completely unlined. It's dirty, sure, grimy and greasy-looking, but the man's eyes are bright and wide open, taking everything in. He stops a couple of steps from the bottom and puts his hands on his hips.

In one hand he carries a dirty leather satchel, its contents bulging the sides out though there does not appear to be anything of any significant weight in there as it swings by his side effortlessly. He stands around five eight, five nine, a long black coat coming down to his shins, its sleeves rolled up to make thick cuffs which even then, with his arms bent, cover most of his hands. On the coat, either pinned into place or stitched – he's standing too far away for the quintet at the table to be sure – are a series of signs and shapes, some of which are clearly moons, crescent moons, and stars, the kind of stars you see in children's story books, five points and a fat centre. The only thing that's missing on these are faces, though McCoy wonders to himself if they weren't there, once upon a time, and have merely been stolen by the city and the night.

Around the man's waist is a makeshift belt which appears to have been constructed by several neckties of various designs and colours, its knot lavishly fashioned into an elaborate bow. Beneath the coat hangs a pair of trousers, grey and flecked, which culminate in a series of ruffles at the man's ankles, resting on a pair of scuffed training shoes bearing the unmistakable motif of *Nike* on the side. But it is his headgear that makes for the most striking item of his clothing.

For on top of that veritable explosion of lank and matted hair sits a cross between a tall, conical hat and an old leather flying helmet, its tapered end bent so that the point hangs at a right angle to the rest of it, ear-flaps hanging loosely at the sides of his face and the whole affair similarly lavished with symbols and drawings, all of which are faded and scuffed and somehow altogether tired looking.

"*Bonsoir, mes amis,*" the man's voice booms, and he lifts his hands as though he is a benign ruler addressing his people. Taking the final three stairs onto the floor of Jack Fedogan's tavern, he sees the five people all holding their hands flat on the table and says, "Hey, don't tell me ... 'Seance on a Wet Afternoon', right?"

They stare at him in silence.

"Okay, maybe you're enacting one of those shlocky slice 'n' dice features ... like maybe 'Evil Dead 7' or 'Halloween 24', something like that?" He waves his hands in the air and looks to the ceiling. "Is there anybody there?" he says in a deep wavering voice, dragging the words out to three and four times their length. "Aunt Jemima, tell Uncle Frank I'm gonna look after his stamp collection."

Jack stands up from the table and starts towards the man, waving his hands slowly in front of him. "I don't know what you're looking for pal," Jack tells the man, "but you ain't likely to find it in here."

"Me?" The man's face frowns and he places both of his hands on his own chest. "It is not I who am looking for anything, but you yourselves."

"*Us?*" Edgar manages to say the word correctly and almost surprises himself that the drunkenness seems to have passed, at least for a while.

"For sure," says the man, turning to Edgar Nornhoevan. "For is that not why I have been summoned?"

"We didn't summon nobody," says Jack. "And, like I say, we don't allow no bums in here," he adds, reaching a hand out to take hold of the man's arm.

"Ah, fear not friends ... that is quite normal," says the man, and he lifts a hand to straighten his hat. "Rather it is the City itself that seeks my help on your behalf," he says, imbuing the word 'city' with a strange significance. He looks to the upturned faces and says, "It does that all the time."

Shifting around in her chair, Rosemary Fenwick asks the man who he is, something that most of the others have also been wanting to find out.

"Me?" the man booms, "I am Gandalph Cohen."

"Gandalph Cohen?" says Edgar.

"What kind of a name is that?" asks Jim Leafman.

The man turns a withering glance at Jim and says, softly, "It's Jewish."

"I think he meant 'Gandalph'," says Rosemary.

"Ah, of course, an unusual name I grant you." The man smiles at Jack and shakes his elbow free. Pointing to the table, he says, "Might I join you?"

Without waiting for a response, the man pulls a chair from one of the other tables, drags it across to sit between Rosemary and Edgar, and plops down with a sigh. Jack shrugs and walks across to the bar where he pours a fresh pitcher of beer which, along with a clean glass, he brings back to the table. The man accepts the glass and McCoy pours the beer.

"My parents, God rest their souls, were Tolkien freaks," he says, slurping the froth from his beard loudly. "The saga of the Ring and of the hobbits' epic journey figured largely in their lives. When I came along, almost thirty-nine years ago, the choice of a name was of no concern. The only problem was that the Rabbi misspelled it, so I'm Gandalph with a pee-aitch instead of with an eff. The full name is Gandalph Ara*gone For*do Cohen. The man was a Philistine where fantastic literature was concerned but at least he spelled Cohen correctly."

The man takes another drink and, resting his glass back on the table, lifts his left side – the one next to Edgar – from the chair and lets rip a loud fart. "*Pardonnez moi*," he says.

Astonished, Rosemary Fenwick bursts into uncontrolled laughter, quickly joined by Jim Leafman, McCoy Brewer and Edgar himself, though, placing a hand across his nose, he backs away from the man.

"Jesus Chri—" Jack Fedogan begins before he too starts to laugh.

"Why did you *say* that?" says Rosemary, still sniggering.

"What?"

"That 'pardonay mwah' stuff?"

The man shrugs. "Just being polite. It's always polite to excuse yourself when you pass wind in public."

"No, I mean saying it in French," says Rosemary, unable to keep the exasperation out of her tone.

Another shrug. "I used to be French."

"*Used* to be?" says McCoy.

"Uh huh. I've been all kinds of nationality – French, German, Hindu, Russian ... you name it, I've been it. The French has stuck, though. Hard to shake off."

"I thought you said you were Jewish," Edgar says.

"Nope. I said my *name* was Jewish."

"So what are you? What are you now?" asks Jack.

"Jewish. Been Jewish all my life ... this one, anyways." He takes another slug of beer.

"You just said—"

"Sorry," Gandalph Cohen says to Jack Fedogan, "playing the old semantics game. The other nationalities were other lives ... existences before this one. This time around I am most assuredly Jewish ... but a little French here and there never hurt anyone."

Jack, Edgar, Jim, McCoy and Rosemary sit looking at each other, exchanging frowns, grimaces and rolled-up eyes, side-glancing at the new arrival as he leans on the back of his chair and scans the interior of the Working Day.

"Nice place," says Gandalph Cohen at last, turning back to face the others but nodding at Jack Fedogan. "Bet it's expensive to run, yes?"

Jack regains his composure and nods. The truth of the matter is, that it's very expensive. Jack is currently fighting a foreclosure order from the bank, something he tries to keep to himself. But not for long. He figures he's got one week.

"Ah, well," says the newcomer, "it's only money, yes?"

He turns to Edgar. "And you need to urinate and can't do it so well, yes?" He leans forward and sniffs. "Cancer of the prostate, if I'm not mistaken." He nods to himself, satisfied with his diagnosis. "Invariably fatal, I believe but—" He sniffs again. "I think this one will respond to treatment. A few visits to the radiography area will put it to rest ... plus you'll be able to start up electrical household objects from twenty paces."

Turning to Rosemary, he places a grubby hand on her knee and squeezes once before removing it. "And you, my dear, are worrying about your husband and your little boy..." He pauses and closes his eyes. "New England?" He opens his eyes and sees Rosemary staring at him, her mouth hanging limply open. "Nice place ... but terrible winters." He pats the knee again. "You'll see them again, my dear ... but leave it until the spring." He glances away quickly, trying to convince himself that one lie might ease a burden where the truth would only increase it.

"And you, sir," he says across the table to Jim Leafman. "Woman trouble, I believe, is what ails you."

"Who—" Jim's voice sounds about three octaves too high, like a choirboy's, and he clears his throat before continuing. "Who said I was ailing?"

Gandalph Cohen laughs. "Ah, we're all ailing, *mon ami*," he says to Jim, "it's only the reasons that are different. Your future lies away from your wife – is it Clarice?"

Jim nods.

"Yes? Nice name. Well, your path goes in another direction from hers. But be happy with it. It's a good path."

"What about my bar?" asks Jack Fedogan. "You never said. You just said, 'It's only money'."

"No, you'll never lose the bar," says Gandalph Cohen. "But you'll lose its present location. And it won't be the same."

"Shit," says Jack, and then, "pardon my French, Rosemary."

"French?" says Gandalph Cohen. "That would be *merde* surely?"

"Of course it won't be the same," says Jack, annoyed. "But where will it be if it ain't here?"

"There'll always be a Land at the End of the Working Day," comes the reply, "just as there will always be a proprietor. Right now, it's here and it's you. A few years back, it was a Laundromat in Queens. Before that, a hot dog stand down near Battery Park ... a video store in Jackson Heights – that was the one before you..."

"A Laundromat, a hot dog stand and a video store all called The Land at the End of the Working Day?" says Jim Leafman.

"*Mais non*, my little garbage collecting friend," says Gandalph Cohen. "'Squeeky Clean' – with a double 'e' – 'Frank's Franks' and 'The Big Picture'. The name isn't important."

"Never mind the name," says Jack, "what do you mean 'before me'? I don't think I'm following you? Just who are you?"

"I told you," says Gandalph Cohen. "I'm Gandalph Cohen."

"How do you know so much, I think is what he means," says Rosemary, pulling a cigarette out of her pack.

Gandalph Cohen shrugs. "I just know, that's all. I know that the City creates its own amusements. It's like an offshoot of the Gaia theory ... you know? Where the planet is a thinking entity that looks after itself?"

Edgar nods and takes a drink. Suddenly he's feeling a whole lot better than he's felt in days. In fact, he's feeling downright good.

"And," Gandalph Cohen continues, "it needs something to appease the people who live in it. Kind of like a pressure valve, through which temperatures are allowed to cool off. But it moves it around."

"It moves it around?" Jack Fedogan shakes his head. "*What* moves *what* around?"

"The City," says Gandalph Cohen. "The City moves its pressure valve around. On a whim," he says, brandishing an arm theatrically, "for no good reason other than sheer caprice. And tonight's the night it goes from here."

McCoy has been silent for a while, thinking over what has been said. He clears his throat now and says, "Where does it go from here?"

The man in the strange hat shrugs. "Don't know yet. Don't ever know. Thing is, I don't need to know. People only need the valve when they're close to bursting. Some folks are close to bursting most of the time and they become regulars ... kind of like therapy, you know? Some folks are so *very* close to bursting they never find it – like not seeing the wood for the trees? – and they end up blowing away a couple families in their local McDonalds or decapitating their neighbours for not returning a half-used carton of barbecue-lighting fluid.

"Me, I've been at fourteen of these handovers over the years. I suspect it was someone else before me, someone the City picks."

"What ... you know, what do you actually *do*?" asks Jim.

"You *believing* all this?" says Jack, slapping Jim's arm.

"I don't actually *do* anything," Gandalph Cohen says, ignoring Jack Fedogan's remark. "I'm what you might call a conduit. It's through me that the necessary levels are attained so that the ... the force, I guess you could call it – though I am aware that someone else already thought up that particular usage of term – so that the force can be freed." He drains his glass and pours some more beer. "Where it'll go from here is anybody's guess. How long it'll stay there, the same." He reaches into his coat pocket and removes the sandwich.

"You never said," says Rosemary, grimacing as she watches the man take a bite out of the soggy-looking baguette, "how you know so much about us ... our names ... and everything else."

"And you never said what was going to happen to *me* ... you 'did' everyone else," says McCoy.

"You," Gandalph Cohen says to McCoy Brewer, speaking around a mouthful of sandwich, "you are out of a job. Tomorrow you will *still* be out of a job. But a job is just a job, yes? Tonight, *mon ami*, you have a mission ... a quest, even ... and a quest has always been more important than a job. More than that I cannot say ... though I will say that you will be immensely helpful to Jack here, over the months and years ahead. As, it must be said, he will be to you.

"And in response to *your* question," he says to Rosemary, "the rhythms of the City are complex." He offers her a huge smile which exposes brown teeth. "But it is possible to follow them. Those rhythms are the people that live here ... like fleas on a dog. It's too difficult to explain any more than that." He takes another slug of beer and wipes his sleeve across his beard.

"The people know that the force is moving on," he continues. "That is why there are none of them here tonight. They wouldn't say that if you asked them, of course. They would simply say that they had other things to do ... like dinner parties, movies, bowling – do people still go bowling?"

Everyone shrugs.

"No matter. But the point is that the City is keeping them away."

"Why?" McCoy asks quietly. "Why does it want to do that?" Even as the last word of the question leaves his mouth, McCoy Brewer wonders whether he has had too much to drink.

"It doesn't need them."

McCoy says, "But it needs us?"

Gandalph Cohen nods. "It needs them that need it the most. Tonight, you five need the City in the worst way. Tomorrow night, it'll be other people; last night it was others still. And so it goes on." He slaps the table. "But, enough talk ... we have work to do."

"What work?" asks Jim Leafman.

"We have to enjoy ourselves and perform the handover."

"Hey," says Rosemary, holding her hands palm out above the table. "Can you feel it?"

"*Feel* it ... I can *see* it!" says Edgar.

And, sure enough, the table seems to be shuddering, tiny, infinitesimally small vibrations that make it seem as though it's alive, alive with expectation.

"What do we do?" asks Jack Fedogan.

"Well, *mon ami*," says Gandalph Cohen, "I suggest you get us another couple pitchers of beer – and maybe a few pretzels or nuts? That would be good – and we'll just sit around like the friends we are and we'll make each other smile.

"Tell me," says Gandalph Cohen, leaning onto the vibrating table in The Land at the End of the Working Day, "has anyone heard the one about the guy from the mid-west who goes on holiday to Scotland? He goes into this bread and cakes store and he says to the assistant, pointing at this cake-thing in the display case, 'Is that a doughnut or a meringue?' And the assistant, she says—" He puts on a Scottish accent, "Och, no, you're right – it's a doughnut.'"

Jack exchanges a quizzical expression with Edgar, and then his eyes light up and he starts to laugh. Then Rosemary starts to giggle, her eyebrows raised high in sudden understanding ... and then McCoy Brewer. Only Jim maintains a frown. "I don't think I get that one," he says quietly.

"Doesn't matter," says Gandalph Cohen. "Keep it going. Every joke you ever heard ... every funny story, every anecdote."

"Okay," says Edgar. "How about this one..."

As the night wears on, and the beer flows thick and fast, the stories come out ... some stories the teller heard just the other week and some are dredged up from their deepest memory. Sometimes the stories get a laugh and sometimes they don't ... but the City accepts the laughter from all of them, drinking it in gratefully like a man lost in the desert drinking in droplets of soda from a discarded can. Eventually, a little after eleven p.m...

Resting his hands on the table and sensing something has changed, Jim Leafman says, "The table feels different. Has it happened?"

Gandalph Cohen nods and places his empty glass on the table.

"It feels sad," says Rosemary. "It feels like I just sat up all night with a sick friend and now ... now she's gone."

"Not gone," says Gandalph Cohen. "Just moved on to where she's needed more. *Écoutez...*" he says. Out in the darkness, outside the two-flight walk-down on the corner of 23rd and Fifth, a wind seems to have gotten up.

"So tell me," says Jim Leafman, watching the others cocking their heads to one side, listening ... smiling to themselves ... watching them get to their feet and stretching, seeing them embrace and shake each other's hands, "what *is* a meringue? Could someone tell me that?"

RINGFENCED

Lynn M Cochrane

SO I PHOTOGRAPHED Sam that sunny afternoon, leaning against the gatepost at the entrance to the field, his hair blowing in the wind, eyes sparkling, laughter written in every crease of his face. Later, and there was a later, I would look at that image and not know whether to destroy it or linger in the beatific warmth of his gaze.

Holidays get you like that, don't they? You slave all year for a few measly days in a better place – oh, and enough to put the roof over your head and the food on the table the rest of the year – then you zoom off somewhere else and remind your camera what it's supposed to do. And it reminds you of what it can't. So you recharge the battery and try again. Only by the time I'd got the camera functioning, it was our last day on holiday and I went trigger-happy.

"Do you fancy the beach, again?" I asked Sam.

"Not for the second day in a row," he said. "Let's head for the country. I could do with some green fields around me and the wind across the hilltops blowing the cobwebs out from between my ears."

I chased him round the hotel bedroom until he turned and caught me and kissed me into submission, both of us laughing all the time. Then, we picked up our cameras and packed lunch and headed for the local bus and a trip into the country.

The bus was the town-link service, one of a hundred or so in the local livery. I have never blamed the bus. It took dangerous bends fast. It stopped at short notice to collect people hiding in the tall hedges that lined the single-track roads. It raced where I would have been cautious and dawdled where I would have rushed; even stopping once while the driver went into the news-agents and again while he delivered a couple of bags of shopping to a small cottage set back from the road.

"Your Mum all right?" one of the locals asked him as he climbed back into his cab.

"She is now she's got the bread and coffee she forgot yesterday," he answered.

"Ah! Breakfast is served," called one of the other passengers.

"Delivered, more like," said someone else.

Sam and I sat there, grinning like idiots, enjoying this glimpse into the local community.

We were almost sad to leave them when we got to our stop and started up the steep footpath towards the top of the hill and the long walk back to the hotel.

The scenery was stunning. Sky and sea were blue with the horizon a darker blue line with occasional sails or sets of funnels moving along it. The grass along the path seemed a brighter-than-usual green. Gulls wheeled overhead, glaring white against the sky. Both of us went trigger-happy, catching fleeting glimpses of butterflies and birds, dragonflies and bees, unusual angles on standard holiday scenes.

Near the road, the hill had been quite steep. We reached what we had thought of as the top – and wasn't. There was a dip before the hill went on up, in a long incline that robbed both of us of breath. At the end, the slope went convex once more, bulging out to meet us as we climbed up between pairs of stones that were almost lost in the ubiquitous hedges.

Gasping, Sam leaned against the right-hand post of the gate that barred our way. Sam had ran out of memory on his camera; I had a few shots left available on mine. Laughing, I snapped one of those last few images, capturing the effects of that climb on the man I loved.

When we had finally regained our breath, we opened the gate, slipped through, and closed it behind us. Sam briefly laid a hand on the stone of the gate-post.

"Someone must have brought this here," he said. "Why? How?"

"Don't ask me," I said. "Let's find a place to sit out of the wind and investigate the Hotel's packed lunch."

We found a sheltered nook with a decent view of the sea and opened the packed lunch. I found my share inedible and scattered it around for the wildlife to find. Sam, he of the cast iron stomach, chomped his way through day-old sandwiches, a yellow -ing pork-pie and cakes so stale they disintegrated into crumbs at a touch. Rested, but not refreshed, we carried on along the path.

I felt it first as an itch between my shoulder-blades, right where I couldn't scratch. Then the hairs on the back of my neck all stood up – closely followed by the hairs on my arms and legs. I shuddered, not liking the sensation.

"You, too, huh?" muttered Sam. He stopped, looking round, eyes growing wide.

Confused and worried, I looked round as well. The path was running across a wide open area with hedges forming a circle around it – a circle marked out by standing stones that formed dots in the dashes of the greenery.

"Wow!" said Sam. "I wonder if anyone knows about this."

Trust him to react that way. I was, perhaps, a bit more observant. We were the only visible life forms in the circle. The clean, green grass was short but there was no evidence of what had shortened it. No rabbits, then. Birds flew in the air all around but none crossed the hedge and stone boundary to fly over the velvet green lawn. Bees and butterflies had been our companions all the way from the bus but there were none here in what should have been an insect paradise. Even the grass felt like Astro Turf.

I found the lack of wildlife worrying. I glanced up at the sun – suddenly hidden behind milky white cloud. I looked around again before consulting my watch. The afternoon was wearing away faster than I liked.

"Sam, we need to go *now*," I said, emphasising the last word.

"*Ssssaaaaammmm,*" came the sussurant echo from one side of the circle, replicated and returned until I heard, as a faint whisper, "*Ssssussstainn.*"

It was, honestly, an attempt to get Sam to hurry that had me pacing to the far edge of the stone circle. I kept clear of the twin menhirs that formed the gateway, although the couple of scraps of wood that hung from the one had long since ceased to be a barrier across the path. I side stepped to avoid the last wagging finger of rotting timber before I stopped and turned and looked back to see where Sam was. After all, a grown man doesn't need a minder, does he?

Perhaps he does. Sam stood in the centre of the circle, head thrown back and arms outstretched. He seemed bathed in light, somehow, the morning star against the midnight blue of the open area.

"Sam!" I yelled. "Come on! Look at the time!"

Sam looked up at the sun, which struck me as odd. He'd usually check the time on his mobile phone, even when we were at home in the garden. Then he shrugged, gave me a thumbs-up and started plodding across the circle to join me.

By the time he reached the gateway, he was stumbling. He

reached out to the nearest stone and used it to balance himself. It was some moments before he let go and stepped away to join me on the path.

But it wasn't Sam. Not the Sam I knew. Not the gentle, teasing lover I had chased round the bedroom that morning. Plodding just behind me to my left was the outward appearance of the man, but none of the vivacity that made up Sam.

He was staggering by the time the path became wide enough for two. I paused to let him regain his balance until I heard whispers on the track behind us, sounding like approaching snakes. I put Sam's right hand onto my left shoulder and led him further down slope, along the path. Three pauses later I was holding him round the waist, trying to keep him more-or-less upright but at least the hotel was in sight. I almost carried him into reception.

Thinking back, I was surprised to see our cases waiting for us by the reception desk. At the time, I was more concerned about getting medical help for Sam. The receptionist nodded but didn't seem to do anything. She just watched us.

The ambulance, blue lights flashing, drew up outside. Two burly paramedics came into reception. One of them took Sam from me and began to walk him out to the ambulance. The other indicated our cases. I nodded. He picked up the luggage and indicated that I should precede him. Behind the desk, the girl hadn't moved.

In the ambulance, Sam was already lying on the stretcher, looking exhausted. I was ushered onto a seat on the other side of the vehicle and our cases were strapped down nearby.

"What's going on?" I asked.

The paramedic who had carried the cases looked shocked. "You can still talk!" he said.

"Yes," I said. "Why not?"

"This is a small community," he answered. "You were seen going up to the circle by the receptionist's sister. She was on the bus with you yesterday morning. Then you were so very late back. You should have returned yesterday afternoon. The people here are superstitious. They think that anyone who spends the night in the stone circle is dead but doesn't know it yet. When you were seen approaching the hotel, your cases were brought out and we were called. It usually goes down as an accident and nothing is said ... but you can still talk. Tell me what happened."

So I told him. It seemed the best thing to do, really. Behind him, the other paramedic was sucking his teeth and shaking his head. Eventually, he turned round and asked for his colleague's help. The paramedic I was talking to stood up and looked at Sam.

"I'll drive," he said.

It was the last ride I took with Sam while he was alive. Not that I could see much. The ambulance windows were dark, small and way above my head and the paramedic kneeling beside Sam blocked my view.

At the hospital, I was ushered out of the ambulance and sent into A&E to give all the relevant details for both of us. Sam was brought in on the stretcher and nodded through into the main part of A&E. By the time I was called for, it was too late. Sam had simply stopped functioning.

I'm told I cried. I don't remember. As far as I was concerned the world had stopped

They did a post mortem, of course. They gave the cause of death as major organ failure, but no reason was stated as to *why* everything had ground to a halt.

They seemed more concerned about me, keeping me in for observation for several days, almost as if they were waiting for me to die, too. In which case, I disappointed them.

They wanted me to take Sam's body away with me. When I

suggested he should be cremated and his ashes scattered in the stone circle it was greeted with horror. No one in their right mind, I was told, would go within a hundred metres of the place.

We compromised. It was Sam's ashes that accompanied me home. I scattered them sadly round our garden.

It was much later that I downloaded both cameras onto the laptop. Many of Sam's shots were blurred, as if the memory was somehow corrupted. Most of mine were clear enough – a couple of my thumb, a beautiful shot of my left shoe and many of insects and birds.

And one of Sam; leaning against the gatepost at the entrance to the field, his hair blowing in the wind, eyes sparkling, laughter written in every crease of his face. From the top of the standing stone that formed the gatepost rose a ray of light, blueish-white against the sky: light of the same colour that had bathed Sam's cruciform pose in the middle of the circle.

ITHICA OR BUST

Bryn Fortey

SO IT CAME that Troy was obliterated, leaving only an empty orbit around the twin suns. A destruction that had finally ended the latest of the Great Galactic Wars. Such was the unleashed power necessary to reduce a whole world to nothing, that even the victorious battle fleet were scattered far and wide throughout space. A few managed to make straight forward journeys home, but many were forced into strange and tortuous complications.

The Fleet Commander, man-metal hybrid Space Admiral Agamemnon, was one of those able to overcome navigational problems. By allowing his robot half ascendancy he could plot a direct warp-route home. Unfortunately, during his long absence the planet Mycenae had banned all flesh, becoming the first world inhabited entirely by robot-evolved creations.

"Death awaits," intoned his Cassandra-box, but the conqueror of Troy was too used to his duality. So he landed as a Hero upon the purple plain, accepting the acclaim that was his due. Then roared old fashioned defiance as his flame was extinguished.

So died Agamemnon, joining those who had perished while the war had raged.

Palamedes was dead.

Protesilaus was dead.

Achilles was dead.

Ajax was dead.

Anticlus was dead.

And many, many more, but Odysseus, architect of the victory, still lived.

FOUR-LEGGED, FOUR-armed, two-headed Odysseus: bravest of the brave, most cunning and clever of them all, now so far away from his home planet of Ithica. His warp drive still worked but the direction finder had ceased to function. His ship would plunge through the depths of non-space but there were no guarantees as to where it might emerge.

"Well, that's us finished," said the subservient second head.

The dominant first head frowned. "That's enough of that," he ordered.

"I told you the sub-particle intensifier would be too strong."

"It destroyed Troy didn't it?"

"But at what cost, tell me that?"

However smart, awkward or pettifogging the second head might be, the dominant partner always had the definitive option. He could direct enforced sleep cycles during which the subservient head would sink in its shoulder socket, leaving Number One with a better all round view and the ability to act without interference.

Odysseus knew that a major failing with his species was a tendency to impulsive over-reaction, which had made the double-head system so important in their development from primitive to now. Number Two's function was to offer advice, suggest caution, to worry over fine detail. No Ithican would be without his second head, but it was good to be able to shut them up now and then.

If the direction finder no longer worked it might be best to engage the warp drive in short hop sequences only. He had tried one massive jump and had ended up where they were now, in an unrecognised corner of space with unknown star constellations so distant they were only faint glimmerings.

Number Two had, of course, warned against such a big jump. So, short hops only from now on. He entered the relevant instructions into the propulsion guidance network, then gave the order for the first of the shortened flights through non-space.

It wasn't long before Head Two woke and rose from its shoulder socket. "You're using the warp drive again," he stated.

"Only for short hops."

Number Two said no more, but smirked that know-it-all, I-was-right-all-along expression so disliked by all Number Ones.

Four hops later, a life bearing planet was found, according to all retrievable data.

"Maybe at a pre-radio stage," suggested Two when none of their available bands solicited any sort of response. Visuals were out too. Not being able to penetrate a fog-like blanket that circled the world,

"Guess I'll have to go down," decided Head One.

"I?" grumbled Two. "I? Shouldn't that be *we*?"

"By the Great Godheads of ancient times!" thundered One. "If I go, you go. It's a biological necessity. So no more nit-picking!"

After locking the battle cruiser into an unequivocal orbit, Odysseus summoned a ship to surface transporter and set off to investigate. Once through the vapour layer he could see what appeared to be a world of rich grasslands, dense forests and high mountain ranges. There were also strange triangular buildings dotted here and there, though not in any profusion.

Landing on flat grasses, he put on full battle gear and left the craft while nodding vigorous agreement to the subservient head's whispered entreaties for care to be taken. There being no immediate signs of life, he moved at a steady four-legged pace towards a nearby area of forest.

The people of Ithica stood an average five metres tall with a body sturdy enough to cope with their four legs, four arms and two heads. Indeed, of the sentient races making up the combined attacking force sent against Troy, none were bigger. Odysseus was used to standing tall, so when a large lizard-like creature over twice his height stepped out from the trees he adopted a speedy defence posture. Weapons primed and ready for use.

"Hang on, old chap," called the creature. "What is one supposed to say in these circumstances? I come in peace. Will that do? Or shouldn't you be the one saying it?"

"He's right," whispered Head Two. "We are the intruder."

"Shut up!" hissed Number One.

"Pardon?" asked the lizard.

"No, not you."

"I should think not."

Odysseus had heard of such giant creatures, but not of them being intelligent. Some such wild breeds were said to have roamed the jungle regions of Troy. "I do come in peace," he called, "but how can I be sure of your intentions?"

"I am a Deinonychus. I am fast as the wind and have teeth that could pierce your puny armour as easy as cracking coconuts, which I find very easy. If I had meant you any harm, you would already have been seen to."

"I knew we should have sent an unmanned drone," whimpered the subservient head, but Odysseus was willing to let his dominant part meet force with force, if necessary. "I am Odysseus, Lord of the planet Ithica, Galactic Prince, destroyer of Troy," he shouted. "I have weapons to match your natural advantages. As you'll find out if you make one false move."

The Deinonychus laughed at that. A deep laugh which seemed to contain echoes of its ancestral past. "Let us not put it to the test, friend. My meat-eating days are long gone. My companions converted me to vegetarianism more years ago than I care to remember. I have shown myself merely to greet you. Visitors are very rare in this long forgotten corner of space."

"That I can well believe," muttered Number Two.

"Ignore my lesser head," said Odysseus quickly through his dominant side. While he would take this giant lizard at its word, he would also keep weapons primed, just in case. "There are many questions I would like to ask," he continued, "but tell me first, what world is this?"

"This is Machu Picchu, Cloud Planet of the Fourth Quadrant. The cloud bit is obvious, but don't ask me what the rest means. According to local legends, there are individuals here who are the last surviving members of what would otherwise be extinct species. Some even from other planets! Rather odd, don't you agree?"

"Odd indeed."

"And by the way, my friends call me Denny. So much easier than my full mouthful."

Denny the Deinonychus. A talking lizard. Big! Odysseus had never come across anything like it before.

"A four-legged, four-armed, two-headed intelligent being," said Denny with a rumble that passed for a chuckle. "I've never seen anything like you before."

"Nor I you, Denny. You must be the biggest creature in all the universe."

"Oh my. You definitely don't know dinosaurs. Just wait till you meet my friend, Sunny. He's a Supersaurus, all fifty tonne of him."

"Fifty tonnes?"

"That's what I said, and thirty metres long. Don't worry, he's always been a vegetarian. Let's go and find him. I'll walk slowly so you can keep up."

Odysseus would normally have challenged such a slight, but even his dominant head realised that though he could march for days on end, the big lizard would certainly be able to out speed him. So he adopted hike mode and trudged along without comment.

They saw Sunny long before they reached him. Or at least, as they followed the edge of the forest and approached a bend in the outline, they saw a head towering above the tallest trees.

"Sunny! Sunny!" shouted the Deinonychus, jumping up and down and waving. But the monster carried on eating the succulent tree-top leaves. "He's not the most clear-sighted being on the planet," explained the lizard.

"He is the biggest, though, isn't he?" asked a flabbergasted Odysseus, who was relieved to hear that he most certainly was. But nothing had really prepared him for his first sight of the creature's size when they finally turned the bend.

The huge body.

The pillar-like legs.

The long, long neck.

"Put me to sleep, please," begged Head Number Two.

"No way," replied One. "We need full input on this,"

The Supersaurus lowered his head to see them better. "Well, well, Denny. Who have we here? Not another near extinction?" The voice was not as loud as might have been expected from such a large being, but was loud enough.

"No, just a visitor," explained Denny. "Odysseus by name, from the planet Ithica."

"Welcome to Machu Picchu, Odysseus," said the Supersaurus, swinging his long neck to bring his head in line with the newcomer. "What brings you to our quiet little world?"

"To be honest, a faulty direction finder on my warp drive,"

said Odysseus. "I'm executing short hops through non-space until I emerge near a planet where I can get repairs carried out."

"No luck here then," said Sunny.

"We are not industrialised," added Denny.

Odysseus's two heads looked at each other, wide-eyed, hardly able to credit that he was in a conversation with two dinosaurs.

"I hope you will stay a while though," continued the Deinonychus. "I would value your opinion on my collection of moving pictures. And you must try our broccoli pie."

"Oh him and his broccoli pie," smiled Sunny indulgently. "He would live on it if he could."

"Scrumptious!" exclaimed Denny. "And here's the master chef."

Coming out from the trees was a thickset two-legged, two-armed, one-headed being, with that single head being flattish on top and with a sharply receding chin. Odysseus was relieved to see a being shorter than himself.

"Come and meet our guest," called Denny.

"Guest? Not staying for lunch I hope. Broccoli pie! Broccoli pie! That's all I do. All I cook. Enough broccoli pie to feed a dinosaur."

"Consider yourself lucky I prefer my tree-top leaves," said Sunny.

"This is Keb Moust, last of the Neanderthals," introduced Denny.

"I am Odysseus, Lord of Ithica," said head Number One.

"And we would quite fancy a slice of your broccoli pie," added Two.

"More mouths to feed," grumbled the Neanderthal. "And he's got two of them!" And off he stomped.

The Supersaurus returned to tree-top munching then, while the Deinonychus showed their visitor around. "I christened him

Sunny because he gets nearer the sun than anyone else I've ever known," he confided.

The strange triangular shaped buildings turned out to be called pyramids and contained tunnels and chambers, so it had been reported; Sunny and Denny being far too large to explore themselves. Some had already been there before the dinosaur's arrival. Others had been built since, by beings who stayed only until their particular construction had been completed.

"That one is the King Minos Pyramid," pointed out Denny. "It's filled with what Keb refers to as treasure. Shiny. Yellowy. Pretty in its way but of no interest to Sunny and myself."

Another was called the Knights Templar Pyramid, but that only held a single artefact, according to Keb, in what he called the Star Chamber. In both cases the aliens had arrived in numbers and had deemed Machu Picchu a suitable place for the building and guardianship of what they left behind.

Odysseus also saw a number of other near extinct species, including a bad tempered and rather ugly bird called a Dodo.

"No wonder they fell away in numbers," suggested Head Two. "I wouldn't want to wake up next to a face like that every morning."

"Now you know how I feel," said One.

Then it was time to eat, and broccoli pie was the only thing on the menu. Head Number One saw food as merely a means to an end, as fuel for the body, so ate whatever was put before him. The lesser head though, had more in the way of taste buds, and actually did find the dish to be most enjoyable.

The entertainment that followed, however, was strange indeed for Odysseus. On Ithica, sporting achievement and physical power were held as ideals to strive for. The tiny minority who tried to write books other than instruction manuals, who wanted to recite something they called poetry, who wanted to stand on a platform and pretend to be someone they weren't, were not tolerated. They were condemned, sneered at, even physically abused. So for him to watch these images of different species indulging in what Denny described as acting, well, his reactions veered from revulsion to a guilty interest.

The Deinonychus sat transfixed throughout, even though he had obviously viewed it all many times before. "I don't suppose you have any of these entertainments in your space vehicle?" he asked. "Any you could spare?"

Odysseus assured him that such things were unknown on his home planet. "Otherwise I would have willingly let you have them."

"Well thank you for that at least," responded the lizard.

Denny and Sunny were both disappointed but gracious when Odysseus told them his search for a repair planet would have to continue. They walked to his transporter craft to see him off. Keb Moust even brought some broccoli pie as a farewell gift, for which he thanked the Neanderthal most sincerely.

Later, back on board the battle cruiser, Odysseus prepared for the next short hop. "I think there may be many strange places ahead, before getting back to Ithica," said the dominant head.

Number Two finished eating a piece of broccoli pie. "Tell me, if they should ever make a – what did Denny call them? – flim, movings, flickers? One of those. If they should ever make one of our journey, who could pretend to be us?"

Number One considered for a moment. "Not that I was really taking notice, but there was a being in samples from a planet called Earth who caught my eye."

"Planet Earth?" Number Two was shocked. "But they were mere bipeds! How could one of those convince as a mighty Ithican?"

"I know, I know," muttered head Number One, feeling more

than a little ashamed. "But that Kirk Douglas being did seem to have the right attitude."

With a shrug, Odysseus tried to dismiss the thought, giving the order for his next short hop into non-space.

THE SOUND OF DISTANT GUNFIRE

Adrian Cole

"ARE YOU SURE your brother will be all right on his own?"

Manning glanced at his wife and their eyes met in a brief, shared moment of concern. He eased it aside with feigned exasperation. "Sure he will. It's what he's here for. Besides, he doesn't have to go far. Just a few miles. To the cafe and back. In this weather, there'll be loads of other cyclists along the trackway."

"It's a shame you can't go with him." She looked uneasy.

"Darling, he needs time to himself. It's part of the process. I'm damn sure he doesn't want me constantly dogging his heels. I can't think of anything more relaxing than that ride."

"Yes, well you cycle out there all the time." She remained rueful.

"So I know what I'm talking about. Vaughan will be fine. He will."

She would have said more, but Vaughan had materialised from the hall. He knocked gently on the kitchen door as if wary of disturbing them.

"Come in, mate," said Manning. "No need to be so formal." He laughed.

Vaughan managed a smile. It seemed an unfamiliar thing on that gaunt face. He was barely thirty, but looked ten years older, Manning thought, and the war in the desert lands had desiccated him and set a remote, cold look in his eyes. He came into the room silently, as if it took a great effort.

Linda pushed a small pack across the table. "I thought you might want to take some sandwiches. To have with your tea at the cafe."

"That's very kind of you," said Vaughan, staring at the pack as though unsure whether to trust it and pick it up. Eventually he did.

"So, you ready to roll?" said his brother. "I'll show you the bicycle. It's not top of the range, but it knows the route backwards. When did you last ride one?"

Vaughan never answered promptly these days. Whereas he had once been as talkative and animated as the next man, now he was far more taciturn, introspective. It was a symptom of his condition, Manning knew, though it was taking a lot of getting used to.

"I'm more familiar with tanks and armoured cars," the soldier said eventually, frowning at the memory. "But I can handle a bike. It's not something you forget."

"You could always wait until tomorrow," said Linda. "Mike's free then. He could go with you."

Vaughan shook his head. "No. I have to do things for myself, Linda. I'm fine. Really."

Mike ushered him out into the yard, with a last exaggerated glare at his wife. She poked her tongue out at him.

Vaughan studied the bicycle intently. He nodded in his slow, deliberate way, as though ticking off its credentials. In the desert, life depended on equipment. Every nut had to be tightened, every cog had to turn. Death waited all too eagerly for the careless.

"You've got a great day for it," said Mike. "You've brought the sun with you. These last couple of days have been the best we've seen this year."

Vaughan stared at him uncomfortably for a moment, as if Mike had said something harsh.

"So, you know where you're headed?"

Vaughan nodded, apparently satisfied with the machine. "I'll just ride. How far does the track go?"

"Altogether? Nearly twenty miles. The first eight miles is well used. After that it heads on up a slow incline to the foothills of the moors. The railway was mainly to serve the clay pits out there. If you do go that far, be careful. Seriously, mate, the pits are dangerous. Filled in now – lakes. But if you stay on the track, you'll be fine."

"I'll do that. I just want some exercise."

"Take it easy. Your biggest problem will be your backside." Mike grinned. "You'll feel it when you get back, if you go a long way out. It's easy enough. The incline is gradual. Had to be for the train. But the further part of the track hasn't had tarmac down, so it's a bumpy ride."

Vaughan studied the bike again, then, as if making an abrupt decision, gripped the straight handlebars and pushed it toward the gate at the far end of the yard. Mike opened the creaking door for him and Vaughan rolled the bike outside, getting astride it.

"Just go down to the bottom of the hill and you'll see the old station. There's a path. You can't miss it. Once you're on the track, you're away. Follow your nose."

Vaughan simply nodded, got on the bike and kicked off. Mike watched him disappear. A movement at his elbow made him jump. It was Linda. She put her arm through his.

"The war has changed him," she said.

"Three of his best mates were blown apart by a land mine. I

can't begin to imagine what that's like."

VAUGHAN FOLLOWED HIS brother's instructions and within the space of a few minutes was up on the disused railway track, now a smooth tarmac path. He looked around him. The small rural town had receded and so had most of its sounds. Apart from an occasional car in the streets below, it was silent. Behind him was the old railway station, a testament to days gone by, when its concrete platform would have been thronging. Although it was locked up, the windows shuttered against inevitable vandals, someone had cared enough to keep it in good condition, its paint new, its unique woodwork preserved so that it seemed to stand outside time.

Ahead of him, in an almost straight line for as much as half a mile, the tarmac track ran on, hemmed in by low bushes and banks of trimmed bramble. Overhead the sky was completely free of clouds, the sun gathering mid-morning strength, though it was not the pitiless fireball Vaughan knew from his days in the desert. That stifling, blistering heat could turn a man's mind, that and the relentless, ubiquitous sand.

Here the sun was something to be enjoyed, not endured. There was a light breeze, bringing with it the fishy odours of the nearby river and its mud flats: the tide was low. Gulls flapped overhead, snapping the silence with their shouts. Vaughan pedalled with a gentle ease, the old mastery of the machine awakened within moments so that he began to enjoy the sensation of movement, almost gliding across the landscape.

Half a mile slid by comfortably, a mile, two. The track curled slowly through forest, across a steel bridge that spanned the river and more mud flats and onwards into tunnels of trees that summer had thickened out with foliage. Banks of fern rose up on either side and the air was cool, rich with the tang of wild garlic.

Vaughan moved effortlessly, the machine well oiled, and the air flowed past him as though he was slipping like a seal through clear water. The world that he knew – the nightmares he had known – dropped away further and further.

He wore a watch but deliberately avoided looking at it, instead focusing on the way ahead and its steady curves. Long stretches of the track were very straight and he imagined the old steam engine pounding along, its carriages rattling over the rails. Long gone. Occasionally a figure, or group of them, appeared up ahead, fellow cyclists. They quickly came toward him, most waving cheerfully before disappearing behind him and on to their own destinations. He was in a timeless zone, the world moving yet somehow not moving.

Ahead of him now, cut into a block of land that jutted across the track like a huge stone wall, was a tunnel. It had been partly obscured by overhanging boughs and long grass as Vaughan was approaching it, but now he knew it for what it was. Twenty feet high, black as midnight, although he could discern a row of overhead lights disappearing down that long gullet. He slowed and then braked gently, straddling the bike. He could feel his pulse thumping. Mike hadn't said anything about a tunnel. Vaughan felt a trickle of perspiration running down the side of his face. He slapped at it as if it were a fly.

From the darkness ahead, shrill voices unnerved him. Almost at once the tunnel disgorged a man, woman and two young children, all on bikes: they rang their little bells. They called to him gleefully as they came out into the sunlight and then were gone on and away. Vaughan took a deep breath, re-mounted and pedalled into the tunnel. It was not the oppressively dark hole he had anticipated. The lights were a gaudy orange, giving off enough illumination to point the way. The old brick walls were sooty black, slick and shiny, although the way ahead to the end of the tunnel was clear enough, two hundred yards in the distance.

He pedalled slowly, not wanting to risk veering into a wall, especially at a point where one of the overhead lights was out, clotting the darkness. He mastered panic, eyes fixed on the brilliant white of the exit. Somewhere behind him there was a sound, a vague *crump* that reminded him of something. He felt cold as he realised what he thought it had been. An explosion, distantly faint. Instinct made him brake, stop and look back.

The tunnel mouth was now a hundred yards behind him, shrunk down to a curved space of white light. As Vaughan looked, he saw a shape forming in the light, a silhouette, dark against the external sun's brilliance. Another cyclist, evidently, but it was impossible to see any detail. The shadow-shape could have been a man wrapped in a thick duffel coat, head merged into the bulk of the figure, surely a distortion of the light. It had stopped in the entrance and as Vaughan squinted at it, it became motionless. For a few moments Vaughan and the distant shape remained strangely static. He had no way of knowing if the rider – if rider it was – was waiting for him to move on, or waiting for a companion to catch up. Maybe they didn't feel comfortable about entering the tunnel either.

Then he was pedalling once more, a shade more quickly, the exit rushing towards him. In no time he was out into the sunlight and warm air again, the track forging on through thick strands of trees. To his left they plunged down towards the river. He could see its wide, gleaming course and hear its running waters. There were brilliant green fields beyond, and more forest, deepening with every mile.

Rounding yet another sweeping curve, he saw a whole gaggle of cyclists approaching and for a moment the familiar panic welled up again. He fought against it: they were just youngsters out to enjoy a ride. He saw now that there was at least one adult with them: maybe they were school kids on a trip. A few yards ahead, to his left, he noticed a large, open platform set into the side of the bank. It afforded spectacular views of the river valley below. A sign proudly proclaimed that it had been built using Lottery funding. He turned on to it, resting his bike against the wooden side and leaned on the far rail to study the river, though his attention remained fixed on the kids. He realised now that they were coming to the platform, too. At least some of them. And he felt his entire body trembling as if with a sudden, biting cold.

He had been right about the adult. The man was clearly their teacher. He stood close to Vaughan, ignoring him and indicated the valley below to his audience, beginning a rehearsed mono-logue about its history and the people who had once roamed there. Vaughan caught snatches of it, partly muffled by the noise of the kids. Some were paying attention; others were mock-squabbling out on the track.

"Saxons?" one kid repeated, picking up something the teacher had said. "Were there any battles here, sir?"

"Loads," said another kid. "Them fields must be full of bones."

There was laughter, but Vaughan felt his fingers gripping the wooden rail. In his own mind he could see the wolf pack as the raiders thrust their craft up the river, cutting a swathe through anyone opposing them. A sudden flurry of movement blurred the image: the kids were back on their bikes, the party readying to go back towards the town.

"You okay?" said a lone voice. The last of the kids, a burly lad of probably fifteen was studying Vaughan, coarse hands wrapped around his handlebars as if ready to take off. In his eyes there was a kind of sympathy, as if somehow he read Vaughan's uneasiness.

Vaughan forced himself to smile. "Sure. I was miles away. Thanks."

The boy nodded as if they had shared some deep secret, then was off, rejoining his companions, where the noise of mild rebellion ebbed and flowed gently.

Vaughan continued his journey, more quickly now. The route remained almost flat, allowing him to fly along. He had travelled five miles when he saw another old station up ahead. Like the one in the town, it had been preserved, part of its buildings modernised as a pub. Across the track from it was a rundown engine shed, its planks flaking, rotting in places. A sign announced that this housed the promised cafe. He swung off the track into a deserted car park and rested the bike up against the wall of the dilapidated building.

Inside, at a counter piled with chocolate bars, biscuits and various sweets, a man in a tee- shirt welcomed him. Vaughan asked for a mug of tea, paid for it and went out into the sunlight to one of three tables. He unwrapped the pack of sandwiches Linda had given him and bit into the first. A thought occurred to him. He put the sandwich down in the paper and got up. He walked slowly to the track and looked back the way he had come.

Someone was coming, half a mile away, framed like an insect in the curve of an overhead bridge. Vaughan watched, waiting for the figure to draw closer. But it seemed to be caught in time, motionless. He couldn't make it out.

"Your tea," called the man from the cafe, jerking him back to his present surroundings. Vaughan went to the table and sat down, splitting a sugar sachet and spilling its contents into the mug that the man had set there.

"First time on this ride?" the man asked affably.

Vaughan nodded. "Yes. Very pleasant."

"Where you headed?" The man was wiping his hands on a

stained rag, his shirt and trousers daubed with oil. Behind him in the shadows a score of bicycles were lined up, above them a sign offering hire rates.

Vaughan shrugged, stirring his tea. "I guess I'll just keep riding."

"About eight miles on, the track crosses a road that goes uphill to a small village. Can't miss it, sits on the skyline. Best pub lunch around. Nice pint, too. You might like to try it."

"Thanks, I might do that." Vaughan sipped his tea.

The man pulled a spanner from a deep pocket and wiped it. "Other than that, there's the monument. Lot of people enjoy the climb up to it. That's another mile on from the village turning. Signposted, so you'll find it easy enough."

"Monument?"

"Yes, standing stone. Oldest one around. You get a nice view up there. Probably why it was put there. I've got a brochure somewhere. I'll find it for you." The man slipped back into the cool of the building. When he came back he had several sheets and brochures.

Vaughan took them mechanically. The man tapped one of the brochures; it had a photo of a standing stone on its cover, a tall menhir, with a bike nearby to give an idea of its size, which was about eight feet.

"What do I owe you for these?"

"Keep them." The man grinned. He realised that Vaughan was not going to engage in conversation, so left him to his tea.

Vaughan flicked through the literature. He found himself drawn back to the monument. In the brochure it talked about Neolithic times and the people who had lived in the local landscape. There were several legends about the monument, the most popular being that it was a gift from the old gods, a protective talisman that watched over the area. A Saxon warlord, Brunna, had met a sticky end there, tracked and cut down by local tribesmen as a reward for his brutal treatment of them.

Vaughan finished his sandwiches and tea and got back on the bike. He coasted to the track and again looked back the way he had come. Although the day remained brilliantly hot and cloudless, there were shadows along the route, under the distant overhead bridge. Something clung to those shadows, man-sized but indefinable. He pulled his gaze from it and kicked off.

The man in the cafe watched him indifferently. He gathered up the brochures and papers and took them back into the cafe and put them with the others before returning to his world of gears and chains and wheels.

Vaughan rode steadily for another half an hour, seeing less fellow cyclists now as he began to penetrate the deeper forest where only the more enthusiastic went. The sense of timelessness and tranquillity enfolded him even more completely; the town he had left earlier could have been a hundred miles away. A stream tumbled through the woods on one side of him and a wall of pines closed in from the other. The track rose slowly and he twisted the handlebar grip to drop a gear.

Ahead of him, on the left, he could see a bench, one of a number that had been set aside periodically. But someone was sitting on this one, head bowed as if in deep thought. Vaughan watched apprehensively as he neared the figure and then realised as he drew closer why it had mildly disturbed him. It was a sculpture, made entirely from wood, its arms and knees slightly green with age. As he rode past, Vaughan had the strangest sensation that it would look up and hail him.

It didn't, of course.

A hundred yards further along, he stopped and looked back. The wooden figure remained in place, but behind it, emerging from the curve of the track, a lone walker was approaching.

Vaughan tried to study its detail, obscured by a clutch of shadows. He waited. But it had become strangely motionless, like the sculpture. Almost as if it were waiting.

An abrupt burst of sound jarred his nerves, bells jingling madly behind him. He swung round, terrified, only to see two very young girls come pedalling past him, grinning like miniature demons. Beyond them, their mother looked askance at him, apologising profusely for their abandoned behaviour.

Unable to speak, he stood rigidly to one side as the group sped on, receding in an instant, leaving him in a muck-sweat. He clawed with blind instinct at his belt for a weapon, a gun. If he had been armed he would have flicked off the safety catch, swung the muzzle around and unleashed a withering storm. For a moment he was in the desert, snared by the horrors of war, every sound a threat, every heartbeat a gunshot.

It all receded as quickly as it had burst on him and the forest closed in again. Vaughan wiped streaks of perspiration from his face, watching the trio of cyclists disappearing, the last ting of a bell snuffed out by distance. It was a while before he was able to continue, riding at a steady pace once more, his body again fused with the machine, effortlessly rolling forward.

He passed an old station platform, almost hidden by weeds and huge tufts of grass, with a broken sign that revealed part of a name. There were no buildings here, just trees and a rotted fence, more evidence of distant life. Beyond the next turning, something partially blocked the track. It looked at first to be a large sack, its contents spilling from a long rupture. But as Vaughan approached he knew it for something else. A corpse. A cloud of flies swarmed noisily up from it as he neared it. He knew the rotten smell of a carcass. This was a large animal, probably a badger. But he sped by quickly, flapping at the hail of flies. They hummed about him like bullets.

He was rising now, the landscape beyond the woods to his left steepening as it became the foothills of the tors. Again he thought of the steam train, burrowing with metal determination through the forest, easing up the incline, relentless. He pushed himself harder, blowing out air and with it the memory of the dead creature. Eventually he came to a gate. There was a road crossing the track, with another gate beyond, but this could not be the one that the man in the cafe had spoken about. He would ride on. He crossed the road and as he closed the second gate, he looked back the way he had come. For a long time he watched the curve of track. Someone was coming. At any moment they would appear. He would wait, damn them, until they showed themselves.

Minutes passed. The world had frozen, focused on the path. Nothing moved. Then, from somewhere up above the valley, a sound reached out for him. A rattle of gunfire, far away. A farmer maybe, scattering crows. The sound broke his concentration on the path and shook him out of his torpor. At once he swung on to the bike and was off, the ground softer here, no tarmac covering it, the fallen leaves and small branches forming a mulch in places that threatened to skid the wheels. He was glad to concentrate on riding.

By the time he eventually reached the crossroad that he'd been told to look for, the one that led to the village and the promised pub, he was ready for a cool drink; the sun close to its zenith, urged him to sanctuary. But as he was about to turn on to the road and its twisting incline, his instincts warned him to wait. In the desert, in action, nothing had been left to chance. No one walked forward without taking everything in. Even then, there was no certainty of safety. Men died. Those mines—

He drew back. This was rural England. There were no land mines here. It was a remote country road, empty, hardly a shadow crossing it. Yet as he stared at it, he could not bring himself to ride on. Perhaps his experiences had developed in him a super-sense, a prescience. He swung back on to the old railway track. What was it the man at the cafe had said? A monument. There was something about a mile further on.

The trees closed around him and he was riding down a tunnel, the path arrowing directly ahead for half a mile. The air in here was cool, refreshing as he rode faster. There was a distinct sense of relief at not having taken to the road. Maybe he just didn't want human company. It would have been inevitable at the pub, however remote.

Soon he was out in sunlight again, the track branching slightly over to the fields and tors above them. He was pedalling steadily and almost missed the sign. It leaned over, pointing more to the ground than the fields. But it read *The Monument*. He braked, crunching gravel and faced a stile in the low hedgerow, with a small iron gate beside it. He could see from tyre tracks that it was regularly used by cyclists.

Through the gate, he looked up at the curve of a bleached field. The track was faded but wove its way up to the brow of the hill. There was an open space here and part of an old iron fence which seemed to serve as a hitching rail for visiting cyclists. Soft laughter made him start, but it was just a couple whom he hadn't noticed, a young man and woman, back-packers. The man bent down and unlocked the two cycles that Vaughan now saw by the fence. The woman approached him with a wave.

"Hi," she called cheerily. "Are you going up to the monument? It's not far."

He pulled himself together. "Yes."

"It's lovely up there." She gazed up at the hill crest, smiling at whatever private secrets it held for her. "Really magical."

Beside her, pushing the two cycles, the man beamed at Vaughan. "Hi. You can leave your bike here. Don't worry if you haven't got a lock. It's secure enough." He tugged a plastic bottle from his belt. "Do you have water?" He held it out invitingly.

Vaughan shook his head. "No, that's fine. Have you seen the monument?"

"Yes, it's a menhir. A tall standing stone. Must be eight feet tall," said the man, taking a pull at his water bottle.

"It's supposed to be a gift from the gods," said the girl. "Sent to protect the land from evil spirits."

"I read something about it in the brochure." Vaughan nodded, digging into his pockets. But he remembered he had left the brochure with the other stuff back at the cafe.

The man exchanged a final, slightly embarrassed grin and then he and his girl were through the gate and gone, melting into the woodland. Vaughan was left alone with a deep silence, broken only by the drone of a bee.

He leaned his bike against the old fence and began the walk up the path, glad to stretch himself. His body had quickly become used to the exercise again after such a prolonged recuperation. His awareness – his former *desert sense* – had sharpened acutely. Surprising how quickly it all came back. Like riding the bike, he supposed.

The climb was not steep, winding gently across the thick grass. This field had not been planted with wheat, rape or any other crop for some time, he imagined, probably because of its erratic contours. The grass up here grew waist high beside the track. He paused and looked back. Already the landscape of the railway valley was spreading out below in a long line from left to right, stained by its trees. His bike was a miniature metal trinket far away, the sun glinting on its tiny frame.

By the gate, a solitary figure hopped over the stile. Not a cyclist. Vaughan squinted at it. It was not moving. It had an odd shape, as if it wore a thick coat, totally inappropriate for the searing heat of midday. Why wasn't it moving? He turned away, climbing swiftly again. When he paused, another twenty yards further on, he looked back. The figure had moved on to the track, but as he studied it, he could see that it had again stopped moving. *It only moves when I'm not looking at it*, he thought irrationally.

Drenched in perspiration and suppressing a wave of panic, he made his way on up the path. He could see the tor clearly now and its stone guardian. A last look back showed him only the lush expanse of grass, the lower path – and its other occupant – hidden by the shoulder of the hill. For the second time that day he reached for weapons he was not carrying. He wiped stinging perspiration from his eyes. Quickening his pace, he strode on up to the edge of the tor. The grass petered out and became a cropped carpet of moss and scrub, small chunks of granite poking through it. Now the tall stone, a single, isolated block of dark grey, was no more than fifty yards away. It looked as if it belonged at Stonehenge, or some other ancient circle.

He turned again, studying the lake of grass that lapped silently, almost sensuously at the tor. Where was the figure? Surely it must be coming into view soon. He waited, mouth dry, wishing he had accepted the young man's offer of a drink.

There! Some distance from the track, in the grass. It was airless up here in spite of the height. Not even a breeze. Yet the grass was moving. In more than one place. At least three patches of grass were being disturbed. Vaughan could just about discern hunched shapes. What were they? Kids? Yes, that must be it. Stupid, fucking kids playing a game. A war game. Sneaking up on him.

His attention was tugged back to the path. As if it had risen up from the deep grass, the figure was there. Muffled, heavily clothed, as if against a winter blast, not summer heat. Or protected against the ferocity of the desert. No, that was ridiculous. Around it, the smaller shapes hopped like broken insects. Impossible to see them properly.

Vaughan spun round and broke into a gentle run up the last of the slope. Suddenly the menhir loomed over him like a huge fist. The sun was behind it, making its silhouette more foreboding. And yet, didn't they all say that it was protection against evil? He stood in its shadow, heedless at first of how unnaturally *cold* it was. Behind him he heard the same far-off sound he had heard earlier. Farmer shooting crows.

Except that farmers didn't use machine guns. He swung round. Where? Where had that sound come from? Way off in the distance he could see smoke, curling up in a number of places. Bonfires. They reminded him all too easily of the fires of war, spewed up from the fall of bombs. His eyes focused again on the grass. At last the figure was emerging. Vaughan could see now what it was wearing. It was not an overcoat or any kind of western dress. It was what they called a mufti. The man was an Arab.

He did move now. Stumbling, holding his stomach as if it pained him. His robes were light coloured, except for the area he was holding, which was a vivid scarlet. On either side of him, other figures held back, still obscured by the grass.

Vaughan swore. He had seen this man before, months ago. Seen him and – shot him. In the madness of war. The village. In the bloody mayhem, the snarling of the machine guns. The insurgents. The men, their wives – *their children.* War levelled all. No rules, no mercy, no rational thought.

He felt his back bump up against the monument. As soon as his body was in contact with it, he felt himself *pulled* to it, as if a huge magnet had attracted a chunk of metal. Hands clawing at the air impotently, he could not pull loose. Like a fly stuck on wallpaper, he wriggled, but the monument had him. The creature on the path staggered forward, leaking blood, the bullet-torn body impossibly alive. In the grass, the others waited like coiled snakes for the command.

THE CAULDRON
OF CAMULOS

William Meikle

DAWN ROSE OVER Camulodunum as the battle came to its close.

The field in front of the town gate had been reduced to a bloody morass full of dead and dying. A lone man was left facing five men. Long braids, thick with blood, swung in time with the strokes of a large double-headed axe as he kept his attackers at a far-enough distance that they could not use their swords. He knew that it was only a matter of time before they brought in a spear, and when that happened, his advantage would be gone, and the tiredness he felt in every bone and muscle would surely then tell.

But for now, he fought, and they died. Two more fell.

Hentra split the skull of another attacker, though it took the last of his strength to do so. Suddenly the tiredness washed over him like a wave. His axe became too heavy to hold and fell unnoticed in the mud. Hentra dropped to his knees in a patch of ground strewn with the dead of his enemy, and waited for the blow that would send him to join his brothers in the shining fields of Neorxnawang.

The blow never came. More tribesmen of the Trinovantes

arrived on the field, newly emboldened now that Hentra had finally fallen. They surrounded him, subduing him with the weight and press of their bodies. He did not have to strength to resist as they trussed him like a pig and carried him bodily through the streets of the city. They threw him into a damp hole in the ground and he lay there unable to move as they took turns *pishing* on him.

It was not supposed to end like this. My Wyrd has failed me.

The raid had begun well enough. Aelfer, their leader, had taken no chances. Before taking the fleet out of safe haven he had called for Hentra and the sight from the Wyrd.

And Hentra had seen a victory. He had seen Saxons at peace, farming and raising children all over the lands vacated by the Romans. With the Sight in his mind, he had no hesitation in joining the Aelfer on the boats. Even a stormy voyage over rough seas had done little to dull their enthusiasm, and by the time they marched over the fens and onto the road leading to the city, their spirits were high and thoughts of plunder foremost in their minds.

They had not expected the Trinovantes to be there already. The Wyrd had not shown Hentra that. Neither had it shown him the battle that lasted nearly two days and ended with his ignominious defeat in this dank hole in the ground.

He was the last Saxon remaining, bereft of both companionship of his brothers and the surety of his Sight.

He lay in the hole and wept for what he had wrought on his people.

THEY GAVE HIM plenty of time to dwell on his pity. He lay in the hole for three days. On the second day it rained, but that was not as bad as it could have been as it kept them away from taunting him, and allowed the smell of piss to be washed away.

He was finally taken to a large stone hall that had once been a

Roman temple. Broken statuary lay all around and the trappings of ritual had been replaced by steaming cauldrons and long trestles filled with meat and fruit. A feast was underway, and by the look of the throng gathered there, it had been going on for quite some time. Most of the people were drunk, or most of the way there. Couples rutted like dogs on the floor and the place stank of stale ale and cooking meat, overlaid with the tang of piss and shit.

He readied himself for the indignities that would surely come, and was surprised to be led to a trestle. They untied one of his hands and motioned towards a pile of food and a flagon of ale. Hentra needed no second telling. He set to it with gusto.

The ham was undercooked and too bloody, but he ripped into it anyway, sending it down with plenty of bread and ale until his belly was tight as a drum. Finally he sat back and belched.

A small red-haired boy sat nearby staring at him with wide-eyed curiosity.

"What is the matter lad?" Hentra asked. "Have you never seen a *real* man eat?

The boy turned on his heels and ran as if chased by a bear.

An old woman sat down at Hentra's side and helped herself to some of his ale.

"He did not understand you," she said. "To him, you do indeed sound like a bear."

Hentra was momentarily nonplussed to hear his thoughts echo back at him, and in his own tongue, but one look at the woman told him he should not be surprised. This one also had more than a touch of the Wyrd about her.

She had been a beauty in her day – he could see that in the sparkle in her eyes and the bow of her lips. But that day had been some years ago, and the Wyrd had taken its toll. Her eyes were haunted. He knew the look well – it came from having seen too much of what fate decreed would come to pass. She, like him, had seen, and been unable to do anything about it. That knowledge takes a heavy toll from a person.

She nodded when she saw him looking at her.

"Yes," she said. "We know one another. And that is why you are still alive. I do not have the strength myself. I need another of the Wyrd."

He sank a long gulp of ale and kept quiet.

Now is perhaps not the time to mention that the Wyrd seems to have deserted me.

His mind was full of questions, but he wasn't given time to ask. A herald at the main table called for silence and a grey-haired man that Hentra guessed must be the leader of the tribe started to speak. He did not understand a word of it, and contended himself with getting more ale inside him.

After the man's speech an old bent man took over and started to intone. Hentra recognised the form – it was a saga, one of the tales of old. But again he understood none of it – until the woman put a hand on his arm.

Words filled his mind

ONE MORNING CAMULOS went into the forest with his dogs, intent on a hunt. The dogs led him to a small copse but as soon as he set the dogs to flush out what may lie there they withdrew swiftly, trembling and fearful, and came back towards Camulos with their tails between their legs.

But Camulos felt no such fear – he drew towards the copse. Suddenly a shining white boar arose out of the ground. The dogs rushed towards it, all fear forgotten. The boar stood its ground against the dogs without retreating until, when Camulos drew near, it withdrew once again, and ran.

For three days Camulos and his dogs followed the boar,

through forest and over moor and fen, none of them taking any rest, until at last the white beast led them to a high caer. The boar was making for it swiftly. The dogs ran ahead, outpacing Camulos in their lust for the hunt, and followed the boar into the caer.

There was something about the caer that gave Camulos pause, for the hunt had taken him to unfamiliar lands, yet he had never heard tell of anyone living here.

"I will not give up my dogs," he said, and followed his beasts.

When he got to the caer, he could see neither the boar, nor the dogs, nor any dwelling inside the caer. There was only an empty courtyard, and in the middle of the courtyard a cauldron with marble stonework around it. Four heavy chains anchored the cauldron to the marble slab – with the chains also reaching up into the air, and he could not see the end of them.

The hunt had brought on him a great thirst and he came up to where the cauldron was, and laid hold of it. As soon as he did so, his left hand stuck to it, and his feet became rooted to the slab on which he was standing. The power of speech was taken from him so he could not utter a single word.

He hacked at the marble slab that was even now starting to ooze and flow around his ankles. The sword sank into the stone that hardened around the blade so that when he tried to draw the weapon back he found it held fast.

He withdrew his hand from the sword and placed it on the cauldron, intent on dragging the pot from its place. The ground shook and trembled such that people all across the land left their houses and stared in fear at the skies, fearing the end of days. But Camulos, for all his strength, was stuck firm even as the marble flowed around his nethers and loins, even as it gripped at his chest, even as it filled his mouth.

And thus he stood, unable to move from the spot, unable to call for aid.

Soon all that could be seen was the cauldron, and the hilt of the great sword standing proud from the rugged stone.

And thereupon, as soon as it was night, there came was a peal of thunder, and a fall of mist and with that the caer disappeared, taking the cauldron, and Camulos with it.

They were never again seen by men, but the spot has forever after been named in his honor, Caer Camulos.

Our home.

THE OLD WOMAN let go of Hentra's arm as the crowd cheered and set to drinking and fucking with renewed gusto.

"This place is sacred to us," the old woman said. "It has been since long before the Romans came and stole our name. It was a place of strength and power – the place of a god, of Camulos. Our mothers and their mothers before them knew it.

"And now I have seen that power arisen anew. But I am too old for what is required."

Hentra felt a sinking feeling in the pit of his stomach. He hoped it was only the ale.

"Nothing happens without a reason," the old woman said. "You have been sent to us at our time of need. We cannot naysay the will of Fate. Come. Let me show you why you have been brought here."

She waved her hand and his bonds fell away.

She has far more of the Wyrd in her than I. I must be careful here.

Two tribesmen at the nearest table stood, daggers drawn, alarmed at the prospect of the Saxon's freedom. The old woman waved them down.

"The big man will be no trouble," she said. "Not tonight at least."

Hentra realised she was right. His interest had been taken by the tale, and now he was anxious to see whatever she wanted to show him.

For has it not often been said, the Wyrd knows no tribes, no kinsman, no master. The Wyrd is as it always was and always will be.

He had that thought at the forefront of his mind as she led him deep into the temple.

EVERYTHING THAT HAD been Roman was tumbled and broken. Huge marble statues lay smashed and defiled on the floors, and an intricate mosaic floor had been partially dug up and the rest smeared with blood and shit. Drunken tribesmen lay slumped in alcoves previously reserved for votive offerings, and there were more couples rutting in dark corners.

Soon the sounds of the feast were left behind as the old woman led him to the central chamber of the temple. A huge statue lay broken on the floor, some fifteen feet in length. It had once depicted a warrior, clad Roman style and brandishing a sword. Someone had attacked the facial features with a hammer, and all trace of what it might have represented had been obliterated.

"This is not what I brought you to see," the old woman said. "Come."

At the far side of the chamber a large rock had been pulled aside to reveal a set of steps led down into the ground. The air was drier here, a thick, musty odour. And the steps were old – far older than the Roman occupation of this land.

His Wyrd chose that moment to return. Suddenly he had no more desire to see what was at the bottom of this passageway. He had left a flagon of ale back at the feast, and was more than eager to get back to it. He stopped, and would indeed have started to retreat if the old woman had not put her hand on his arm once more.

"The only way you will leave this city alive is if you come with me," she said. "Without my protection they will fall on you in their scores. You will be dead. And you will never know the glory that might have been."

She headed down the stairs, and his shame at a woman going where he would not led him to follow.

The light grew dimmer, and he was afeared that they might soon be in darkness when he saw a reddish glow beneath them. She led him into a rough-hewn chamber lit by torches in sconces high on the walls.

The chamber seemed empty – but his Wyrd told him otherwise. There was power here. He could almost feel it *sing* in his head. He raised his hand and felt his fingertips tingle.

"You feel it?" she whispered. "It is him, I am sure of it."

"Camulos?"

She did not reply. She took the Saxon's left hand in hers and started to chant in a high singsong language that Hentra had never before heard. The spell that lay in front of them started to become visible, a spider's web of black strands woven tightly around a core to make a seemingly impenetrable ball some ten feet across.

The old woman stopped chanting and urged Hentra forward.

"Quickly. Reach inside. We have little time."

He reached into the lattice with his right hand and immediately met resistance. His hand tingled, as if he'd been sleeping on it all night.

"Can you feel it?" she said. "Can you feel the sword?"

It was only then that he realised why he'd been brought here. She wanted him to draw a weapon from the spell – a weapon that would then be used to strengthen the tribe – his enemy. He started to withdraw his hand.

At the same second his fingers brushed against something. But this was no sword hilt. This was rough hair, almost bristly, like a long-unwashed beard. He felt hot breath on his palm.

"Fetch it out then lad," the old woman shouted. "Fetch it out now."

Hentra smiled, took a tight grip of a handful of bristly hair, and *pulled.*

The fabric of the holding spell ripped with the sound of tearing cloth. Hentra was knocked roughly aside as something huge and fast came through from the other side. He smelled acrid sweat and felt the heat of a warm beast. All he saw as he was thrust roughly against the chamber wall was a flash of greyish-white.

His head hit the rock hard and he stumbled, almost falling and momentarily blinded. The old woman screamed – but not for long. The noise cut off into a gurgling choking sound he recognised all too well.

When Hentra regained his footing he looked up. The chamber was empty, the spell having receded back to wherever it had previously been hidden. There was no sign of any Beast – just the writhing body of an old woman on the floor. Her belly was a mess of guts and gore, torn asunder in the time it had taken Hentra to stand.

The gurgling sound was the crone drowning in her own blood.

The gurgling was joined by screams echoing down into the chamber from high above.

I can make my escape.

He headed for the entrance that led back up to the temple but was stopped as a hand slippery with blood grabbed at his ankle.

"What have you done?" she whispered through bubbles of blood.

In truth, he did not know whether he had *done* anything. He smiled grimly down at the dying woman.

"*You* brought me here. If anything has been done, it is of your own doing."

The grip on his ankle tightened.

"The Beast will know its master," she said. "Only the chosen may drink."

Before he could glean her meaning, the life went out of her eyes and the bloody hand fell away, limp and dead.

More screams from above told him that many were being sent to join her.

He headed for the steps, cautiously at first, then more assured. He met no resistance.

THE MAIN TEMPLE looked as if a madman had run riot with red paint. A copulating couple, still locked together, lay against a wall in a pool of gore that steamed in the chill air. More blood ran from a man sitting at the base of a column, staring at the ruin of his leg as he sprayed the floor for six feet all around. The man looked up at Hentra, but he was too near death for the Saxon to offer any aid.

Besides, aid was the furthest thing from the big man's thoughts at that moment.

Woden, send me a weapon, and a clear run at a door. That is all I ask.

As he approached the hall where the feast had been taking place the screams grew ever louder. He thought he was prepared for anything, but the sight that met his eyes made him step back behind a pillar, unsure as to his next move.

A white beast rampaged to and fro through the hall. At first he took it for one of the great snow-bears that sometimes ventured south from the northern lands. Then it raised its head and he saw the two long tusks on either side of the snout, and the fiery red eyes that seemed to burn in the head.

A boar!

But a boar unlike any he had ever previously seen. It stood four feet high at the shoulders, was nearly twelve feet from snout to tail, and was built like a stout barrel on legs. Its coat was off-white and made of thick tough bristles, smeared red along the length of both flanks. The tusks were two feet long and dripped with blood and gore.

Bodies lay broken and strewn the length and breadth of the hall, which smelled even worse than it had previously. Many of the bodies showed the tell-tales signs of goring, and others had clearly simply been thrown aside to smash their bones against walls and trestles. The *snuffling* of the boar could be heard over groans of the injured as it rooted in spilled guts for the choicest parts.

A group of men stood by the main door that led outside, blocking the boar's escape. Each of them held a long spear, but none of them looked like they wanted to be there. The boar had not taken any notice of them yet, being content to snuffle among the dead, but sometime soon more carnage would ensue.

Hentra did not intend to wait that long.

He found a two-headed axe among the strewn debris. Just the weight of it in his hand made him feel more secure. Keeping his back to the wall, he started to sidle around the hall, making for the doorway.

He nearly made it, but, while he was still twenty feet from his goal, his foot slipped in a gory nest of guts and blood and he had to put a hand out to steady himself. The axe head *clanged* against stone.

The boar's head came up. Beady red eyes stared at him. It snorted, steam rising from its gore-covered snout. With no other warning it lowered its head and attacked.

Hentra had only a second to decide whether to stand or run. A mental picture of a tusk taking him up the backside settled the matter. He hefted the ace two-handed and made sure he had steady footing.

The boar came at him hard and fast, and he had time for only one blow. He brought the axe down hard, cutting deep into the beast's shoulder and bringing a bellow of pain. The huge head swung at him. A tusk scored a shallow gash across his belly then the sheer weight of the head threw him aside in a tangle of arms and legs. He landed on his back on a trestle, the wood breaking beneath him and sending him to the ground in a tumble of splintered beams and spilled ale.

The boar was on him before he could right himself. Its head ducked and dove, seeking an opening where it could thrust a tusk in his belly. He grabbed a tusk in each hand and held the beast at bay, but it took all his strength, and he knew he would not be able to hold it off for long.

"To me," he shouted. "Help me."

He did not know if any of the tribe even knew his language, and indeed had little hope that they would come to his aid if they did.

The boar's head lowed inexorably towards his chest despite all his efforts. The stench of its hot breath stung in his nostrils and at the back of his throat. Soon he was eye to eye with the beast, pinned by its weight. It tugged its head back, breaking his hold, and then lunged forward.

Hentra watched his fate come for him.

A yell came from his left and a spear took the beast full in the snout, sending a wash of hot blood over the Saxon. The boar fell back with a yelp and Hentra looked up to see a red-haired boy standing over him, bloodied spear in his hand and a determined look on his face. It was the same boy who had watched him so intently earlier.

Hentra got slowly to his feet and retrieved the axe. He stood beside the boy as they both watched the boar. But it had lost interest in them. It was already barrelling towards the entrance.

The men guarding the spot fell before it. Bodies flew. Bones broke and blood spilled. The beast stopped in its rush just long enough to *stomp* one man into a bloody mush then it was gone.

The only sound in the room was the groans of the dying.

"THANK YOU," HENTRA said to the boy at his side, but the lad only looked at him quizzically, then shook his head.

He does not understand me. Yet he came to my aid. I owe this boy my life.

They made their way to the doorway. Screams rose from somewhere in the city. The beast was still rampaging.

Hentra started to walk in the direction opposite to the commotion.

The boy tugged at his sleeve to get his attention then made *stabbing* motions with the spear towards the screams.

He means to hunt the beast down.

Hentra took a look along the path he had been on and sighed.

I owe the lad my life. The least I can do is prevent him from getting himself killed.

He motioned with the axe towards the screams.

"Lead on," he said.

The boy's face broke into a wide smile.

He will charm many women when he is grown ... if he gets that far.

The boy led and Hentra followed. They would not need any hunting skill to find the beast – the sound of screams was evidence of its whereabouts.

Several townspeople balked at Hentra's presence among them, but the boy, calm at all times, spoke on the Saxon's behalf, and no one stopped them.

Not only a charmer, but also a born leader.

The screams were louder now, women and children's voices raised alongside those of the men. The boy led Hentra through a courtyard to a more open area where the tribe had pitched a small village of wooden huts. Most of the huts were now trampled ruins and the boar ran amok among them, throwing wattle and thatch aside like kindling, goring anybody too slow to get out of its path and snorting happily every time it found fresh meat.

The boy did not hesitate. He stepped forward into the beast's path.

I cannot allow this. I owe this lad my life.

Hentra jumped ahead of the boy, raising the axe above his head. He knew he would only have time for one stroke.

I have to make it a killing blow.

He timed the blow and brought the axe down, intending to cleave the beast's head, but it made a lunging move at the last. The left-side tusk went clean through Hentra's thigh and the axe only succeeded in cutting a deep gouge above the boar's ear.

The wound only served to enrage the beast further. With a flick of the head it once again sent Hentra sprawling. He landed, face first, in the wreckage of a hut, feeling twigs and broken wood lash against his face. His leg felt warm where blood poured from the thigh wound, but it was not a spout.

I will live. For now.

He got to his feet and turned, just in time to see the boy step between him and the boar, spear raised high.

"No!" he shouted, and broke into a stumbling run. He knew he was going to be too late. The beast had already girded itself for an attack. It was about to bear down on the lad when it stopped, seemingly confused.

It sniffed at the air, three times, head rocking from side to side. The boy raised the spear higher.

The boar walked towards him, slowly, never taking its eyes from his. When it was six feet from the boy it stopped and *sniffed* again. Then, to Hentra's astonishment, it lowered its head and sank to the ground on its knees.

It kneels to him. It pays obedience to the lad.

Hentra limped forward, axe raised for a killing blow, but the boy stopped him, putting a hand on his arm.

He could see the same confusion in the lad's eyes as he himself felt, but there was something else there.

It is as if the boy almost expected this to happen.

A crowd was starting to gather. At first they merely gaped in astonishment at the spectacle in front of them, before starting to remember the carnage that had occurred from this very beast.

"Kill it," one cried, and made a move to step forward.

The red-haired boy looked pleadingly at Hentra.

The Saxon stood between the crowd and the spot where the boar knelt at the boy's feet. They might not understand his tongue, but when he hefted the double-headed axe, no one was in any doubt about his intentions.

The mob stared sullenly at him. He stared back, smiling.

"There is nothing I would like better than for some of you to attack."

No one showed any desire to take him up on the offer.

He became aware of movement behind him. The boar got slowly to its feet. Hentra turned, axe raised, but the beast merely nuzzled at the boy's hand then walked away, looking back. When the boy did not move it repeated the movement.

It wants the lad to follow it.

The boy understood and, taking hold of the bristly hair at the beast's shoulder, he walked alongside it. Hentra followed just behind, making sure to keep himself between the mob and the beast.

His leg flared in white-hot pain with every step. Blood still seeped from the wound, his breeches on that leg soaked through. Each pace brought a damp squelch from where the blood had pooled in his boot.

But I do not have far to walk.

He knew already where the boar would take the lad. Even if the Wyrd had not shown it to him, he would have known.

Five minutes later they descended the steps from the Roman temple and entered the rough-hewn chamber.

The crone lay dead on the floor. The boar moved the body to one side with its head then raised its snout and roared.

The black spider-web spell slowly appeared in the centre of the room. A large rent in the fabric showed where the boar had come through. The hole widened as the beast approached. Once again Hentra's fingers tingled, but when the boar led the boy into the spell he followed, amused to note that the mob behind them stayed well back, ready to flee the chamber at the slightest provocation.

THE WYRD WAS strong here.

They stood in an open courtyard surrounded on all four sides by thick stone walls that towered high above. There was no obvious sign of egress, merely a shadowy patch on one of the walls where Hentra saw the ghostly faces of the tribesmen peering in awe into the spell.

In the centre of the courtyard, beams of sunlight played on a great cauldron, a black iron pot nearly four feet in diameter. Rock moulded itself all along the left-hand side, a length of stone that might almost seem man-shaped. Just below this stone the marble plinth on which the cauldron sat had buckled and bent. The hilt of a sword showed proud from a ragged piece of rock. As the boy approached, the sun caught a gem at the very heel of the sword, sending dazzling light dancing all across the yard.

The boy stepped up and dipped a hand in the cauldron, raising clear glistening water to his lips.

Only the chosen may drink.

The boar nuzzled at the sword then looked the boy in the eye.

The lad needed no second telling.

He put a hand on the hilt and with one smooth pull raised the whole length of the sword from the stone, raising it high overhead where it shone silver like the brightest star.

And at the same moment the Wyrd gripped at Hentra as it had never done before, laying the future out before him as clear and bright as one of the Roman mosaics

The boy, grown to a man but still with the same wide grin sits at the head of a table as he is crowned. The hall is full of hard-eyed warriors, all swearing allegiance.

The boy turned the sword in the air. Each time it caught the sun, another vision seared into Hentra's mind.

With the sword raised high the new king drives the Saxon before him, all the way to the sea where they are forced into ignominious retreat.

Another turn of the sword brought a new picture.

The man sits at a round table where the best and the wisest are gathered. Outside the land is tilled and fertile and the people give praise to their king and their prosperity while the Saxon skulk in their boats, afraid to make any attack on this mighty warrior.

The boy gave the sword a final flourish.

The man, greying at the temples and stooped with age, drinks from the great cauldron and stands up, straight and young again, the fire once more in his eyes as he lifts the sword and declares that the land and the king are one again.

Hentra stumbled, almost fell, the power of the Wyrd overwhelming him. He staggered back, leaning against the marble.

The boy stepped off the plinth. The spell fell apart around them. It left behind a black flurry of dust as the only sign it had been there. The boar was gone.

But the great cauldron remained behind, sitting in the centre of the rough-hewn chamber on its bed of marble.

THE BOY SHOWED the sword to his people.

Not all were happy to see it. Hentra did not understand the arguments that were thrown around, but he understood the gist.

They will not follow a boy. Never mind that all of Wyrd itself has shown them the truth of it.

He tried to stand, to go to the boy's side but found himself too weak. His wounded leg would no longer hold his weight. He stumbled and fell back against the marble. He put out a hand to steady himself. It sunk into the rock, the stone itself *sucking* at him.

He was held tight in the rock's embrace and could only watch, as the mob grew uglier.

The boy's face was set in grim concentration. Two men tried to take the sword from him. He ducked away, but was in danger of being cornered. Rather than give up the sword to the men he dodged between a sea of arms and ran for the cauldron. Without a pause he *slammed* the sword back into the stone. It sat there, vibrating, sending off a deep hum as it settled.

The mob was in uproar. A tall heavily built man strode forward, almost knocking the boy to the ground. He tugged at the sword, but it was held tight. He put both hands to the task, muscles bunching under his tunic. The sword held to its place, even as the man went red in the face. He stayed there, tugging and pulling, until he was spent.

Man after man, almost every one present took his turn. None

were able to shift the sword by as much as an inch.

Finally, when all others had taken their turn, the boy strode forward again. He played the crowd, pausing for effect before, one handed, sliding the sword from the stone with no effort. He showed the crowd the sword and stood in front of them, that wide, impish grin painted across his face.

The boy turned back to Hentra, dismayed to see where the Saxon's hand was embedded in the rock. Try as they might, neither of them could shift it. The boy even tried to pour water from the cauldron around the stone, in the vain hope that it might *soften*.

And that is when Hentra knew what must be done.

This boy will be king. He has the sword, and my people will not be able to stand against him.

But he does not yet have the cauldron.

Hentra put his free hand against the cold black iron and called on the Wyrd.

Almost immediately the tribes-people in the room became shadowy figures, as if seen through a thick fog. Hentra wove a hiding spell, using all the strength he had in him and moulding reality to *his* will.

The marble flowed and shifted, taking first his legs then his torso. But Hentra kept his hand on the cauldron, moving it, and him, to the furthest corner of the Wyrd, to a place where no one could find it. He bound it with cryptic puzzles and glamour, and hid it among stories from other places, other times.

At the end, just as the stone finally took him, the Wyrd showed him one last vision. It was of an aged king, bent and worn by many cares, searching in vain for a cauldron to renew him, even as the Saxon armies once more arrived on his shores – this time to stay.

The boy might have won the sword.

But Hentra had won the war.

TIME AND THE CITY

John Howard

THE CITY BEARS no name, or at least they have never been able to discover it. So it is the City. There is a map, but there are no names inscribed on it. The precise material the map is made from remains uncertain. And it is not even possible to determine how it was produced: whether it was drawn, or printed by a process long since lost – and lost so long ago that the loss itself is not remembered.

From the start they are able to make out the course of the river, together with the surrounding hills and valleys, and the barest skeletal outline of the City. The lattice of its plan reveals itself: twining and intersecting threads of varying widths laid down over the charted landscape, the many forums, squares, arenas, and other spaces marked only by the absence of lines. Many of the City's streets and ways clearly take the natural paths of contour lines; others are part of a formal geometry imposed on the land, lines knotted together in an encompassing net that could catch anyone who chances to come upon it. That is all.

Kayler decides to dedicate himself to exploring the map and seeking the city it reveals. He experiences the icy exhilaration of gazing down into deep time – as he stares at the ancient city, contemplating it, he feels as if he is standing at the edge of an abyss. Layer upon layer of strata fall away before him, as if tumbling with him into the millennia. At other times, as he concentrates on a particular area of the City, or a certain feature, it is like staring into a yawning shaft, a wondrous vertigo seizing him as the depths rush up to meet him, inexorably coming into resolution around him. To Kayler the nameless city becomes truly the only City. He sinks into the pit of time; he embraces and returns its chill grip.

HE STANDS AT what was once the centre of a world. Sunlight slants over roofs covered with golden tiles. Shadows grow long as the sun goes down behind the temples piled up against the City's low hills. Ahead of him, on both sides of Triumphal Way, rows of marble columns march towards infinity, striking into the empty sky. If the pillars were ever capped by statues, there are none left now. As Kayler strolls towards the Central Forum the procession of topless columns sow in him a sense of incompleteness and jeopardy: as if a gigantic knife has sliced a layer off the top of the City, and might sweep back again at any time.

Soaring above the Central Forum and crowning the City's highest hill is the Verdigris Dome. The metal flashes and glints in the setting sun. He starts to walk across the patterned red and black marble slabs towards the mighty staircase that mounts the hillside rising towards the Dome. Space opens out on all sides of him. During all of his time in the City he has met no-one, seen no -one. There is no sign of any life. The City seems deserted, as if scoured clean by the winds that gust in from the surrounding plains.

KAYLER SNAPS OUT of his reverie as the train clatters into the station. From memories of wandering across the vast open space of the Central Forum, the Verdigris Dome swelling into the sky in the distance, Kayler recalls himself to the swaying carriage.

Advertisements flash past on the tunnel walls. Soon he is standing on the platform gazing at grimy tiles. A fresh blast of warm wind pushes its way into the tunnel as another train roars towards the station.

Outside at street level Kayler smells the fumes and hears the rumble of traffic and the endless subdued muttering of the people crowding the pavements. He is jostled; he looks around him for the row of columns, but lamp posts are no substitute. Litter frolics around his feet. He hesitates, thinking that next time he will walk to a quay and get into one of the empty boats, but a train is crawling slowly over the first bridge he comes to, and the river is the wrong one. He shakes his head, trying to fully return himself to the present.

He thinks of the map of the City and how the River Mercuriel meanders through the grid of streets. So far he has crossed the river once, on the Segmental Bridge; he saw the ranks of boats tied up at the empty quays, and vowed to follow the slow and drowsy flow of the river from one side of the City to the other. He sits on a bench, feeling the solid wood pushing up in reaction against his weight. This time in the City he knelt on the terracotta paving of Three Fountains Square and had been able to feel the gritty material as he rubbed his palm over its surface. For the first time it was as if the City had declared something of itself to him. It isn't far to Melas' office.

He tells Melas that he is beginning to hear the sound of the wind and to smell the grass. "The resolution of the Bistre Quarter has improved significantly, then?" Melas says.

Kayler nods. "Yes. Triumphal Way is forming out well. It will be interesting to see if statues do grow on top of the pillars."

Melas smiles. "Couldn't you choose more evocative names? Maybe I should be more careful how I put you under, try and influence you while you're … away. Back there."

Kayler invents the names. Every street and building in the City that a name has been bestowed on is given it because it seemed right, because it seemed to fit. "Those names choose themselves," he says. "The map is filling itself in, isn't it? It wouldn't if the names weren't accurate."

"I expect you're right. Let me know when you want to look at the map again," she says softly. "If you think you really need to."

"Soon," Kayler says. He remains seated and closes his eyes. The City is there in the nebulous distances within.

HE CROSSES THE expanse of the Central Forum and stands in front of the Arch of the Dawn. The Forum's paving pushes up against the soles of his feet. Kayler feels the distance walked, and the slight ache increases as he contemplates the switch-backing steps rising from beyond the Arch as they climb the heights towards the Verdigris Dome.

If the orientation of the City is what it seems, the rising sun will shine directly through the Arch of the Dawn on the spring and autumn equinoxes. Shadows, miles in length, would be cast along the white marble slabs of the Avenue of the East, which is aligned precisely with a notch in distant mountains now becoming visible to Kayler for the first time. He breathes in deeply. The morning air of the City is becoming richer: now he smells smoke and the occasional tang of salt from the sea he knows is there. Under them there are traces of animal smells and a multitude of odours that can only come from cooking. They become stronger even as Kayler stands in front of the tremendous Arch breathing them in. He is alert for sounds, too. Surely they will soon intrude – or, rather, claim his attention as is their right. He imagines parades and processions converging on the Arch from the three broad ways leading into the Central Forum. He sees the glitter of gold and silver and the multi-coloured twinkling of gems, flashing armour and swishing robes and cloaks. He sees chariots and carts; elephants, oxen, and horses. In the silent morning Kayler hears trumpets and the steady beat of drums, matching the marching soldiers and the creaking wheels. There are shouts and cheers as the head of the procession passes under the Arch of the Dawn and comes to a halt. The very stones would be calling out acclamations in exultation.

Kayler walks into the shadow of the Arch and through the main portal. He takes another look around: still no sign of anyone, anything. Nothing moves. Then he spreads himself against the warm marble, its veins and flecks little further away than the ends of his eyelashes. He grasps and smells the building blocks of the City. His tongue flickers out and for a moment touches his condensing dream.

MELAS ASKS HIM about the people.

"If I'd seen any I'd have told you," Kayler says. "But I can feel them more and more each time. The sheer depth of the past – our past, not theirs, of course – terrifies me and yet makes me glad. Can you imagine it, Melas? How much I've travelled in the City, how far I've penetrated into its secrets, yet still knowing so very little! I will hurt myself if I were to stumble and fall, now. There is the white and grey stone, the marble, the terracotta and polished wood, the cloudy glass and green bronze. And, yes, its people. The City, Melas, the City!" Kayler shivers. "And aeon after aeon! Now put me under."

KAYLER SLOWLY TOILS up the first set of the great ranks of steps. The Arch of the Dawn is behind and below him. He remembers the golden coffered vaulting of the main portal, and the narrow staircases channelled into the thickness of its piers, tempting him to climb. But he ignored the small staircases.

Reaching the first terrace Kayler sits on a wide stone bench that follows its course around the side of the hill. The hill now seems entirely encased in stone and covered with marble buildings. The colossal mass gleams in the sun and hurts his eyes. In front of him the City unrolls itself, a stone carpet flung out to the low ramparts of its surrounding hills. Kayler can easily see the Central Forum and Triumphal Way; the expected – or intended – statues are beginning to grow on top of the rows of columns. He sees the City stretching out over gently undulating land, covering its smooth rising and falling in a succession of frozen waves of architecture. Domes bubble and towers leap up from the dusty colours of the packed buildings below him. Kayler sees the glint of the river, its bridges holding the City together like stitches knitting a deep cut. The sun is a circular smear in a white sky, too bright to look at but impossible to ignore. Kayler absorbs its heat just as the City does. He turns away and looks towards the next section of the steps. From where he is standing the Verdigris Dome is hidden by the blinding ranks of pillars and porticos, pediments, towers, terraces, and row upon row of arches sweeping up before him. He starts climbing again.

KAYLER RUSHES TOWARDS Melas' office. The pavement is crowded – the complete opposite to the streets and boulevards of the City, which remain deserted. The people around him, moving with the same tide as him, or weaving against it, are reassuringly solid. They cast shadows. They make noises. They touch each other and brush against him. Kayler thrusts his hands deeper into his pockets. Suddenly someone steps in front of him and asks a question. Kayler blunders on, straight into the man and past, out the other side. He still feels the contact, but it's like emerging from a stiff revolving door. The voice trails away in anger behind him. The crowd looks less substantial now. Kayler reaches

Melas' building and bounds up the steps.

She tells him that the map now shows a definite wall girdling the City. "The City is almost circular, as if it was built at the centre of a shallow saucer hundreds of miles across. Is that how it really seems?"

"Yes," Kayler says. He prepares himself to return.

AT THE NEXT terrace Kayler turns and surveys the City again. He gasps at what he sees. In the Central Forum and boulevards feeding into it there are now hundreds – thousands – of minute specks. Some are moving, milling around each other; some are still. Kayler blinks several times, in case the spots are inside his eyes. He shakes his head in wonder. There are boats on the River Mercuriel – small craft showing tiny squares of sail. The City's people are returning.

For a moment Kayler considers descending again, but in his experience so far when something has resolved itself into life, it remains. The people will still be there when he comes down from the Verdigris Dome. Kayler lets his gaze linger on a grid of streets and open spaces nestling close to the wall, and distorted due to his angle of sight and the distance. The area is bisected by a canal, which leads straight towards an enormous arena or open theatre in the centre of – he names the district Sunline. Even as he does so its resolution sharpens and he sees its inhabitants strolling along the wide pavements or sitting on stone benches built into the embankments of the blue canal. He hears the thin buzz and flutter of conversation and laughter. Wheels rattle. Children run across an open space emerald with grass and trees. Flowers blaze out in their beds next to the yellow and white marble pathways. Melas will be pleased. He smiles and turns away, back to the waiting heights.

Kayler ascends stairway upon stairway, crosses terrace after terrace. As he gets higher the air grows thicker; he tastes it with every intake of breath. Columns of smoke rise from innumerable chimneys, and he smells the bluntness of stone warmed by the sun. Some of the buildings soaring above him now have windows instead of porticos. The crystal glass flashes in the sun and reflects the tall cloudless sky. Kayler imagines jumping up into one of the half acre windows and feeling it sucking him in, drowning him on the other side. When he tilts his head back the cupola crowning the Verdigris Dome is just visible above the terraces and pediments mounting up in front of him.

Two great stairways carved from what looks like a single piece of pale pink onyx curve away from either side of a pillared archway. Kayler walks towards the shadowed entrance and stands in front of a vast pair of doors sheathed in copper and worked with an intricate design of curving incised lines picked out in brass and silver. He reaches out and touches, only lightly, one of the large circular bosses or studs raised at head height on the inner edge of each door. Without any sound the doors swing open smoothly, blossoming open in front of him and drawing him onwards.

MELAS FROWNS AT him. "I heard them shouting at you in the corridor," she says. "What were you thinking of, Kayler? Why were you so rude and thoughtless? This isn't like you." She looks at him closely. "And you almost walked into me just now. Don't you see us?"

"I rise up through the millennia each time you bring me back," Kayler says. "This city and all of you … all of you … are like so many misty figures. Soon I will sink down into the pavement and be able to put my hand through any wall I choose. I pull the years into myself every time you put me under to go back to the City. I am years, decades, centuries – whole epochs – they stack up like the palaces and obelisks ranged around Gold Glory Hill. The magnificence of the City, the magnitude and power of its achievements! And that's not all, Melas. For the first time I glimpsed the machines.

"There were immense mechanisms, or maybe they were all one great sublime machine. It was all acres of glittering steel and shiny brass, with its own sets of staircases and balconies where there were switches and levers made from crystal and ivory and ebony. There were rows and rows of light twinkling and sparking inside jewels of a million colours. There were mirrors and lenses. And it rose up from the floor of the hall as far as it could go. You should've seen the size of the base supports and the flying buttresses of dull iron that held it all together. They were massive from where I stood and yet I think they were the best part of a mile below. And the sunlight poured in through the windows, and everything was warm and solid, with a heft and a – a purpose that made me shudder."

"Surely you couldn't know what that thing was for? What it was doing there."

"Oh, that's just it," Kayler says. "Yes, it *endures*. There was a raw purpose and power locked in those shining tubes. But I didn't – I don't – know what it is, what it's capable of. But it's stupendous – and so very old. I felt the air vibrate with something like the deepest note of an organ, almost too deep to hear, but not to feel, trembling at the border of my senses. Even the City itself is a modern suburb of boxy houses when compared to that machinery in that hall. Something, some power, is chained, kept in check. And I don't know whether that's by the machine, or for it – something hoarded for release through the machine. Oh, Melas, I'm sure those forces could tear through the ages, rip the world apart from then to eternity as surely as I could pull that new paper map off the wall and shred it into a thousand pieces."

Melas gets up from her chair and starts to play with the single plain gold ring she wears. She paces up and down in front of the wide window. "That must be the reason for the symbol that's appeared in the middle of the map of the City," she says quietly.

SPACE, ENORMOUS EMPTY volume, explodes around Kayler as the copper doors open and he walks forward. A marble balustrade appears in front of him, forming a low barrier around the intricate glittering structure thrusting up from the centre of what he has always imagined to be a domed hall. Kayler thinks the object is a sculpture. Then he realises he is standing on a gallery, halfway up the inner surface of a perfect sphere like the inside of a small planet. Although it must be hundreds of feet away, at least, he sees the sculpture is clearly a mechanism. It thrusts on up past him towards the distant curve of the hemisphere suspended above. Something catches his eye: a ring of jewel-like lights is now flashing, with no apparent set sequence and at an increasing speed. The lights encircle a burnished metal depression, at the centre of which is a sphere of delicate silver, woven in a web. His eye moves to set itself on something that seems to be revolving or oscillating inside the silver sphere. With a shock Kayler realises that it must be a minimum of a hundred feet across. But he cannot quite follow whatever it is that moves; the motion of each full cycle is always interrupted, fading out and reappearing again in its orbit. He cannot tear his eyes away either. They follow the motion: a flickering like a bird imprisoned in a cage and fluttering in vain against the wire.

A shaft of sunlight lances down from the heights, channelled by mirrors into a waterfall of light. Kayler gasps as the radiant beam flows around the silvery sphere before being swallowed up inside it. The oscillations within continue, but his eyes ache violently from still trying to keep track of them. He feels his mind being pulled away, out into the void and towards the glittering web; at last he succeeds in wrenching his attention away and staggers backwards.

Eventually he is able to look up again, and notices what look like several narrow bands wrapped around the surface of the hemisphere, each progressively smaller in diameter the further away – up – they are. Kayler sits on the lowest step of a spiral staircase made of stone so smooth and seamless that it looks as if it were moulded in one piece with the colossal sphere. He gets up and continues his ascent, following the twisting way bored into the thickness of the dome.

The thin wind whips at his hair, which he pushes back from his forehead. The pale green of the Verdigris Dome drops away from where he stands, arcing down towards the City and its pattern of buildings and streets sprawling out so far below. The air is thinner and cooler; the sun seems warmer than he remembers from when he last stood on solid ground. The Central Forum is black with the mass of people crowding into the gigantic space. The streets leading to it are seething. Kayler knows that the inhabitants of the City are moving towards him in endless columns pouring like rivers of ink out of their streets, climbing towards him, following in his footsteps to where he stands. Now that he has reached the top of the Verdigris Dome, Kayler examines the white marble globe. The carved outlines seem familiar, but are certainly not the ones he knows, or thinks he knows. There is a globe on a stand in Melas' room; Kayler tries to visualise it clearly, but it wavers. The base of the marble globe is green metal, a baroque growth embossed with the symbol Melas had attempted to describe. He grips the metal railing. The faraway City draws itself into sharper resolution, names filtering out of newly-minted time. The City fits the map Kayler remembers. He dreads the memories of the awful gulfs separating him from the map – from all he knows. *There!* He is done.

KAYLER RECLINES IN a deep armchair in Melas' office, occasionally reaching out for the cups of hot sweet tea she has her staff making for him.

"Are you feeling better now?" she asks.

He shakes his head. "I will never feel better." Kayler looks around the bland and pale office with its window overlooking the busy street. Yet again he sees the rendered walls and wooden shelves, framed photographs and glowing computer screens. "Which end of the vortex have I arrived in?" he says. Melas leans in to hear.

"I knew I'd be lost if I let myself be taken by that –whatever it is – in the machinery, that *movement* in the silver sphere. Wherever or whenever it endlessly loops to," Kayler says. "It and the City are lost in the deep past, so far back that there's no physical trace left or even a hint in human memory now. But are they also lost in futurity, so far ahead that time itself is wearing out and allowing shifts we cannot imagine? Back then I raised my arms to the sun and the sleeves of an embroidered robe slipped back, exposing my arms to the light. I wore bands of silver and amber. The last things I saw were the map and the City as one, the muffled commotion, the first people reaching the place where I stood, when everything decayed like a film running backwards and the City toppled and shrank in on itself, the hills wore away, the river overflowed and spread out over the land until even that dried up and all became a flat plain. Somehow I saw all that. And maybe I will see it again. I do know one thing, though. Now we've found the City, it's always with us."

THE GREAT AND POWERFUL…

Selina Lock

THE CARVED DOOR stands open, the key still in the lock. Brass inlays glint in the weak sunlight emanating from inside the room. The varnish on the rose petal bas reliefs is cracked and flaking away. Dust motes float in the air, disturbed by the first human visitor in a long time. The interior of the room is even more fantastic than the entranceway. Two rows of pedestals line a central walkway. Perched on each are stone objects: here, the remains of a sculptured hand; there, what might have been a torso.

At the far end, the room is watched over by a massive stone head, easily three metres tall. A heavy set brow above its unseeing eyes. A wide nose with one side missing, and a full-lipped mouth curved upwards in a benign smile. Despite its size, the face is welcoming, with its podgy, dimpled cheeks and quizzical eyebrows. The outer ears are worn down, possibly by the weather of its native land, but the raised semi-circles show where the head once listened to distant winds.

What did it hear then? What does it hear now?

A woman stands a metre away from the gigantic head, just to the right of its nose. Her head is cricked to one side, gazing into its wide eyes. She shifts her weight to her right hip. Scuffed red Doc Martens on her feet. Creased black jeans and a plain black t-shirt which bulges slightly over her stomach. Silver and black earrings dangle below her short, floppy hair. She clutches a small camera in one hand; a tatty green rucksack is slung over the opposite shoulder.

"You are magnificent. Where did you come from?" she whispers. "Who made you? Were you their god? Their protector? A symbol of love?"

The woman happily keeps up a running commentary to the inanimate object; she is used to talking to herself, to having no-one around. She reaches out with her left hand, hesitates and glances around the room. Satisfied it's deserted, she steps forward and reverentially places her palm on the left cheek of the stone head.

The serenity of the room is split by a clanging from the floor below. She starts, her hand falling from the statue.

"They've found me."

Fear flashes across her face, followed by dismay.

"I thought I'd have more time. I wish I could stay here with you – it's so peaceful and beautiful. There's so little beauty and love left in the world now. No time to marvel at wonders – or create them."

The noises get louder. Glass smashing. Voices, whooping like demented birds. Wood splintering. She tugs her rucksack on her back, pockets the camera and stalks towards the carved wooden entranceway. Running footsteps echo in the corridor outside, and a teenage boy races into the room, breathing heavily.

"Marie, they're here. We have to go!" he says.

"Calm down, Gordie. I'm here. We're going now."

Marie catches Gordie's arm, pulling him into the corridor. They start running to the stairs at the far end. There is a thumping stamp of boots. A blue and white china vase smashes to the floor ahead of them, followed by a hail of other antique objects from around the world – a clay mug, fertility statues; a shower of the precious past disintegrating before their eyes.

Marie and Gordie slide to a halt before the onslaught and desperately look for another exit, but it's the stairs or the room she'd just left. Marie considers the huge, arched window behind them; but they are on the third floor and the chances of both surviving the leap are slim.

Spiky green hair rises up the stairway, followed by a snarling face of a youth. He is dressed in torn leathers. Others surge up behind him. All are in their early twenties, with piercings and rainbow-coloured hair. Tattoos of pairs of burning eyes on right cheeks signify their allegiance to the Annihilators. Their credo is violence, vandalism and devastation. After all, what else is there left to do in this dying world?

"Arm yourself, Gordie."

Marie glances at the wood-panelled walls around her, and spies an ancient longsword hanging high up. Springing onto a wooden cabinet, she lunges for the weapon. Grabbing the hilt, she swings in the air for a second before the display fixings give way and she crashes down. The blade clangs on the floor, missing her thigh by millimetres. She drags the sword towards her and pushes upright. Once standing, she grasps the hilt with both hands and manages to lift the tip a metre off the floor.

The gang members pause to laugh and jeer at her efforts.

Gordie acquires the remains of a mace, mostly the chain and handle. He swings it wildly above his head.

"Get back!" Marie says, pointing her sword towards the Annihilators. They smirk and move forward, picking up shards of pottery and glass as they come.

"Gordie, get back down the corridor – grab the door key.

We'll lock ourselves in."

"No. I'll fight." he replies.

Marie grimaces. "You'll get to fight soon enough. Now move."

Gordie glances at the green-haired goon. He bares his teeth in a feral grin and Gordie decides retreat is the better part of valour. Marie allows herself a moment of relief and then slowly backs after him, all the while swinging the sword toward the gang. The heft of the weapon strains her arms, making them tremble.

The gang surges forward, some of them attempting to close in from the sides. She heaves the blade in a semi-circle. It pierces the gang leader's thigh leaving a jagged gash. He howls and falls back. A pink-haired girl darts forward. Marie feels a sharp stab of pain in her side, as the girl jabs her with a shard of pottery; she yelps, nearly dropping the sword. Marie struggles to swing the blade again, panting with exertion. The flat of the steel connects with the back of the girl's knees. Pink Hair pitches forward, becoming entangled with another gang member as she falls, becoming a thrashing heap of limbs.

"Marie – quickly," Gordie shouts from the doorway to the sculpture room. The remaining gang members pause to assist their fallen comrades. Marie throws the sword at them and runs towards Gordie.

"Get them!" Green Hair yells, as another youth is tripped by the flying blade.

Adrenaline surges as Marie races towards the room. The pain in her side makes her stumble just as she reaches the carved doorway. Gordie pulls her inside, slams the door and turns the big, wrought iron key in the lock. They lean on the door, caught between relief and fear.

"Won't hold long. What we gonna do?" Gordie asks.

"I don't know," Marie replies. "Help me to the far end." She gestures with her head.

He places her arm over his slender bony shoulders and half drags her back towards the large stone head. Her other hand clutches the wound at her waist. Reaching the statue she removes her hand: it is covered with blood. She reaches forward, to the stone head, to steady herself, and slides down its side to the floor. Leaning against its strong jaw, she leaves her blood smeared across its dimpled cheeks.

"Sorry I couldn't keep you safe," she says, smiling weakly at Gordie.

"No-one could. Least you tried."

"Sit with me?" she asks, patting the floor beside her.

He perches, cross-legged and takes her hand. They sit in silence, listening to the muffled sounds of the gang attacking the door.

Marie looks up at the genteel face of the stone head and once again whispers to it. "I wish I had more time."

As she lowers her face, it seems that the smear of blood on the statue's cheek is absorbed into the stone. A red light flickers in its cold, grey eyes.

A sharp, loud crack signals the wooden door giving way to the Annihilators' onslaught.

Marie's head snaps up and Gordie's grip tightens on her hand. From her perspective, it looks like the gang bursts through the door in slow motion. Even so, they are all rage and glee and noise. Green Hair brandishes the sword Marie had abandoned, his eyes full of pain and anger as he limps towards them.

Marie's vision starts to blur from the blood loss. She catches a whiff of salt water and feels a light breeze across her face. Shaking her head, she tries to focus, pushing against the statue in an effort to stand. She refuses to die sitting.

Although the Annihilators are coming closer, they seem less

clear, like reflections in a puddle. It's as if they are approaching against a back drop of blue sky. Waist-high grass sways in a breeze, but a breeze that is growing stronger by the second, ruffling her hair – despite the fact that she knows they are still in that musty old room.

"What's happening?" Gordie asks, as the wind buffets them, pressing them back against the stone of the statue.

"I don't know." She grips his hand in both of hers. The wind rises, roars to a crescendo, and her ears pop, like attaining a high altitude. She starts trembling as pain and adrenaline surge through her system. Were they church bells? *How odd,* she thinks as her vision darkens. *What will happen now?* She slips into uncon-sciousness. The last thing she feels is Gordie stroking her arm and calling her name. *I'm okay,* she thinks, *just a bit tired.*

MARIE OPENS HER eyes. The gang, the room – in fact, the whole damn building – has disappeared, replaced by lush blue-green grass, a sprinkling of white flowers. Topped by the brightest blue sky she has ever seen: a sky not possible in her smog-choked, polluted world. But then she doubts she is in that world right now.

"Where are we?" Gordie asks.

"Well, we're not in Kansas any more, Toto." she replies.

"Eh?"

"Oh, it's something Mother used to say." She looks around. "I have no idea where we are."

Pain slices through her side. She is still crouching so she slides to the ground; warm stone scrapes against her back. The giant head from the museum is behind her, exactly as before...

"Wherever we are, it's here too," she says, jerking her head towards the statue.

A low rumbling sound startles her; it's in time with the

vibrations she notices running through the statue and the surrounding earth. The noise bubbles up, becomes louder, and the head starts to shake. Marie and Gordie scramble away from it, falling into the grass nearby. Just in time … to witness the rocky lips open and hear the booming laugh burst forth

Blue and green lights flicker in its eyes, looking straight at them. The laughter quietens and the lips settle into a smile. Marie stares at the now-animated head. She is definitely hallucinating, Marie thinks. *Chalk that up to the amount of blood I've lost. Either that or I'm going mad, or dead, or all three.* The extra pain from Gordie squeezing her shoulders a little too tightly suggests maybe not – unless they are both sharing the same hallucination.

"Of course I'm here, too, young lady. This is my domain, after all. Where else would I be? Well, apart from that museum, and a few other museums, and actually, my awareness is stretched a little thin among all my representations to be honest, so forget I asked that." the head rumbles.

"You … you're talking," Gordie states, pointing a trembling finger at the stone figure.

It raises an eyebrow in response. *"Not too quick on the uptake, that one, is he?"* the head says. *"Then again, I'm sure being whisked through a few dimensions and suchlike would have an effect on* zee little grey cells." The final few words are intoned in a rather odd attempt at a different accent.

Marie and Gordie stare at the stone head.

Its expression drops slightly. *"Not* Poirot *fans either, then? Should have guessed … you don't even know* The Wizard of Oz. *What has happened to culture in your time?"*

"You're the Wizard of Oz?" Marie asks. "Did you bring us here with some kind of … magic?"

They both jump as the booming laugh washes over them again.

"HA HA HA HA. Me, the Wizard of Oz? Ha ha haaa! No, no. The Wizard of Oz was … well, never mind. That would be far too complicated to explain. But you can call me Oz if you want, it's as good a name as any, and you probably couldn't pronounce half of my other ones."

"Where are we … Oz? Why did you bring us here?" Marie asks. "Not that we're ungrateful – better than being killed." She points her face into the gentle summery breeze for a moment. The land is peaceful, now that Oz has stopped sending ripples through the ground with his laughter. Gordie sits down behind her, though one hand still rests on her shoulder.

"I told you where you are, my dear girl. My domain." Oz replies. *"And as to why I rescued you, why, it seemed only fair after your flattering comments. I'm rather partial to being called magnificent. Plus, you made the appropriate offering."*

Marie's bloody smear briefly reappears on Oz's cheek before soaking into the stone again. She shivers, despite the warmth.

"You whispered many wishes in my ear." Oz continues. *"For time, peace, beauty, love, to marvel at wonders and to create them. To stay with me. Well, I could grant the last request easily. As for the boy – you seem rather fond of him, so it would be rather churlish to leave him behind."*

Its full stone lips quirk upwards and the light in its eyes starts to dim.

"For now, my attention is needed elsewhere and you need to rest. You'll find everything you need in the hut behind you. See you later, alligator."

The blue-green light flickers out and the stone eyes stare straight ahead.

"Oz? Oz?" Gordie says.

"It … he's gone," Marie replies. "Or rather he's not answering. Come on, rest sounds good."

THE HUT IS constructed of woven grass. Inside, they find a couple of grass-stuffed pallets and a crude wooden table. A number of wooden bowls sit on the tabletop. Several contain nuts, berries and fruit. Another contains water and a final one a grey paste. Little handmade paper notes are propped up against the bowls, each with instructions, written in an ornate hand.

EAT ME, says the food note. *DRINK ME*, says the water note. *PUT ME ON YOUR WOUND*, says the paste note.

"I don't remember the last one from *Alice*." Marie mutters. As she says this, on the final note more writing appears, in a smaller, more hurried script.

Hurrah, you have at least read Alice's Adventures. There is hope for you yet. I had to improvise as Alice did not sport a wound like yours...

While Marie is reading, Gordie eagerly grabs a handful of nuts, but then hesitates. "Do you think it's safe to eat them?" he asks.

"I expect so. Seems a bit of a waste of time to rescue us and then to poison us."

THEY EAT AND drink their fill. Marie dresses her injury with the grey paste; it numbs her wound quickly. Then they both collapse on the grass pallets. Sleep comes quickly, lulled by the sounds of waves lapping and the sweet scents of summer flowers.

The next morning, they wake refreshed. Gordie heads straight to the table. Marie yawns and stretches, pausing to check her side, lifting her t-shirt to peer at the wound. The skin has healed into a slightly puckered scar, which feels tender and tight – but no actual pain. *Miraculous, indeed.*

"There's no new food. I thought it would magically refill," Gordie complains.

Marie smiles.

"Well, I'm glad the magic worked on my injury," she says, indicating her side, "but I guess we can't rely on magic for everything ... let's go explore."

They spend the rest of the day wandering around. It turns out to be an island only a few miles across. Their hut is the only habitation. Otherwise it's just plants and rocks, apart from Oz's statue, which is visible from nearly everywhere. Despite frequent treks past the head, and yelling at it a few times, there is no reaction from the entity. A stream provides fresh water, the sea a warm bath and patches of trees and bushes plenty more berries to refill the wooden bowls. This becomes their routine over the next few days, as they slowly relax, luxuriating in a freedom from fear that she – and Gordie – has not experienced for a long time.

Gordie laughs more, splashes in the sea and eats everything in sight. Marie sleeps, floats in the sea, and collects pebbles and flowers. The deep coil of tension within her slowly unravels. Each day Marie sits in the shade of the stone head, talking to Oz. She tells it about her life, the little she knows of Gordie's experiences, the few books she used to read, the things she misses and since the deterioration of her world.

Hoping for an answer – even just a quick quip to indicate that Oz is still aware of them.

GORDIE SHAKES HER awake, lines creasing his forehead and his breathing heavy.

"Marie! Marie! The berry bushes have gone."

"Uurgh. Whaddaya mean?" she says, rubbing her eyes.

"The bushes have gone—"

"What? You mean the wind has torn them up – or something?"

"No," Gordie replies, jabbing his hand towards the entrance.

"There's no sign of them. It's like they never existed."

They spend the day searching the island, noticing changes. By midday some of the trees have gone and it takes five minutes less to walk across the island. Then a further five minutes less the next hour. By the evening only their hut and Oz's head remain on an island a few hundred yards in diameter. Waves lap the shores surrounding them.

"Oz! Oz! Answer us, damn you." Marie shouts. "Where are you? What's happening?"

Tears of frustration run down her cheeks, and she hugs Gordie to her. After a few minutes staring at the statue she slowly pushes him away and wipes her eyes. She takes a deep breath and tightens her shoulders. "Okay. We'll try it another way." she says, looking directly into the stone eyes. Picking up a sharp rock from the ground she scrapes it across her lower arm, grimacing in pain. Gordie grabs the hand holding the rock.

"What are you doing?" he yells.

"Blood got his attention last time. Perhaps it will again. We have to do something, before we … we wake up in the sea." She squeezes Gordie's hand and carefully removes it from her own. She scrapes the jagged rock against her arm again, this time drawing a little blood. She drops the rock and wipes the blood off with her forefinger. She dabs her bloody finger on the warm stone cheek of the statue, hoping for a reaction.

Green-blue light flares in Oz's eyes and a sighing breeze escapes the stone lips.

"More blood? What now?" it asks, eyebrows drawing together.

"The island's disappearing," Marie shouts.

"Don't be ridiculous," Oz replies.

"We're not," Gordie says. "Look around."

There is a grinding noise as the stone head slowly swivels from side to side. The flickering eyes take in their surroundings.

"Ah. That's not good. No, indeed," Oz states. *"Houston, we*

have a problem."

"A problem! *A problem!"* Marie's eyes widen. "I thought we were safe here. You're a god, for God's sakes. Do something!" She slaps Oz's cheek, stinging her hand.

"Hey, hey! No need to get violent." Oz's stone lips purse. *"I never said I was a God. You just presumed that."*

"What are you, then? More importantly, what're you going to do?"

"What I am would take a little long to explain. Let's just say that ... that I'm a powerful being, rather like the Wizard of Oz. Your blood gave me a power boost, but obviously that's worn off while I've been distracted. I thought you'd be fine here."

Marie and Gordie stare at the head, its green-blue eyes dimming a little under their scrutiny.

"What I do is easy. I grant your next wish. So, what will it be? Time, peace, beauty, love, to marvel at wonders or to create them?"

"What?" Marie asks, now realising their idyll was always too good to be true.

"Where do you want to go? What do you want to do?"

"What do I want?" she shouts, while Gordie hides behind her. "I want to live, I want Gordie to live. In fact, I want us to do more than live. I want us to have lives. Lives that aren't all about fear and hiding, and sieving the ruins for scraps. I thought you'd given us that, but it was all a big trick, wasn't it?"

The stone head draws back a little at her onslaught and then grins. *"You are a feisty one, all right. No wonder I like you. It isn't a trick, merely a respite while you heal. I could never keep you here forever. Your path is always back in your own world. It's just a case of seeing what path you would choose."* The light in its eyes flares red. Its mouth opens wide. *"You do not wish destruction, therefore you choose creation."* it shouts. The roar of its voice knocks them over and the waves wash right up to their bodies.

Marie's vision dims. *This is all starting to feel familiar*, she thinks, as the darkness envelopes her.

GORDIE IS SHAKING her awake. She keeps her eyes closed, wondering where they'll be. The museum or the island? Sounds of shouting and clanging impinge on her thoughts. The Annihilators! Gordie! She opens her eyes, jumps to her feet, grabs her friend's arm to steady herself. Sweat drips down her forehead as the heat and humidity threaten to overwhelm her. She stares at the massive jungle trees towering overhead. Glancing behind, she sees the familiar stone head, overgrown with plants. Its full lips and dimpled cheeks peep out from a fringe of creepers. *Definitely no gang in sight.*

Marie and Gordie exchange glances and then turn their attention towards the origin of the commotion, the voices. A little way off, a clearing is a hive of activity. A group of walking wounded is tending the cooking fires. A gaggle of children chop unfamiliar looking vegetables. Further back, behind the cooking area, men and women are busy measuring and sawing wood. Some wear jeans and t-shirts, and others skirts or tunics. All show signs of wear and tear. A half-constructed building rises up in the centre of the community.

A young girl standing at the clearing's perimeter spies them, waves and gestures forward.

Gordie takes a step, then hesitates and looks at Marie. She nods and smiles.

"They seem friendly enough," she says and follows him.

The girl offers them food and water. They eat and drink , and the people down tools and gather around. An older woman, with wrinkled brown skin and a ready smile, sits down next to Marie and Gordie. She is clutching something in her right hand. She opens it to reveal a miniature statue of Oz.

"He says you've got one helluva story to tell us," the woman says, patting Marie on the knee. "So go on honey, we're all dying to hear it."

"A story? Umm, okay." Marie looks around at the expectant faces and wonders where to begin. All at once, pictures, people, and landscapes flood into her mind.

She starts to speak and a world is created from her words.

YS

Aliette de Bodard

SEPTEMBER, AND THE wind blows Françoise back to Quimper, to roam the cramped streets of the Old City amidst squalls of rain.

She shops for clothes, planning the colours of the baby's room; ambles along the deserted bridges over the canals, breathing in the smell of brine and wet ivy. But all the while she's aware that she's only playing a game with herself – she knows she's only pretending that she hasn't seen the goddess.

It's hard to forget the goddess – that cold radiance that blew salt into Françoise's hair, the dress that shimmered with all the colours of sunlight on water – the sharp glimmer of steel in her hand.

You carry my child, the goddess had said, and it was so. It had always been so.

Except, of course, that Stéphane hadn't understood. He'd seen it as a betrayal – blaming her for not taking the pill as she should have – oh, not overtly, he was too stiff-necked and too well-educated for that, but all the same, she'd heard the words he wasn't saying, in every gesture, in every pained smile.

So she left. So she came back here, hoping to see Gaëtan – if there's anyone who knows about goddesses and myths, it's

Gaëtan, who used to go from house to house writing down legends from Brittany. But Gaëtan isn't here, isn't answering her calls. Maybe he's off on another humanitarian mission – incommunicado again, as he's so often been.

Françoise's cell phone rings – but it's only the alarm clock, reminding her that she has to work out at the gym before her appointment with the gynaecologist.

With a sigh, she turns towards the nearest bus stop, fighting a rising wave of nausea.

"IT'S A BOY," the gynaecologist says, staring at the sonographs laid on his desk.

Françoise, who has been readjusting the straps of her bra, hears the reserve in his voice. "There's something else I should know?"

He doesn't answer for a while. At last he looks up, his grey eyes carefully devoid of all feelings. His bad-news face, she guesses. "Have you – held back on something, Ms. Martin? In your family's medical history?"

A hollow forms in her stomach, draining the warmth from her limbs. "What do you mean?"

"Nothing to worry about," he says, slowly, and she can hear the *not yet* he's not telling her. "You'll have to take an appointment with a cardiologist. For a foetal echocardiograph."

She's not stupid. She's read books about pregnancies, when it became obvious that she couldn't bring herself to abort – to kill an innocent child. She knows about echocardiographs, and that the prognosis is not good. "Birth defect?" she asks, from some remote place in her mind.

He sits, all prim and stiff – what she wouldn't give to shake him out of his complacency. "Congenital heart defect. Most probably a difformed organ – it won't pump enough blood into the veins."

"But you're not sure." He's sending her for further tests. It means there's a way out, doesn't it? It means...

He doesn't answer, but she reads his reply in his gaze all the same. He's ninety-percent sure, but he still will do the tests – to confirm.

She leaves the surgery, feeling – cold. Empty. In her hands is a thick cream envelope: her sonographs, and the radiologist's diagnosis neatly typed and folded alongside.

Possibility of heart deformation, the paper notes, dry, uncaring.

Back in her apartment, she takes the sonographs out, spreads them on the bed. They look ... well, it's hard to tell. There's the trapeze shape of the womb, and the white outline of the baby – the huge head, the body curled up. Everything looks normal.

If only she could fool herself. If only she was dumb enough to believe her own stories.

Evening falls over Quimper – she hears the bells of the nearby church tolling for Vespers. She settles at her working table, and starts on her sketches again.

It started as something to occupy her, and now it's turned into an obsession. With pencil and charcoal she rubs in new details, with the precision she used to apply to her blueprints – and then withdraws, to stare at the paper.

The goddess stares back at her, white and terrible and smelling of things below the waves. The goddess as she appeared, hovering over the sand of Douarmenez Bay, limned by the morning sun: great and terrible and alien.

Françoise's hands are shaking. She clenches her fingers, unclenches them, and waits until the tremors have passed.

This is real. This is now, and the baby is a boy, and it's not normal. It's never been normal.

THAT NIGHT, AS on every night, Francoise dreams that she walks once more on the beach at Douarnenez – hearing the drowned bells tolling the midnight hour. The sand is cold, crunching under her bare feet.

She stands before the sea, and the waves part, revealing stone buildings eaten by kelp and algae, breached seawalls where lobsters and crabs scuttle. Everything is still dripping with brine, and the wind in her ears is the voice of the storm.

The goddess is waiting for her, within the largest building – in a place that must once have been a throne room. She sits in a chair of rotten wood, lounging on it like a sated cat. Beside her is a greater chair, made of stone, but it's empty.

"You have been chosen," she says, her words the roar of the waves. "Few mortals can claim such a distinction."

I don't want to be chosen, Francoise thinks, as she thinks on every night. But it's useless. She can't speak – she hasn't been brought here for that. Just so that the goddess can look at her, trace the minute evolutions in her body, the progress of the pregnancy.

In the silence, she hears the baby's heartbeat – a pulse that's so quick it's bound to falter. She hears the gynaecologist's voice: *the heart is deformed.*

"My child," the goddess says, and she's smiling. "The city of Ys will have its heir at last."

An heir to nothing. An heir to rotten wood, to algae-encrusted panels, to a city of fish and octopi and bleached skeletons. An heir with no heart.

He won't be born, Francoise thinks. *He won't live.* She tries to scream at the goddess, but it's not working. She can't open her mouth; her lips are stuck – frozen.

"Your reward will be great, never fear," the goddess says. Her face is as pale as those of drowned sailors, and her lips purple, as if she were perpetually cold.

I fear. But the words still won't come.

The goddess waves a hand, dismissive. She's seen all that she needs to see; and Françoise can go back, back into the waking world.

SHE WAKES UP to a bleary light filtering through the slits of her shutters. Someone is insistently knocking on the door – and a glance at the alarm clock tells her it's eleven a.m., and that once more she's overslept. She ought to be too nauseous with the pregnancy to get much sleep, but the dreams with the goddess are screwing up her body's rhythm.

She gets up – too fast, the world is spinning around her. She steadies herself on the bedside table, waiting for the feeling to subside. Her stomach aches fiercely.

"A minute!" she calls, as she puts on her dressing-gown, and sheaths her feet into slippers.

Through the Judas hole of the door, she can only see a dark silhouette, but she'd know that posture anywhere – a little embarrassed, as if he were intruding in a party he's not been invited to.

Gaëtan.

She throws the door open. "You're back," she says.

"I just got your message—" he stops, abruptly. His grey eyes stare at her, taking in, no doubt, the bulge of her belly and her puffy face. "I'd hoped you were joking." His voice is bleak.

"You know me better than that, don't you?" Françoise asks.

Gaëtan shrugs, steps inside – his beige trench coat dripping water on the floor. It looks as if it's raining again. Not an unusual occurrence in Brittany. "Been a long time," he says.

He sits on the sofa, twirling a glass of brandy between his fingers, while she tries to explain what has happened – when she gets to Douarnenez and the goddess walking out of the sea, her voice stumbles, trails off. Gaëtan looks at her, his face gentle: the same face he must show to the malnourished Africans who come to him as their last hope. He doesn't judge – doesn't scream or accuse her like Stéphane – and somewhere in her she finds the strength to go on.

After she's done, Gaëtan slowly puts the glass on the table, and steeples his fingers together, raising them to his mouth. "Ys," he says. "What have you got yourself into?"

"Like I had a choice." Françoise can't quite keep the acidity out of her voice.

"Sorry." Gaëtan hasn't moved – he's still thinking, it seems. It's never been like him to act or speak rashly. "It's an old tale around here, you know."

Françoise knows. That's the reason why she came back here. "You haven't seen this," she says. She goes to her working desk, and picks up the sketches of the goddess – with the drowned city in the background.

Gaëtan lays them on the low table before him, carefully sliding his glass out of the way. "I see." He runs his fingers on the goddess's face, very carefully. "You always had a talent for drawing. You shouldn't have chosen the machines over the landscapes and animals, you know."

It's an old, old tale; an old, old decision made ten years ago, and that she's never regretted. Except – except that the mere remembrance of the goddess's face is enough to scatter the formulas she made her living by; to render any blueprint, no matter how detailed, utterly meaningless. "Not the point," she says, finally – knowing that whatever happens next, she cannot go back to being an engineer.

"No, I guess not. Still..." He looks up at her, sharply. "You haven't talked about Stéphane."

"Stéphane – took it badly," she says, finally.

Gaëtan's face goes as still as sculptured stone. He doesn't say anything; he doesn't need to.

"You never liked him," Françoise says, to fill the silence – a silence that seems to have the edge of a drawn blade.

"No," Gaëtan says. "Let's leave it at that, shall we?" He turns his gaze back to the sketches, with visible difficulty. "You know who your goddess is."

Françoise shrugs. She's looked around on the Internet, but there wasn't much about the city of Ys. Or rather, it was always the same legend. "The Princess of Ys," she said. "She who took a new lover every night – and who had them killed every morning. She whose arrogance drowned the city beneath the waves."

Gaëtan nods. "Ahez," he says.

"To me she's the goddess." And it's true. Such things as her don't seem as though they should have a name, a handle back to the familiar. She cannot be tamed; she cannot be vanquished. She will not be cheated.

Gaëtan is tapping his fingers against the sketches, repeatedly jabbing his index into the eyes of the goddess. "They say Princess Ahez became a spirit of the sea after she drowned." He's speaking carefully, inserting every word with the meticulous care of a builder constructing an edifice on unstable ground. "They say you can still hear her voice in the Bay of Douarnenez, singing a lament for Ys – damn it, this kind of thing just shouldn't be happening, Françoise!"

Françoise shrugs. She rubs her hands on her belly, wondering if she's imagining the heartbeat coursing through her extended skin – a beat that's already slowing down, already faltering.

"Tell that to him, will you?" she says. "Tell him he shouldn't be alive." Not that it will ever get to be much of a problem, anyway – it's not as if he has much chance of surviving his birth.

Gaëtan says nothing for a while. "You want my advice?" he says.

Françoise sits on a chair, facing him. "Why not?" At least it will be constructive – not like Stéphane's anger.

"Go away," Gaëtan says. "Get as far as you can from Quimper – as far as you can from the sea. Ahez's power lies in the sea. You should be safe."

Should. She stares at him, and sees what he's not telling her. "You're not sure."

"No," Gaëtan says. He shrugs, a little helplessly. "I'm not an expert in magic and ghosts, and beings risen from the sea. I'm just a doctor."

"You're all I have," Francoise says, finally – the words she never told him after she started going out with Stéphane.

"Yeah," Gaëtan says. "Some leftovers."

Francoise rubs a hand on her belly again – feeling, distinctly, the chill that emanates from it: the coldness of beings drowned beneath the waves. "Even if it worked – I can't run away from the sea all my life, Gaëtan."

"You mean you don't want to run away, full stop."

A hard certainty rises within her – the same harshness that she felt when the gynaecologist told her about the congenital heart defect. "No," she says. "I don't want to run away."

"Then what do you intend to do?" Gaëtan's voice is brimming with anger. "She's immortal, Françoise. She was a sorceress who could summon the devil himself in the heyday of Ys. You're—"

She knows what she is; all of it. Or does she? Once she was a student, then an engineer and a bride. Now she's none of this – just a woman pregnant with a baby that's not hers. "I'm what I am," she says, finally. "But I know one other thing she is, Gaëtan, one power she doesn't have: she's barren."

Gaëtan cocks his head. "Not quite barren," he says. "She can create life."

"Life needs to be sustained," Françoise says, a growing certainty within her. She remembers the rotting planks of the palace in Ys – remembers the cold, cold radiance of the goddess. "She can't do that. She can't nurture anything." Hell, she cannot even create – not a proper baby with a functioning heart.

"She can still blast you out of existence if she feels like it."

Françoise says nothing.

At length Gaëtan says, "You're crazy, you know." But he's capitulated already – she hears it in his voice. He doesn't speak for a while. "Your dreams – you can't speak in them."

"No. I can't do anything."

"She's summoned you," Gaëtan says. He's not the doctor anymore, but the folklorist, the boy who'd seek out old wives and listen to their talk for hours on end. "That's why. You come to Ys only at her bidding – you have no power of your own."

Françoise stares at him. She says, slowly, the idea taking shape as she's speaking, "Then I'll come to her. I'll summon her myself."

His face twists. "She'll still be – she's power incarnate, Françoise. Maybe you'll be able to speak, but that's not going to change the outcome."

Françoise thinks of the sonographs and of Stéphane's angry words – of her blueprints folded away in her Paris flat, the meaningless remnants of her old life. "There's no choice. I can't go on like this, Gaëtan. I can't—" She's crying now – tears running down her face, leaving tingling marks on her cheeks. "I can't – go – on."

Gaëtan's arms close around her; he holds her against his chest, briefly, awkwardly – a bulwark against the great sobs that shake her chest.

"I'm sorry," she says, finally, when she's spent all her tears. "I don't know what came over me."

Gaëtan pulls away from her. His gaze is fathomless. "You've hoarded them for too long," he says.

"I'm sorry," Françoise says, again. She spreads out her hands – feeling empty, drained of tears and of every other emotion. "But if there's a way out – and that's the only one there seems to be – I'll take it. I have to."

"You're assuming I can tell you how to summon Ahez," Gaëtan says, carefully.

She can read the signs; she knows what he's dangling before her: a possibility that he can give her, but that he doesn't approve of. It's clear in the set of his jaw, in the slightly aloof way he holds himself. "But you can, can't you?"

He won't meet her gaze. "I can tell you what I learnt of Ys," he says at last. "There's a song and a pattern to be drawn in the sand, for those who would open the gates of the drowned city..." He checks himself with a start. "It's old wives' tales, Françoise. I've never seen it work."

"Ys is old wives' tales. And so is Ahez. And I've seen them both. Please, Gaëtan. At worst, it won't work and I'll look like a fool."

Gaëtan's voice is sombre. "The worst is if it works. You'll be dead." But his gaze is still angry, and his hands clenched in his lap; and she knows she's won, that he'll give her what she wants.

ANGRY OR NOT, Gaëtan still insists on coming with her – he drives her in his battered old Citroën on the small country roads to Douarnenez, and parks the car below a flickering lamplight.

Françoise walks down the dunes, keeping her gaze on the vast expanse of the ocean. In her hands she holds her only weapons: in her left hand, the paper with the pattern Gaëtan made her trace two hours ago; in her right hand, the sonographs the radiologist gave her this morning – the last scrap of science and reason that's left to her, the only seawall she can build against Ys and the goddess.

It's like being in her dream once more: the cold, white sand crunching under her sandals; the stars and the moon shining on the canvas of the sky; and the roar of the waves filling her ears to bursting. As she reaches the bottom of the beach – the strip of wet sand left by the retreating tide, where it's easier to draw patterns – the baby moves within her, kicking against the skin of her belly.

Soon, she thinks. *Soon.* Either way, it will soon be over, and the knot of fear within her chest will vanish.

Gaëtan is standing by her side, one hand on her shoulder. "You know there's still time—" he starts.

She shakes her head. "It's too late for that. Five months ago was the last time I had a choice in the matter, Gaëtan."

He shrugs, angrily. "Go on, then."

Françoise kneels in the sand, carefully, oh so carefully. She lays the cream envelope with the sonographs by her side; and positions the paper with the pattern so that the moonlight falls full onto it, leaving no shadow on its lines. To draw her pattern, she's brought a Celtic dagger with a *triskell* on the hilt – bought in a souvenir shop on the way to the beach.

Gaëtan is kneeling as well, staring intently at the pattern. His right hand closes over Françoise's hand, just over the dagger's hilt. "This is how you draw," he says.

His fingers moves, drawing Françoise's hand with them. The dagger goes down, sinks into the sand – there's some resistance, but it seems to melt away before Gaëtan's controlled gestures.

He draws line upon line, the beginning of the pattern – curves that meet to form walls and streets. And as he draws, he speaks: "We come here to summon Ys out of the sea. May Saint Corentin, who saved King Gradlon from the waves, watch over us; may the church bells toll not for our deaths. We come here to summon Ys out of the sea."

And, as he finishes his speech, he draws one last line, and completes his half of the pattern. Slowly, carefully, he opens his hand, leaving Françoise alone in holding the dagger.

Her turn.

She whispers, "We come here to summon Ys out of the sea. May Saint Corentin, who saved King Gradlon..." She closes her eyes for a moment, feeling the weight of the dagger in her hand – a last chance to abandon, to leave the ritual incomplete.

But it's too late for that.

With the same meticulousness she once applied to her blueprints – the same controlled gestures that allowed her to draw the goddess from memory – she starts drawing on the sand.

Now there's no other noise but the breath of the sea – and, in counterpoint to it, the soft sounds she makes as she adds line upon line, curves that arc under her to form a triple spiral, curves that branch and split, the pattern blossoming like a flower under her fingers.

She remembers Gaëtan's explanations: here are the seawalls of Ys, and the breach that the waves made when Ahez, drunk with her own power, opened the gates to the ocean's anger; here are the twisting streets and avenues where revellers would dance until night's end, and the palace where Ahez brought her lovers – and, at the end of the spiral, here is the ravine where her trusted servants would throw the lovers' bodies in the morning. Here is...

There's no time anymore where she is; no sense of her own body or of the baby growing within. Her world has shrunk to the pen and the darkened lines she draws, each one falling into place with the inevitability of a bell-toll.

When she begins on the last few lines, Gaëtan's voice starts speaking the words of power: the Breton words that summon

Ahez and Ys from their resting-place beneath the waves.

"Ur pales kaer tost d'ar sklujoù
Eno, en aour hag en perlez,
Evel an heol a bar Ahez."

A beautiful palace by the seawalls
There, in gold and in pearls
Like the sun gleams Ahez

His voice echoes in the silence, as if he were speaking above a bottomless chasm. He starts speaking them again – and again and again, the Breton words echoing each other until they become a string of meaningless syllables.

Françoise has been counting carefully, as he told her to; on the ninth repetition, she joins him. Her voice rises to mingle with Gaëtan's: thin, reedy, as fragile as a stream of smoke carried by the wind – and yet every word vibrates in the air, quivers as if drawing on some immeasurable power.

"Ur pales kaer tost d'ar sklujoù
Eno, en aour hag en perlez,
Evel an heol a bar Ahez."

Their words echo in the silence. At last, at long last, she rises, the pattern under her complete – and she's back in her body now, the sand's coldness seeping into her legs, her heart beating faster and faster within her chest – and there's a second, weaker heart-beat entwined with hers.

Slowly, she rises, tucks the dagger into her trousers pocket. There's utter silence on the beach now, but it's the silence before a storm. Moonlight falls upon the lines she's drawn – and remains trapped within them, until the whole pattern glows white.

"Françoise," Gaëtan says behind her. There's fear in his voice.

She doesn't speak. She picks up the sonographs and goes down to the sea, until the waves lap at her feet – a deeper cold than that of the sand. She waits – knowing what is coming.

Far, far away, bells start tolling: the bells of Ys, answering her call. And in their wake the whole surface of the ocean is trembling, shaking like some great beast trying to dislodge a burden. Dark shadows coalesce under the sea, growing larger with each passing moment.

And then they're no longer shadows, but the bulks of buildings rising above the surface: massive stone walls encrusted with kelp, surrounding broken-down and rotted gates. The faded remnants of tabards adorn both sides of the gates – the drawings so eaten away Françoise can't make out their details.

The wind blows into her face the familiar smell of brine and decay, of algae and rotting wood: the smell of Ys.

Gaëtan, standing beside her, doesn't speak. Shock is etched on every line of his face.

"Let's go," Françoise whispers – for there is something about the drowned city that commands silence, even when you are its summoner.

Gaëtan is looking at her and at the gates; at her and at the shimmering pattern drawn on the sand. "It shouldn't have worked," he says, but his voice is very soft, already defeated. At length he shakes his head, and walks beside her as they enter the city of Ys.

INSIDE, SKELETONS LIE in the streets, their arms still extended as if they could keep the sea at bay. A few crabs and lobsters scuttle away from them, the click-click of their legs on stone the only noise that breaks the silence.

Françoise holds the sonographs under her arms – the cardboard envelope is wet and decomposing, as if the atmosphere of Ys spreads rot to everything it touches. Gaëtan walks slowly, carefully. She can imagine how he feels – he, never one to take unconsidered risks, who now finds himself thrust into the legends of his childhood.

She doesn't think, or dwell overmuch on what could go wrong – that way lies despair, and perdition. But she can't help hearing the baby's faint heartbeat – and imagining his blood draining from his limbs.

There's no one in the streets, no revellers to greet them, no merchants plying their trades on the deserted marketplace – not even ghosts to flitter between the ruined buildings. Ys is a dead city. No, worse than that: the husk of a city, since long deserted by both the dead and the living. But it hums with power: with an insistent beat that seeps through the soles of Françoise's shoes, with a rhythm that is the roar of the waves and the voice of the storm – and also a lament for all the lives lost to the ocean. As she walks, the rhythm penetrates deeper into her body, in-sinuating itself into her womb until it mingles with her baby's heartbeat.

Françoise knows where she's going: all she has to do is retrace her steps of the dream, to follow the streets until they widen into a large plaza; to walk between the six kelp-eaten statues that guard the entrance to the palace, between the gates torn off their hinges by the onslaught of the waves.

And then she and Gaëtan are inside, walking down corridors. The smell of mould is overbearing now, and Françoise can feel the beginnings of nausea in her throat. There's another smell, too: underlying everything, sweet and cloying, like a perfume worn for too long.

She knows who it belongs to. She wonders if the goddess has

seen them come – but of course she has. Nothing in Ys escapes her overbearing power. She'll be at the centre, waiting for them – toying with their growing fear, revelling in their anguish.

No. Françoise mustn't think about this. She'll focus on the song in her mind and in her womb, the insidious song of Ys – and she won't think at all. She won't...

In silence they worm their way deeper into the cankered palace, stepping on moss and algae and the threadbare remnants of tapestries. Till at last they reach one last set of great gates – but those are of rusted metal, and the soldiers and sailors engraved on their panels are still visible, although badly marred by the sea.

The gates are closed – have been closed for a long time, the hinges buried under kelp and rust, the panels hanging askew. Françoise stops, the fatigue she's been ignoring so far creeping into the marrow of her bones.

Gaëtan has stopped too; he's running his fingers on the metal – pushing, desultorily, but the doors won't budge.

"What now?" he mouths.

The song is stronger now, draining Françoise of all thoughts – but at the same time lifting her into a different place, the same haven outside time as when she was drawing the pattern on the beach.

There are no closed doors in that place.

Françoise tucks the envelope with the sonographs under her arm, and lays both hands on the panels and pushes. Something rumbles, deep within the belly of the city – a pain that is somehow in her own womb – and then the gates yield, and open with a loud creak.

Inside, the goddess is waiting for them.

The dream once more: the rotten chairs beside the rotten trestle tables, the warm stones under her feet. And, at the far end of the room, the goddess sitting in the chair on the dais, smiling as Françoise draws nearer.

"You are brave," she says, and her voice is that of the sea before the storm. "And foolish. Few dare to summon Ys from beneath the waves." She smiles again, revealing teeth the colour of nacre. "And fewer still return alive." She moves, with fluid, inhuman speed; comes to stand by Gaëtan, who has frozen, three steps below the empty chair. "But you brought a gift, I see."

Françoise drags her voice from an impossibly faraway place. "He's not yours."

"I choose as I please, and every man that comes into Ys is mine," the goddess says. She walks around Gaëtan, tilting his head upwards, watching him as she might watch a slave on the selling-block. Abruptly there's a mask in her hand – a mask of black silk that seems to waver between her fingers.

That legend, too, Gaëtan told her. At dawn, after the goddess has had her pleasure, the mask will tighten until the man beneath dies of suffocation – one more sacrifice to slake her unending thirst.

Françoise is moving, without conscious thought – extending a hand and catching the mask before the goddess can put it on Gaëtan's face. The mask clings to her fingers: cold and slimy, like the scales of a fish, but writhing against her skin like a maddened snake.

She meets the goddess's cold gaze – the same blinding radiance that silenced her within the dream. But now there's power in Françoise – the remnants of the magic she used to summon Ys – and the light is strong, but she can still see.

"You dare," the goddess hisses. "You whom I picked among mortals to be honoured—"

"I don't want to be honoured," Françoise says, slowly. The mask is crawling upwards, extending coils around the palm of her hand. She's about to say "I don't want your child", but that would be a lie – she kept the baby, after all, clung to him rather than to Stéphane. "What I want you can't give."

The goddess smiles. She hasn't moved – she's still standing there, at the heart of her city, secure in her power. "Who are you to judge what I can and can't give?"

The mask is at her wrist now – it leaves a tingling sensation where it passes, as if it had briefly cut off the flow of blood in her body. Françoise tries not to think of what will happen when it reaches her neck – tries not to fear. Instead, as calmly as she can, she extends the envelope to the goddess. When she moves, the mask doesn't fall off, doesn't move in the slightest – except to continue its inexorable climb upwards.

Mustn't think about it. She knew the consequences when she drew her pattern in the sand; knew them and accepted them.

So she says to the goddess, in a voice that she keeps devoid of all emotions, "This is what you made."

The goddess stares at the envelope as if trying to decide what kind of trap it holds. Then, apparently deciding Françoise cannot harm her, she takes the envelope from Françoise's hands, and opens it.

Slowly, the goddess lifts the sonographs to the light, looks at them, lays them aside on the steps of the dais. From the envelope she takes the last paper – the diagnosis typed by the radiologist, and looks at it.

Silence fills the room, as if the whole city were holding its breath. Even the mask on Françoise's arm has stopped crawling.

"This is a lie," the goddess says, and her voice is the lash of a whip. Shadows move across her face, like storm-clouds blown by the wind.

Françoise shrugs, with a calm she doesn't feel. "Why would I?" She reaches out with one hand towards the mask, attempts to pull it from her arm. Her fingers stick to it, but it will not budge.

Not surprising.

"You would cast my child from your womb."

Françoise shakes her head. "I could have. Much, much earlier. But I didn't." And the part of her that can't choke back its anger and frustration says, "I don't see why the child should pay for the arrogance of his creator."

"You dare judge me?" The goddess's radiance becomes blinding; the mask tightens around Françoise's arm, sending a wave of pain up her arm, pain so strong that Françoise bits her lips not to cry out. She fights an overwhelming urge to crawl into the dirt – it doesn't work, because abruptly she's kneeling on the floor, with only shaking arms to hold up her torso. She has to abase herself before the goddess; before her glory and her magic. She, Françoise, is nothing; a failure, a flawed womb. An artist turning to science out of greed; an engineer drawing meaningless blueprints; a woman who used her friend's feelings for her to bring him into Ys.

"If this child will not survive its birth," the goddess is saying, "you will have another. I will not be cheated." Not by you, she's saying without words. Not by a mere mortal.

A wave of power buffets Françoise, bringing with it the smell of wind and brine; of wet sand and rotten wood. Within her, the power of the goddess is rising – Françoise's belly aches as if fingers of ice were tearing it apart. Her baby is twisting and turning, kicking desperately against the confines of the womb, voicelessly screaming not to be unmade, but it's too late.

She wants to curl up on herself and make the pain go away; she wants to lie down, even if it's on slimy stone, and wait until the contractions of her belly have faded, and nothing remains but numbness. But she can't move. The only way to move is towards the algae-encrusted floor, to grovel before the goddess.

Gaëtan was right. It was folly to come here; folly to hope to stand against Ahez.

Françoise's arms hurt. She's going to have to yield. There's no other choice. She—

Yield.

She's a womb, an empty place for the goddess to fill. She has been chosen, picked out from the crowd of tourists on the beach – chosen for the greatest of honours, and now chosen again, to bear a child that will be perfect. She should be glad beyond reason.

Yield.

The mask is crawling upwards again – it's at her shoulder now, flowing towards her neck, towards her face. She knows, without being able to articulate the thought, that when it covers her face she will be lost – drowned forever under the silk.

Everything is scattering, everything is stripped away by the power of the goddess – the power of the ocean that drowns sailors, of the storm-tossed seas and their irresistible siren song. She can't hold on to anything. She – has to—

There's nothing left at her core now; only a hollow begging to be filled.

And yet ... and yet in the silence, in the emptiness of her mind is the song of Ys, and the pattern she drew in the sand; in the silence of her mind, she is kneeling on the beach with the dagger still in her hand, and watching the drowned city rise from the depths to answer her call.

Slowly, she raises her head, biting her lips not to scream at the pain within her – the pain that sings *yield yield yield*. Blood floods her mouth with the taste of salt, but she's staring at the face of the goddess – and the light isn't blinding, she can see the green eyes dissecting her like an insect. She can–

She can speak.

"I – am – not – your toy," she whispers. Every word is a leaden weight, a stone dragged from some faraway place. "The child – is – not – your – toy."

She reaches for the mask – which is almost at her lips. She feels the power coiled within the silk, the insistent beat that is also the rhythm of the waves, and the song that has kept Ys from crumbling under the sea – and it's within her, pulsing in her belly, singing in her veins and arteries.

The mask flows towards her outstretched fingers, clings to them. It's cold and wet, like rain on parched earth. She shakes her hand, and the mask falls onto the ground, and lies there, inert and harmless: an empty husk.

Like Ys. Like Ahez.

"You dare—" the goddess hisses. Her radiance is wavering, no longer as strong as it was on Douarnenez. She extends a hand: it's empty for a split second, and then the wavering image of a white spear fills it. The goddess lunges towards Françoise. Out of sheer instinct, Françoise throws herself aside. Metal grates on the stones to her left – not ten centimetres from where she is.

Françoise pushes herself upwards, ignoring the nausea that wells up as she abruptly changes positions. The goddess is coming at her again with her spear.

Françoise is out of breath, and the world won't stop spinning around her – she can't avoid the spear forever. The song is deep within her bones, but that doesn't help – it just adds to her out-of-synch feeling.

The spear brushes past her, draws a fiery line of pain on her hand. She has to—

Behind the goddess, Gaëtan still stands frozen. No, not quite, she realises as she sidesteps once more, stumbling – the nausea rising, rising, screaming at her to lie down and yield. Gaëtan is blinking – staring at her, the eyes straining to make sense of what they see.

He raises a hand, slowly – *too slowly, damn it*, she thinks as she throws herself on the floor and rolls over to avoid the spear.

It buries itself into her shoulder – transfixes her. She's always thought she would scream if something like that happened, but she doesn't. She bites her lips so fiercely that blood fills her mouth. Within her, the pattern she drew on the sand is whirling, endlessly.

The pattern. The dagger. She fumbles for it, tries to extract it from her trousers' pocket, but she can't, she's pinned to the ground. She should have thought of it earlier—

"Your death will not be clean," the goddess says, as she withdraws the spear for another thrust.

Françoise screams, then. Not her pain; but a name. "Gaëtan!"

His panicked heartbeat is part of the song within her – the nausea, the power shimmering beyond her reach. He's moving as if through tar, trying to reach her – but he won't, not in time. There's not enough time.

But her scream makes the goddess pause, and look up for a split second, as if she'd forgotten something and only just remembered. For a moment only she's looking away from Françoise, the spear's point hovering within Françoise's reach.

Françoise, giving up on releasing the dagger, grasps the haft of the spear instead. She pulls down, as hard as she can.

She's expected some resistance, but the goddess has no weight – barely enough substance to wield the spear, it seems. Françoise's savage pull topples her onto the floor, felling her like harvested wheat.

But she's already struggling to rise – white arms going for Françoise's throat. At such close quarters, the spear is useless. Françoise makes a sweeping throw with one hand, and hears it clatter on the stones. She fumbles, again, for the dagger – half-out of her pocket this time. But there's no time. No time...

Abruptly, the white arms grow slack. Something enters her

field of view – the point of the spear, hovering above her, and then burying itself in the goddess's shoulder.

"I don't think so," Gaëtan says. His face is pale, his hair dishevelled, but his grip on the spear's haft doesn't waver.

Françoise rolls away from the goddess, heaving – there's bile in her throat, but she can't even vomit. She finally has her dagger out, but it doesn't seem like she will need it.

Doesn't seem...

The goddess hisses like a stricken cat. She twists away, and the spear slides out of her wound as easily as from water. Then, before Gaetan can react, she jumps upwards – both arms extended towards his face.

The spear clatters on the ground. Françoise stifles the scream that rises in her, and runs, her ribs burning. She's going to be too late – she can't possibly—

She's almost there, but the goddess's arms are already closing around Gaëtan's throat. There's no choice. There never was any choice.

Françoise throws the dagger.

She sees everything that happens next take place in slow motion: the dagger, covering the last few hand-spans that separate Françoise from the goddess's back – the hilt, slowly starting to flip upwards – the blade, burying itself at an angle into the bare white skin – blood, blossoming from the wound like an obscene fountain.

The goddess falls, drawing Gaëtan down with her. Françoise, unable to contain herself anymore, screams, and her voice echoes under the vast ceiling of the throne room.

Nothing moves. Then the goddess's body rolls aside, and Gaëtan stands up, shaking. Red welts cover his throat, and he is breathing heavily – but he looks fine. He's alive.

"Françoise?"

She's unable to voice her relief. Beside him, the goddess's body is wrinkled and already crumbling into dust – leaving only the dagger, glinting with drowned light.

Within her, the symphony is rising to a pitch – the baby's heart, her own, mingling in their frantic beat. She hears a voice whispering, *the Princess is dead. Ys is dead. Who shall rule on Ahez's throne?*

Once more she's lifted into that timeless place of the beach, with her pattern shining in moonlight: every street of Ys drawn in painstaking detail.

At the centre of the city, in the palace, is its heart, but it's not beating as it should. Its valves and veins are too narrow, and not pumping enough blood – it cannot stave off the rot nor keep the sea from eating at the skeletons, but neither will it let the city die.

And it's her baby's heart, too – the two inextricably tied, the drowned city, and the baby who should have been its heir.

She has a choice, she sees: she can try to repair the heart, to widen the arteries to let the blood in – perhaps Gaëtan could help, he's a doctor, after all. She can draw new pathways for the blood, with the same precision as a blueprint – and hope they will be enough.

She wants the baby to live – she wants her five months of pregnancy, her loss of Stéphane, not to have been for nothing, not to have been a cruel jest by someone who's forgotten what it was to be human.

But there are skeletons in the streets of Ys; crabs and shells scuttling on the paved stones; kelp covering the frescoed walls; and in the centre of the city, in the throne room, the dais is rotten – to the core.

She hears the heartbeat within her, the blood ebbing and flowing in her womb, and she knows, with absolute certainty, that it will not be enough. That she has to let go.

She doesn't want to. It would be like yielding – did she go all that way for nothing?

But this isn't about her – there's nothing she can offer Ys, or the baby.

She closes her eyes, and sees the pattern splayed on the ground – and the heart at the centre.

And in her mind she takes up the dagger, and drives up to the hilt into the pattern.

There's a scream, deep within her – tendrils of pain twisting within her womb. The pattern contorts and wavers – and it's disappearing, burning away like a piece of paper given to the flames.

She's back in her body – she's fallen to her knees on the floor, both hands going to her belly as if she could contain the pain. But of course she can't.

Around her, the walls of the palace are shaking.

"Françoise, we have to get out of there!" Gaëtan says.

She struggles to speak through a haze of pain. "I—"

Gaëtan's hands drag her upwards, force her to stand. "Come on," he says. "Come on."

She stumbles on, leaning on his shoulder – through the kelp-encrusted corridors, through the deserted streets and the ruined buildings that are now collapsing. One step after another – one foot in front of the other, and she will not think of the pain in her belly, of the heartbeat within her that grows fainter and fainter with every step.

She will not think.

They're out of Ys, standing on the beach at Douarnenez with the stars shining above. The drowned city shivers and shakes and crumbles, and the sea is rising – rising once more to reclaim it.

Then there's nothing left of Ys, only the silvery surface of the ocean, and the waves lapping at their feet. Between Françoise's legs, something wet and sticky is dripping–and she knows what it has to be.

Gaëtan is looking at the sea; Françoise, shaking, has not the strength to do more than lean on his shoulder. She stares ahead, at the blurry stars, willing herself not to cry, not to mourn.

"You OK?" Gaëtan asks.

She shrugs. "Not sure yet," she says. "Come on. Let's go home and grab some sleep."

Later, there'll be time for words: time to explain, time to heal and rebuild. But for now, there is nothing left but silence within her – only one heartbeat she can hear, and it's her own.

I'll be OK, she thinks, blinking furiously, as they walk back to Gaëtan's car. Overhead, the stars are fading – a prelude to sunrise. *I'll be OK.*

But her womb is empty; and in her mind is the song of her unborn son, an endless lament for all that was lost.

ABOUT THE CONTRIBUTORS

James Brogden was born in Manchester, grew up in Australia, and now lives with his wife and two daughters in Bromsgrove, Worcestershire, where he teaches English. His short stories have appeared in the *Big Issue*, the British Fantasy Society's *Dark Horizons*, *Gears Levers Volume One*, and his first novel, *The Narrows* has just been published by Snowbooks. When he's not writing, or trying to teach children how to, he gets out into the mountains exploring the remains of Britain's prehistoric past and hunting for standing stones. Fortunately they don't run very fast.
http://jamesbrogden.blogspot.co.uk/

Aliette de Bodard lives and writes in Paris, France, in a flat with more computers than warm bodies, and two Lovecraftian plants in the process of taking over the living room, one tentacle at a time. In her spare time, she writes speculative fiction: her Aztec noir fantasy *Obsidian and Blood* is published by Angry Robot, and she has been a finalist for the Hugo and Nebula Awards, and has won the British Science Fiction Association Award.
http://aliettedebodard.com

Pauline E Dungate, until recently, was a teacher at the local Museum and Art Gallery. Her stories have appeared in anthologies such as *Skin of the Soul, Narrow Houses, Swords Against the Millennium, Beneath the Ground, Merlin, Victorious*

Villains and *Under the Rose*. She has won prizes for poetry and has been a judge for the Arthur C Clarke Award. She reviews for *SFCrowsnest* and runs workshops covering all areas of creative writing. She lives in Birmingham with husband and fellow writer Chris Morgan.

Lynn M Cochrane lives on the outskirts of Birmingham. She has been writing most of her life and has published three collections of poems. Her short stories have appeared in convention publications and also in *Raw Edge*, the West Midlands Arts publication. She is a member of Cannon Hill Writers' Group, leading writing workshops from time to time, and is currently editor of their showcase anthology *Salvo*.

Adrian Cole, a native of Devon, is the author of twenty-five novels, beginning with *The Dream Lords* in the 1970s, through *The Omaran Saga* and the *Star Requiem* to the *Voidal Saga* in 2011. He is also the author of numerous fantasy and horror short stories, and has been published in *Year's Best Fantasy* and *Year's Best Fantasy and Horror*. Forthcoming from Edge Books is the novel *The Shadow Academy*, and he has a short story in *The Worlds of Cthulhu* anthology due soon from Fedogan and Bremer. Adrian also has a story in *The Alchemy Press Book of Pulp Heroes*.

Peter Crowther is the recipient of numerous awards for writing, editing, and as publisher of the hugely successful PS Publishing (which includes Stanza Press, the Drugstore Indian mass market paperbacks, PS Visual Entertainment and PS Art Books). As well as being widely translated, his short stories have been adapted for TV on both sides of the Atlantic, and collected in *The Longest Single Note, Lonesome Roads, Songs of Leaving, Cold Comforts,*

The Spaces Between the Lines, The Land at the End of the Working Day and the upcoming *Jewels in the Dust*. He is the co-author (with James Lovegrove) of *Escardy Gap* and *The Hand That Feeds*, and has also written the *Forever Twilight* SF/horror cycle. He lives and works with his wife and business partner Nicky Crowther on England's Yorkshire coast. Pete's story "Heroes and Villains" appears in *The Alchemy Press Book of Pulp Heroes.*

www.pspublishing.co.uk

Bryn Fortey appeared in various anthologies during the 1970s, including: *New Writings in Horror & the Supernatural* and *New Writings in SF*. He was also published in various Fontana anthologies edited by Mary Danby. Bryn's beat-styled poetry magazine *Outlaw* was Best UK Small Press Magazine of 2004 in the Purple Patch Awards. In the same year he won the Undercurrent Aber Valley Short Story Competition with "The Dying Game". In 2009 his "A Taxi Driver on Mars" was first in the Data Dump Awards for SF poetry in the UK. Bryn hales from South Wales.

Dominic Harman is an illustrator and graphic designer who is best known for his science fiction, fantasy and horror book jackets and CD covers. He has won many awards for his paintings and designs in the UK and the USA. Dominic's work can be found on the book covers for Harper Collins, Subterranean Press, Quercus, Dell Rey/Ballantine, Macmillian, Simon and Schuster, Penguin, Gollancz, Orion, Orbit and Little, Brown amongst many others.

http://bleedingdreams.com

Misha Herwin has been writing since she could first hold at pen. At twelve she wrote and staged her first play in a theatre made from a cardboard box. Since then her plays for teenagers have been performed in schools by the Stagefright Theatre Company and at the Canadian High Commission in Jamaica. She has published the *Dragonfire Trilogy* for kids and her stories can be found in a number of anthologies and magazines including *Hens, Bitch Lit* and *Ghostly Reflections*.

http://misha-herwin-writer.blogspot.com/

John Howard was born in London. He is the author of the collection *The Silver Voices* and the novella *The Defeat of Grief*. His short fiction has appeared in several anthologies, including *Beneath the Ground, Never Again*, and *The Touch of the Sea*. John has collaborated with Mark Valentine on a number of short stories, six of which featured Valentine's long-running occult detective The Connoisseur, reprinted in *The Collected Connoisseur*. Most recent to appear is *Secret Europe*, (written with Mark Valentine) to which John contributed ten of the twenty -five stories, set in a variety of real and fictional European locations.

Selina Lock is a mild-mannered librarian from Leicester. In her alternative life in comics she edits *The Girly Comic*, and has written strips for *Ink+PAPER #1* and *Sugar Glider Stories #2*. She also helped organise the *Caption* comics convention between 2006-2011. Her short stories have appeared in *Alt Zombie* and *The Terror Scribes Anthology*. She is one half of *Factor Fiction* alongside her partner Jay Eales. Her daily life is spent in service to the god Loki, who currently inhabits the body of a small, black, scruffy terrier.

www.factorfictionpress.co.uk

William Meikle is a Scottish writer with fifteen novels published and over 250 short story credits in thirteen countries. His work has appeared in a number of anthologies; recent short stories were sold to *Nature Futures, Penumbra* and *Daily Science Fiction*. He now lives in a remote corner of Newfoundland, Canada, with icebergs, whales and bald eagles for company. In the winters he gets warm vicariously through the lives of others in cyberspace. William also has a story in *The Alchemy Press Book of Pulp Heroes.*

www.williammeikle.com

Anne Nicholls, author, journalist and counsellor, has had ten books published in SF and the self-help field, with sales from Sweden to Mexico, the USA to China, plus a ten-year Internet presence as agony aunt for Tiscali and the Department for Children, Schools and Families. Her highly acclaimed novels *Mindsail* and *The Brooch of Azure Midnight* appeared under the name of Anne Gay, and *Dancing on the Volcano* was entered for the Arthur C Clarke Award. For four years she was also the editor of LineOne's Science Fiction Zone, which had around 140,000 readers every month. She is currently working on a YA fantasy trilogy. Anne also features in *The Alchemy Press Book of Pulp Heroes.*

Kari Sperring grew up dreaming of joining the musketeers and saving France, only to find they'd been disbanded in 1776. Disappointed, she became a historian and as Kari Maund published six books and many articles on Celtic and Viking history, plus one on the background to her favourite novel, *The Three Musketeers* (with Phil Nanson). She started writing fantasy in her teens, inspired by Tolkien, Dumas and Mallory. She is the author of two novels: *Living with Ghosts*, which won the 2010

Sydney J Bounds Award, was shortlisted for the William L Crawford Award and made the Tiptree Award Honours' List; and *The Grass King's Concubine.*

www.karisperring.com

Adrian Tchaikovsky was born in Lincolnshire, studied and trained in Reading and now lives in Leeds. He is known for the *Shadows of the Apt* fantasy series starting with *Empire in Black and Gold,* and currently up to book eight, *The Air War.* His hobbies include stage-fighting, and tabletop, live and online role-playing.

www.shadowsoftheapt.com

Shannon Connor Winward's writing has appeared in many venues including: *Pedestal Magazine, Flash Fiction Online, Strange Horizons, Illumen, This Modern Writer [Pank Magazine], Hip Mama Zine* and the anthologies *Twisted Fairy Tales: Volume Two, Jack-o'-Spec: Tales of Halloween and Fantasy* and *Spectacular: Fantasy Favorites.* Her poem "All Souls' Day" is nominated for a 2012 Rhysling Award.

http://ladytairngire.livejournal.com

ABOUT THE EDITORS

Jenny Barber is a regular contributor to the *Girls' Guide to Surviving the Apocalypse* blog, runs the *Shiny Shorts* review site, edited *Here & Now* magazine, and has run conventions and edited several publications for the British Fantasy Society. She was one of the judges for the BFS Best Newcomer awards in 2010, 2011 and 2012 and is currently studying for a History BA with the Open University.
  www.jennybarber.co.uk

Jan Edwards was nominated for the British Fantasy Award for Best Short Story in 2011 and 2012, and has won the Winchester Writers' Festival "Slim Volume" Prize. She has a BA (Hons) English Literature, and has more than thirty short stories published in various anthologies and magazines, most inspired by her passion for folklore and mythology. Other work includes scriptwriting for TV spin-offs, reviews, interviews, poetry and articles. Over the past twenty years and more she has been involved with the British Fantasy Society, in various ways, and has chaired its annual conference, FantasyCon. She lives in the Staffordshire Moorlands, on the edge of the Peak District National Park, with her husband Peter Coleborn, three cats and a selection of chickens.
  http://www.janedwards-writer.blogspot.co.uk/

Lightning Source UK Ltd.
Milton Keynes UK
UKOW051449290812

198219UK00002B/29/P